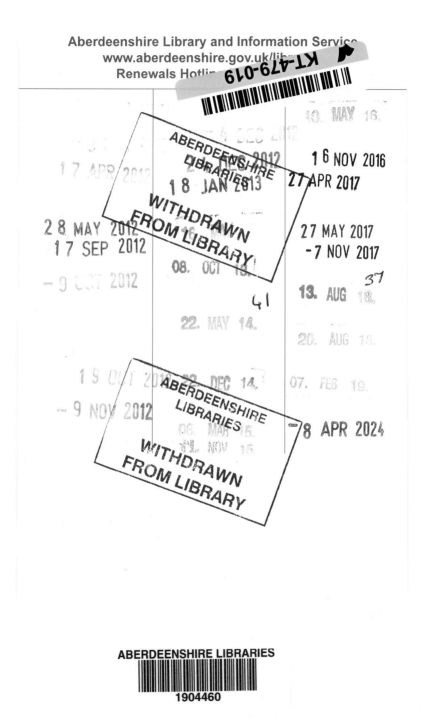
1

2

SHADES OF EVIL

Residents of the sleepy Lancashire village of Kelton Bridge, where forensic psychologist Jill Kennedy has made her home, are looking forward to Christmas. But then the body of a young woman is discovered on the bleak hillside. DCI Max Trentham now begins the hunt for Lauren Cole's killer. And all the evidence points to one man. But Max's chief suspect is Jill's neighbour and she refuses to believe him guilty of the brutal murder. Yet, as they delve into his past, Jill to clear her friend's name and Max to secure a conviction, Jill is forced to question her own judgement. And then another body is found...

SHADES OF EVIL

SHADES OF EVIL

by

Shirley Wells

Magna Large Print Books
Long Preston, North Yorkshire,
BD23 4ND, England.

British Library Cataloguing in Publication Data.

Wells, Shirley
    Shades of evil.

    A catalogue record of this book is
    available from the British Library

    ISBN   978-0-7505-3528-1

First published in Great Britain in 2011 by
Constable & Robinson Ltd.

Copyright © Shirley Wells 2011

Cover illustration by arrangement with Constable & Robinson Ltd.

The right of Shirley Wells to be identified as the author of this work has been asserted by her in accordance with the Copyright, Designs and Patents Act, 1988

Published in Large Print 2012 by arrangement with
Constable & Robinson Ltd.

LP

Magna Large Print is an imprint of Library Magna Books Ltd.

Printed and bound in Great Britain by
T.J. (International) Ltd., Cornwall, PL28 8RW

To Matilda and Murphy, with love

10

Acknowledgements

I'm grateful to all at Constable & Robinson for their hard work in bringing this book to you. In particular I owe thanks to Krystyna Green for having faith in Jill and Max.

A huge thank you also goes to my husband, Nick, who somehow copes with living with a writer whose mind is usually elsewhere.

Finally, I'd like to thank you, the reader. So many of you have taken the time to contact me via my website, www.shirleywells.com, and I'm grateful to each and every one of you. Without you, there would be little point to this.

Chapter One

'Sod you!' Lauren yelled, slamming out of the house. 'You can go to hell!'

She yanked his key from the bunch and hurled it across the garden.

Tears of anger smarted in her eyes as she jumped in her car and fired the engine. She slammed it into reverse, clipped the edge of the wheelie bin, and sent the contents flying across his drive.

'Sod him!'

Charlie was curled up on the passenger seat. His small white body was trembling and his front paws were hiding his face.

'Hey, I'm not angry with you, Charlie.' She took a hand from the steering wheel to ruffle his fur. 'I'm never angry with you.'

She slowed for the T-junction at the bottom of Longman Drive.

'I'm probably not even angry with him, either. But I *am* angry with Josh. And I'm angry with myself. Hell, I'm just bloody angry!'

The fuel gauge was close to empty, but the warning light wasn't glowing yet. She should have enough fuel to get to Kelton Bridge and back.

'Tell you what, Charlie, we'll go to your favourite place. I'll take you for a good run over the hill, OK?'

Charlie looked at her briefly, then returned his

13

face to its hiding place behind his paws.

'Come on,' she said. 'Forgive me, eh?'

She smiled as she spotted a quick twitch of his tail.

She drove out of Harrington, over Deerplay Moor, and took the turn for Kelton Bridge. Once through the village, she parked at the bottom of a rutted track and reached into the footwell for Charlie's lead. It wasn't there. She must have left it at home. They were unlikely to meet anyone so it didn't really matter.

'Come on, Charlie.'

He leapt out of the car and raced around in circles while she locked it and pocketed the keys.

The wind was in her face as she strode past the spinney and on up the hill towards Clough's Shelter.

Decades had passed since the stone building had been used by shepherds and the roof had long gone. These days it only had three walls and they were too dilapidated to offer protection from the harsh weather experienced in the Pennines.

Lauren liked to sit on the low wall, though. From there, she could see the valley below – the village of Kelton Bridge as well as Bacup and Stacksteads.

Charlie ran on ahead, chasing leaves that blew in the wind. Snow had been forecast for later, but there was no sign of it.

When there were no leaves, Charlie chased his tail. No matter how bad things were, her dog always made her smile. Always. Even today, when things were about as bad as they could be.

'If you had a bank account with a few grand in

14

it, Charlie, you'd be perfect.'

He barked happily in response.

Until recently, Lauren hadn't spared God a thought and she'd never believed in spirits or fairy godmothers. As far as she was concerned, life was what you made it. You were on your own to make of it what you could.

Yet she could never explain the way Charlie had found her. It was as if he'd known he was needed, as if he'd been sent to help her through the worst years of her life.

Six years ago, on a Friday that should have been like any other, Lauren had walked into the house, dumped her school bag on the table, made a sandwich and asked her mum how she'd got on at the hospital.

'Not too well,' her mum had said. 'You'd better sit down, Lauren. I need to talk to you.'

At fourteen years of age, Lauren had listened to her mum telling her how kind the staff had been as they'd done the tests, and how they were going to try chemotherapy but how they weren't too hopeful.

Lauren had run from the house. She'd gone to the park and she'd howled. All the while, her mum's words had echoed in her head. *It might be all right, Lauren.*

It might. But then again, it might not. And what if it wasn't? How would they cope?

Walking back home, the tears still wet on her face, she'd been aware that she was being followed. A scruffy white dog, little more than a puppy, was trotting behind her. There was no one in sight and her companion wasn't wearing a collar.

15

'Go home, you'll get lost!'

The dog wagged its tail in response and continued to walk beside her.

'Go on. Scram!'

She'd stopped and tried to shoo the animal away, but, despite her efforts, he'd followed her all the way home.

Her mum, glad of the distraction Lauren supposed, had found some scraps of food and they'd both watched the poor mite eat as if he hadn't swallowed anything for weeks. One of his ears had been bent back as he'd scoffed the food.

'He looks a right Charlie,' her mum had laughed.

He'd been Charlie ever since.

He slept on the foot of Lauren's bed that night. She'd been aware of the weight of his body, and the comforting warmth he provided, and any thoughts of trying to trace his owner had vanished. Instead, she went out the following day to buy collar and lead, food and a bed.

Yes, Charlie had been with her through the best of times and the worst of times. And he was still with her.

She spotted a figure leaning against the stone wall and smiled as recognition dawned.

'Hi, Jimmy,' she said when she neared him.

'H-hi,' he stammered, blushing scarlet.

Jimmy had a crush on her. Even if she'd wanted to, which she didn't, she knew there was no point striking up a conversation. He was too tongue-tied in her presence to make any sense. She guessed he'd watch her, though. He'd probably follow her, too.

As she walked on, she thought of the way she'd stormed out of her dad's house that morning. Even as the door had slammed, she'd regretted it. She had a mental picture of her dad carefully picking up the rubbish from the drive and putting it back in the wheelie bin. It would never be mentioned, she knew that.

Later, when they'd both had a chance to calm down, she'd go back and talk to him. Perhaps she'd suggest they spend Christmas Day together. It was years since they'd been together during the festive season.

Then again, he'd drive her mad with his 'You can't cope, Lauren' chant. That's all he seemed to say to her these days. 'You can't cope, Lauren. You've never coped with your mum's death.'

But she *could* cope. Better than him probably.

Her life was in a mess, true, but her mum had been dead six years. She was over it. If only her dad could see that.

She walked on and, as always, the beauty of the hills calmed her. Her mum had been a keen walker and she'd loved to come here. It was where Lauren felt closest to her. Sometimes, she would even talk to her.

Charlie suddenly barked with excitement and Lauren's spirits sank as she recognized the dog he'd met. The dog was gentle and affectionate. Its owner was a pain in the arse.

Besides, she didn't want company. Not today.

Chapter Two

DCI Max Trentham turned his car into Pennine View where two elderly ladies, clad in wellington boots and standing beneath the streetlamp as they waited for a bus perhaps, waved at him. Given the poor light, they must have recognized the car rather than him, but he waved back.

Although he didn't know them, he could imagine the conversation: 'There's the copper who spends the night with lovely Jill Kennedy now and again. You'd think she could do better for herself, wouldn't you?'

The thing about villages in general, and Kelton Bridge in particular, was that you only had to clear your throat and locals knew your life story.

His car slid on the packed snow and he swore as he righted it. Who in their right mind would choose to live in such a place? Bleak, lonely, isolated.

He thought of the young woman whose body had been found out on the hill late yesterday afternoon. A lone hiker had spotted her. If he hadn't, she could have lain there for days beneath a blanket of snow. The first flakes had fallen in the early hours and it was almost six inches deep now.

He drove a few more yards, but it was hopeless. There was no way his car was going to make it along the lane and he didn't want it stuck in a drift.

Thinking it unlikely that any other vehicle would venture this way, he left it as close to the hedge as he dare and got out. He had a torch in the boot and he walked the rest of the way with the light from that swinging left to right. The snow went over his shoes, and his feet were soon soaked.

He walked on to Jill's driveway where her smug-looking four-wheel drive Suzuki was neatly parked.

In the summer months, with the garden a riot of colour, Lilac Cottage was, quite literally, the stuff of postcards. Even a calendar, produced to show off this corner of east Lancashire, featured her home with the towering Pennines providing a spectacular backdrop. This evening, however, with the garden hidden beneath snow, and only one light visible from inside, it looked a dark, almost forbidding place.

Just as he stepped up to the door, the beam of light from his torch caught something.

'What the–?'

He shone the light straight at it. A cat, attached to a hanging basket bracket with a thin rope, was swinging in the wind.

Max had a knife in the car but, not wanting to tramp back for it, he tried the knot. It was easily undone and the cold, stiff body was released.

Did he tell Jill or not? The good thing, if there was anything good about having an animal hanged by your front door, was that, technically, it wasn't one of hers. It was the old stray that had been calling on her for the last month or so.

He could say he'd found it in the snow, dead from cold or old age. On the other hand, some

19

sick bastard had done this. The cat had been declared terminally ill by the vet, but Max very much doubted it had decided to end it all. He'd have to tell her.

With the animal in his arms, he hammered on the door, then tried the handle. It wasn't locked.

There was no sign of her so he shouted up the stairs.

When she appeared on the landing, she was wearing skin-tight jeans, a chunky blue sweater, wet hair and a scowl that she'd been perfecting over the last week.

'Why the hell is it so difficult to lock–?' He broke off, reminded by the weight in his arms that it wasn't the time for a lecture on security. That could wait until later.

'Yeah.' A hand flew to her mouth. 'Oh, no!'

She ran down the stairs, shock giving way to sadness. 'Oh, no,' she said again, stroking the lifeless head. 'The poor thing. The vet said she might live for months yet.'

But the vet hadn't counted on lunatics with a sense of the macabre.

'Let me fetch her blanket.' She took the corpse from him as if it were a newborn. Tears glistened in her eyes, but he guessed they wouldn't spill over. Not until she was alone, at any rate. 'We'll bury her in the garden. She liked lying under the lilac tree.'

'Bury her–?' Beneath the snow, the ground would be as hard as granite. What else could they do, though?

'I'll start digging,' he said, resigned.

He found the spade in the shed, put it to the

20

ground, and was surprised when he managed, fairly easily, to push it down several inches.

While he dug, he wondered, not for the first time, what people saw in cats. He was inclined to agree with Fly, one of his sons' dogs, that they were neither use nor ornament and should be banished from the face of the earth. There was one advantage to them though; they only required small graves.

Jill had put on wellington boots and a thick coat before joining him. The corpse, wrapped in its pink blanket, was safe in her arms.

'Jill,' he began, as the moon, full and huge, peeped out from behind a cloud.

'What?'

But this wasn't the time or the place. The weather was against him, too. His feet were squelching in sodden shoes and his hands were numb with cold.

'Let's get her buried,' he said.

Ten minutes later, the job done, they headed for the warmth of Jill's cottage.

'Have I got any clothes here?' he asked, the bottoms of his trousers wet and heavy.

She shrugged. 'Who knows?'

'Right.' He wasn't in the mood for sulks, so he went upstairs to her bedroom, opened the drawer that was unofficially his and found a pair of jeans.

When he joined her in the kitchen, she was fussing Sam, her old tabby cat.

A newspaper on the table was open at the racing page and he could see where she'd written the results and the betting odds. A large cardboard box with 'Decorations' scrawled on the lid offered an unwelcome reminder that Christmas was less than three weeks away.

'You OK?' he asked.

'Fine. And thanks for burying her.'

He couldn't put it off any longer.

'Jill, she didn't die from natural causes.'

'How do you mean?'

'Someone had – she'd been hanged. By the front door.'

'She'd been what?'

She was furious, yes. She was shocked, too. Yet, there was something else.

'Any ideas?' he asked curiously.

'No.' Short and to the point. 'But if I lay my hands on the bastard–'

'Not a clue?'

'No.' She shoved her hands in the back pockets of her jeans. 'Although I have had a couple of odd phone calls.'

'Oh for– What sort of odd? When? And how many?'

'Only two. Both late at night, early hours of the morning. The first time, he didn't say anything. Last time, that was Friday night, he laughed and said I'm coming to get you.'

'And you didn't think to mention it?'

'I just did.'

'And you still leave the bloody door unlocked? Christ, why not put up a sign? All lunatics welcome.'

She sighed at that. 'I usually do lock it.'

'Right, we need to look into it. Your job's like mine. You help put people behind bars. They bear grudges.'

That wasn't news to her.

'We need to see who's been released from prison recently—' he began, only to be cut off.

'I've looked. There's no one.'

'Then we'll look somewhere else.' What a bloody day! 'Is there anything alcoholic here?'

'Red wine. And white. Brandy, too, I think.'

There was a god. He was playing some cruel practical jokes at the moment, but at least there was booze.

He went to the cupboard and chose a decent bottle of red.

She put two glasses on the table and he filled them both.

'Thanks.' She took a large swallow.

Max took an equally large one, then reached into his pockets for his cigarettes. He'd given up really, and had only bought a packet for emergency use. He lit one, then looked around for an ashtray.

With a sigh that would have measured a good three on the Richter Scale, she took a heavy glass ashtray from the cupboard and banged it down on the table.

'You don't mind me smoking, do you?'

'I don't have to, do I?'

He thought of extinguishing it, but changed his mind. As he was already in the doghouse, he may as well get his money's worth.

'This isn't a social call,' he said.

'I didn't think it would be.'

He let that go.

'Have you heard about the body found at the back of here?'

'What? God, I saw several patrol cars in the village, but I didn't know–'

'You're currently living near a crime scene. There's an axe murderer on the loose.'

'A what?'

He saw a brief flicker of impatient amusement. He wasn't surprised. Axe murderers had become something of a joke. They didn't exist.

'I know, I know,' he said. 'In all my years as a copper, I've never known anyone to be murdered with an axe. Until now.'

'You're joking.' She dropped down into a chair. 'You're not, are you?'

'Sadly not. The body of a young woman, late teens or early twenties, was found on the hill at the back of here late yesterday afternoon. We haven't managed to identify her yet. A white dog was guarding the body so we're assuming it was hers. She was carrying car and house keys. Other than that, nothing. No ID on her, no mobile phone, the dog wasn't wearing a collar and it hadn't been microchipped. But yes, someone killed her with an axe.'

'Dear God. And when you say at the back of here, where do you mean exactly?'

'Flat Top Hill. There's an old stone building, or what's left of one.'

'Clough's Shelter.'

'That's the one.'

'Good God.'

'I know. How can such things happen in lovely, idyllic Kelton? Move to the countryside, eh? Cats hanged and people axed to death.' He took another swig of wine. 'Sorry.'

'Have you found the murder weapon?'

'It wasn't lost. It was between the victim's eyes.'

She pulled the sleeves of her sweater over her hands and hugged herself for warmth.

'Any ideas?' she asked.

'None.'

'Is she local?' She shook her head at the stupidity of her question. 'Late teens or early twenties, you say? What does – did she look like?'

'Five feet five. Long blonde hair. Wearing jeans and a bright red anorak.'

'And no one's been reported missing?'

'No.' He extinguished his cigarette. 'I don't suppose you've heard anything? Seen anything out of the ordinary?'

'No, but I haven't been here. I've been in Preston all day. Yesterday I was in Manchester and, over the weekend, I was in Liverpool with Mum and Dad.'

Avoiding him, he guessed. Usually, things were good between them. At least, he thought so. He asked her to marry him on a regular basis and she turned him down. They knew where they stood with each other. At the moment, however, things were far from good.

'Are your parents well?' he asked.

'Fine.' Short and to the point. 'Who's in charge of the case? I thought you were still busy looking into the disappearance of Yasmin Smith.'

He was, but the fifteen-year-old had been missing for four months and they'd exhausted all ideas.

'There's no one else available,' he explained. 'People are either on a training course, in hospital or abroad.'

'You're having a bad time of it then,' she said, her voice heavy with sarcasm. 'With the shortage of officers, you'll struggle to make up a decent team.'

'That's true,' he agreed, refusing to rise to the bait.

This atmosphere had hung between them for almost a week now. People believed that Jill, a forensic psychologist, did nothing but build profiles that led the police to criminals. The reality was that she spent much of her time on mundane tasks and staff assessments. As part of this, she had deemed one of his officers, a damn good sergeant in Max's opinion, unfit for work. Max had made his views clear on that, and she'd sulked ever since. He wondered if sulking was a gender thing, and thought it probably was. Men would have a quick argument over a pint and the whole thing would be forgotten.

Jill's other cats, Tojo and Rabble, ambled into the room and he watched her make a fuss of them. She'd be keeping a close eye on them in future. The cat flap would be locked at night, he guessed.

'How busy are you right now?' he asked.

'Too busy. You think people will talk to me because I'm local, but you're wrong. I'm still considered an outsider and I'm too close to the force. Besides,' she added, and he could see her chest rising and falling with anger, 'you've made it quite clear you don't trust my judgement.'

'I didn't say I didn't trust your judgement. I merely–'

'If you'd told me you had no faith in my professional opinion, that would have been one thing. But, oh no. You have to tell everyone else at the blasted nick!'

'Everyone else' was an exaggeration. In Max's opinion, DS Clive White was a damn good officer and keeping him away from a job he loved was ludicrous. If Jill had been within earshot when Max found out, he would have voiced his feelings to her face. As it was, he'd had to content himself with a few choice expletives that had been over-heard by half a dozen officers. Unfortunately, word had flown round headquarters in record time.

'Will you help, please?' he asked. 'We're going to be speaking to everyone in Kelton. I could do with you along.'

'If I can spare the time,' she replied grudgingly. 'I've got a few radio interviews coming up.'

And that was another thing that niggled. As well as being a damn good forensic psychologist, she wrote self-help books. She was getting a name for herself and her books were growing more popular. It took up too much of her time. Not that Max was going to say so at the moment.

'And I'm in court tomorrow,' she reminded him. 'Expert witness on the Jason Lyle case.'

Damn, he'd forgotten that.

'That's fine,' he lied. 'If you can spare some time, I'd be grateful.'

She acknowledged that with a slight inclination of her head.

'Look,' he began, 'I'm sorry, OK? I was angry. If you'd been anywhere near when I found out you'd declared Clive White unfit to do his job, I

27

would have bent your ear. But you weren't. I was angry, and I'm sorry. You shouldn't have heard what I thought about it from someone else.'

'Good God, pigs *do* fly and Trentham *does* know how to apologize. Apology accepted,' she said, adding, 'even if it only came because you want my help and realize it's time to grovel.'

'Oh, I can grovel like a good 'un.' Plenty of practice.

The ghost of a smile touched her mouth, but she looked sad, and he knew the death of that old stray cat had hit her harder than she would ever admit.

He reached for her hand. 'You sure you're OK?'

'Yes. Yes, I'm fine, thanks.'

'Good.' He gave her a quick kiss. 'Sorry, but I'm out of here. I have to get back to the nick.'

While there he'd see if any nutters who might bear Jill a grudge had been released from prison recently. For all they knew, the person who had murdered the young woman could be responsible for stringing up that cat. The dead girl's hair was long whereas Jill's blonde locks were cut short, and the victim was about twenty while Jill was in her thirties. Even so, it could have been a case of mistaken identity. Unlikely, but possible.

'And for God's sake keep the bloody door locked! It's not rocket science, is it?'

Chapter Three

Fortunately, the council's gritting lorries were managing to keep the main roads clear and Max arrived at headquarters twenty minutes later.

The first officer he saw was DC Shepherd.

'Anything new?' Max asked him.

'Yes, we've got an ID on the dead girl. Grace is about to go and see her family.'

'Good. Don't let her leave without me.'

Informing relatives that a family member was dead was never easy, but telling someone their nearest and dearest had been murdered was the worst job in the world. No matter how many times you did it or how many training courses you attended, it never became any easier.

Grace was in the incident room, grabbing her coat, about to leave. Tall and stick thin, she was never still for a moment. Max was glad to have her on his team.

'Who is she then?' he asked her.

'Lauren Cole. Twenty years old. Her address is given as Worcester House, Longman Drive.'

'We're sure it's her?'

'We are, guv. The keys she was carrying belonged to the Ford Ka that was parked out at Kelton. We got a copy of her driving licence sent through. Yes, it's her. Surprisingly, for a driving licence, it's a good photo.'

Lauren Cole. Full of life one minute; lying dead

on a barren hillside the next.

'Someone will need to identify her,' Max said, speaking to himself more than Grace. That was a harrowing ordeal at the best of times and it would take great skill to conceal this killer's handiwork. 'OK, I'll come with you.'

'Yeah?' Grace brightened. It was always better to have moral support at such times. 'As far as I've managed to find out, she lives there with her father. You ready now then?'

'Lead on.'

Grace drove, leaving Max to gaze out at the familiar streets of his town. The few who'd ventured out this evening looked cold and grumpy as they walked carefully on pavements that were topped with about five inches of snow. Half a dozen young men dashed into the warmth of a pub. Several more congregated outside Harrington's finest fish and chip shop. Two women queued behind an elderly man at the bank's cash machine. Lights shone from Asda and it looked, from the number of cars parked outside, that the supermarket was doing a good trade. Every pump was in use at the petrol station.

For most, life went on as normal. For Lauren Cole's family it would never be the same again.

Longman Drive was on the outskirts of town, at the top of a steep hill. The gritting lorries had done their best but the wheels spun as Grace turned the car into the cul-de-sac.

'Worcester House,' she said, slowing the car to a crawl as she checked house numbers and names.

'There.' Max pointed to the end house where a carved stone in the wall showed the house name.

Grace stopped the car and they sat for a moment to look at the building. It was old, large and detached and, courtesy of tall, thick hedges, enjoyed more privacy than most.

'Ready?' Max asked.

'Yeah.'

They left the warmth of the car and began walking carefully through the snow to the front door where, thankfully, a bright security light showed the way.

Some people had cleared their drives of snow but that belonging to Worcester House remained untouched. No tyre tracks or footprints were visible. No heavy-booted postman or milkman had trudged up to the front door.

Grace rang the doorbell and a deep bing-bong echoed through the interior. A light was switched on, a bolt was slid back and a key was turned.

The door was opened by a man in his mid-forties.

'Mr Cole?' Max asked.

'Yes.'

'DCI Trentham and DS Warne, Harrington CID.' They showed him their warrant cards but, like most people, he barely glanced at them. 'May we come in, please?'

'What's going on?' He looked up and down the road as if he thought there must be trouble in the street.

'If we could come inside,' Max said, stepping forward.

Cole moved back, opening the door fully to allow them entry. Without waiting for an invite, Max headed for what he correctly guessed to be the sitting room.

'What's going on?' Cole asked again.

Grace produced the copy of the driving licence with the dead girl's photo. 'We believe this is your daughter?'

'Lauren, yes.' He was a big man, well over six feet tall, yet he seemed to shrink before them. 'What's happened? Where is she?'

'Do you recognize this ring?' Grace said, ignoring his question.

'Of course I do. It's my late wife's wedding ring. Lauren's not had it off her finger since her mum died. What's going on?'

'I'm sorry,' Max said, 'very sorry, but late yesterday afternoon, a walker came across a young woman's body lying on the ground. We believe it's Lauren.'

'No!' He took a step back. 'My Lauren? Dead? How can she be?'

He walked to the window, pulled back the curtain as if Lauren might walk down the drive, then let it drop back before turning to face them.

'How can she be?' he asked again.

Max and Grace sat. After a few moments, Cole did likewise.

'Yesterday afternoon,' Max explained, 'a man out on Flat Top Hill–'

'Kelton Bridge.' Cole nodded. 'Lauren walks her dog there. There's another thing. Where's her dog? Charlie would stick with her.'

'Charlie is at the rescue kennels,' Grace explained. 'Until we could find out who he belonged to, there was nothing else we could do with him.'

'The man out walking,' Max continued, guessing Cole was talking for the sake of it, talking so he didn't have to think that his daughter might be dead, 'found a woman's body. She was wearing dark blue jeans and a red anorak.'

'She – she died?' His voice broke. 'Lauren? It was Lauren out on the hill?' He stood up again. 'I don't believe you. I mean, it can't be.' He took a couple of steps forwards to wag an angry finger in Max's face. 'I want to see her. You've got it wrong, you must have. You can't come here telling me stuff like that!'

'We can take you to see her,' Grace told him. 'Why don't you get a coat, Mr Cole? It's very cold outside.'

Without saying a word, he went upstairs. When he returned, he was wearing a black overcoat. The sight of him, the fear in his eyes, had Max's stomach clenching. No one should ever have to do what he was about to.

It was a long, long drive with Mr Cole becoming increasingly angry. He hadn't been well, he told them, and they had no right to upset him like this. As yet, he hadn't asked how she'd died, and Max was glad of that.

In contrast, the drive back to his house was undertaken in complete silence. Even Grace, prone to language that would make football hooligans blush, simply tapped the steering wheel when an idiot in a blue car almost took off the front wing at a roundabout.

Vincent Cole let them into his house and he was still silent. Max supposed that, as yet, he was too numb to feel anything. That wasn't a bad thing.

Once inside, Cole walked into the sitting room,

threw himself down in a chair and buried his face in his hands.

Max looked at Grace and nodded at the kitchen. She got the message immediately and, while she clattered around looking for cups, Max watched Cole. The man rubbed at his eyes, making them red, but they remained dry.

When Grace returned and pushed a cup of tea at Cole, he looked at her as if he'd never seen her before.

'I've put sugar in it,' she said.

Cole seemed to gather himself and took the cup from her. 'Thank you.'

The room was huge with high ceilings and what looked to be original beams. They were too solid to be modern additions.

Everything in the room was neat. That was the only word Max could think of that described it. Photos and ornaments were arranged with perfect symmetry. Pictures were hung on the walls and it looked as if a spirit level was used to check alignment. A brown rug in front of the inglenook fireplace was a regulation six inches from the hearth.

'Mr Cole,' Max began, 'why didn't you report Lauren missing last night?'

'Why would I?'

Of course, Lauren had been old enough to take care of herself. It was perhaps the norm for her to stay out overnight.

'Can you tell me when you last saw her?'

'Yesterday morning. She called in here–'

'Called in? She wasn't living here?'

'Heavens, no. She has a flat in town. Bank Street,' he added scathingly.

The properties there were old terraced houses, some with the windows boarded up. The uniformed department was called out to Bank Street on a regular basis.

'What number in Bank Street?' Grace wanted to know.

'Three.'

'How long has she lived there?' Max asked. 'According to the DVLA, this is her address.'

'She left about a year ago. No, it's closer to two years now.' He sighed. 'She met some bloke. He was no good. In fact, none of her friends are any good. They all look filthy and they take drugs.'

'Lauren too?' Max asked.

'Yes. She vowed she was off the damn things but–' His expression said he hadn't believed her. 'She had a job at Grant's, that cheap supermarket in town, but she lost that. She always wanted money,' he went on, his expression distant. 'She kept coming to me for money. That's all. She never wanted to see me, just wanted money. And, of course, I kept giving. Drugs. That's what she was spending it on, I knew that.'

'Yesterday morning,' Max said, 'what time did she come here?'

'About eight o'clock. Half eight maybe.'

'Did she have the dog with her?'

'In the car, yes. She has a key and was surprised to find me at home. I'd felt rotten last week, as if I had flu or something, and so I thought I'd have a bit of a break from the office.'

'Which office would that be?' Grace asked, pencil poised.

'Cole and Dawson,' he replied, taking Max by

surprise. 'Insurance,' he added unnecessarily.

Cole and Dawson must be doing well for themselves as they'd recently taken over prestigious town centre premises.

'You're the Cole in Cole and Dawson?' Grace asked.

'Yes. Anyway, as I say, Lauren was surprised to find me at home. If I hadn't been here–'

He broke off.

Max could guess what would have happened if he hadn't been home. Lauren would have hunted round for money or something she could sell. It was common practice for those hooked on any sort of drugs.

'She had a nice car, but sold that. I had to buy her that Ford.' Cole shook his head in despair. 'That would have gone soon, too. She swore to me, promised me that she was off the heroin. She couldn't have been though, could she? If she had been, she wouldn't have come to me for more money.'

'We found no evidence of drugs in her body,' Max assured him.

'Is that right?'

'Yes.'

'She wasn't coping, you see,' Cole went on, his expression distant. 'After her mum died, Lauren couldn't cope with life.'

'I see. And did you argue yesterday morning?' Max asked.

'Not really. Well, in a way. I told her I couldn't afford to give her more money and, when she saw I was serious, she stormed off. Slammed the door behind her, ran to her car, and drove off in a temper. I thought she'd take the dog for a walk and calm down. Funny really, but no matter how low she gets, she takes good care of Charlie. But she's never coped with her mum's death. It's been painful to watch her struggle.'

When he put his cup on the coffee table beside his chair, his hands were shaking.

'We'll be sending someone to be with you,' Max told him.

'Thank you, but I don't need anyone.'

'Someone will come,' Max insisted.

The man had no idea what lay ahead. Dealing with his grief would be bad enough, but someone would have to help him cope with the media interest this case would generate.

'They'll talk to you, tell you what to expect,' Grace explained.

'Do you know who killed her?' Cole asked. 'Any idea at all?'

'Not yet,' Max replied. 'But we will find the person responsible. I give you my word on that.'

His word? What use was that? He'd given his word to Adam Smith. Four months ago, he'd promised Smith that he would find his daughter, fifteen-year-old Yasmin. He was no closer to finding her today than he had been then. It was Smith who was pounding the streets, Smith who was putting up posters, and Smith who was asking everyone he met if they'd seen his little girl.

Grace went into the hall and Max heard her phoning headquarters. From her side of the conversation, he gathered that a family liaison officer would be here in twenty minutes.

'As I said, it was when her mum died that she

went off the rails,' Cole said, his gaze on some distant spot. 'Wendy had cancer. We buried her six years ago.'

'I'm sorry,' Max said.

Grace returned to the room. 'Can you give us the names of her friends?'

'Not really. I saw her in town once with a scruffy youth called Ricky. We weren't introduced or anything but I heard her laughing and calling him that. I don't know his surname or what he does for a living. Not a lot, I expect. Then there was Jo, of course. Short for Joanne, I suppose. Her flatmate. I'm afraid I don't know anything about her either.'

His daughter was a stranger to him. He had no idea where she went or who she spent her time with.

Max hoped the day never came when he knew as little about his sons' lives.

When WPC Morgan, the appointed family liaison officer arrived, they left Cole to his grief.

On the drive back to headquarters, Max thought of phoning his boys. He needed to hear their voices, to know they were safe. But they wouldn't be home. Harry would be at football practice and Tuesday was Ben's night at dog-training classes. He would have to wait till later.

'This investigation will be in Jill's neck of the woods then,' Grace broke into his thoughts. She took her gaze from the road to grin at him. 'Is she speaking to you yet, guv?'

'Not so as you'd notice.'

'The course of true love, eh?'

'Ha.'

Chapter Four

Jill stood in her kitchen, leaning against the hot radiator, watching Max make coffee as if he woke in her cottage every morning.

It was far too early to be out of bed, and she was still trying to decide what had possessed her to let him stay the night. Never mind him spending the night, why had she shared her bed with him?

It was always the same. All he had to do was click his fingers and she melted. She must be mad.

After visiting Lauren Cole's father last night, he'd spent a couple of hours at headquarters and it had been late when he'd called back at her cottage. She'd been touched that he'd come to see if she was OK, and she'd felt for him, knowing just how difficult it was to remain professional while telling a man that his daughter had been murdered.

That was part of the problem, of course. Professionally, she admired him. A lot of people in his job became hard and cynical. Not Max. He could keep the two worlds separate. He was good at his job, he could empathize with people, he could deal with the worst kind of horrors and yet still remain a warm, caring man and a wonderful father to his sons. If some cases monopolized his every waking thought, few would guess at it.

Jill liked to think she was the same. People

often joked that psychologists were crazy, that to see the fine line between sanity and madness, you had to cross the border. Some claimed that you needed to experience some sort of childhood abuse to obtain the necessary qualifications. That was nonsense in Jill's view. Her own childhood had been as happy as anyone could wish for.

She could, however, pinpoint the exact moment the frailty of the human mind first grabbed her interest. As a twelve-year-old, she'd spent hours gazing out of her bedroom window at the big house that was less than a quarter of a mile from the council estate on which she'd been born. She'd imagined the wonderful life the inhabitants must lead. The daughter, about Jill's age, had owned a beautiful pony. Gleaming sports cars had been parked in front of the six-car garage. Marquees had been erected on the lawns on a regular basis. The family had seemed to glide effortlessly from one lavish party to the next.

Then one day, police officers had swarmed around the house like bees. News soon spread that the businessman hadn't been as wealthy or successful as he'd led people to believe. Faced with an avalanche of debts, he'd shot his wife and daughter, and then turned the gun on himself.

Jill's shock had been peppered with fury at such a selfish act. She hadn't minded him killing himself, that was his choice, but she'd been appalled to know that the young girl would never ride out on her beautiful pony again.

Jill would have given a lot to have been able to sit down and talk to him for an hour. Even at twelve years of age, she'd been certain she could have made a difference to his way of thinking.

'You OK?' Max asked, and she came to with a jolt.

'Yes. Fine, thanks.'

And still she wondered why she'd let him spend the night.

Lust had a lot to answer for, she supposed, as did a longing to turn their relationship into something more solid. He infuriated her at times, but she hadn't yet mastered the art of not loving him.

And if she were being totally honest, she would have to say that it was better to have someone in the cottage to answer crank phone calls. She was fairly certain it was nothing more serious than kids playing a joke on her, but all the same–

'What?' he asked, catching her looking at him.

'Nothing.'

'I've said I'm sorry,' he reminded her. 'Oh, and before you hear this from the office grapevine, Dad's spending Christmas with me and the boys.'

'Really? Aw, that's nice.'

He pulled a face at that, and she knew what he was thinking. His father was being difficult right now, and Max couldn't seem to get along with him.

'I hope I get an invite,' she added.

'A what?'

'An invite to see your dad. As odd as it may seem, given that he's related to you, I actually like him.'

'You want an invite?' He folded his arms across his chest. 'God, that's rich. You're the one who insists on living in this godforsaken village. You're

41

the one who's afraid of any sort of commitment. Your choice, Jill. As far as I'm concerned, you have an open invite. Marry me. Move in with me. Bring the cats. Sell the cottage and get out of this bloody village. How's that for an invite?'

An angry retort sprang to her lips, but she bit it back. As far as Max was concerned, the reason their relationship was so volatile was all due to her supposed fear of commitment. It had nothing to do with him spending the night with another woman when they'd lived together. But there was no point bringing that up. It was old news, and they'd moved on. At least, they'd tried to.

Her doorbell rang, startling her out of her gloomy thoughts. It wasn't even seven o'clock, far too early for callers.

She opened her door to see Wilf Appleby standing on her doorstep. Wilf, who owned and farmed most of the land around Lilac Cottage, would have been up for hours. In fact, it was probably late for him.

'The idiot dropped this at my place yesterday,' he said. 'It's plainly addressed to you, but you know what he's like. Bloody hopeless!'

Smiling at the description of their new postman, Jill took the letter from him. 'Thanks, Wilf.'

He could have pushed it through the letterbox, but he wasn't the type. If there was a conversation going spare, you could count Wilf in.

He peered around her. 'Is that copper here?'

'Max? Yes, he is. Did you want him?'

'Dunno. I heard a copper called at my place yesterday afternoon, but he missed me. Then, on the radio this morning, they said a girl were

42

found dead on Monday.'

'That's right. The police are in the village now, asking if people saw or heard anything.'

'Ah, well, I were out in the yard on Monday for most of the day. The farrier were here. I reckon I saw everyone who were about.'

The wind, a raw easterly, was blowing snow into Jill's hallway.

'Come in,' she urged him.

After a brief hesitation, he removed wellington boots, unwound his scarf, and stepped inside.

'We're in the kitchen,' Jill said, leading the way.

She introduced the two men and they shook hands. Wilf was in a heavy waterproof coat with his feet clad in thick woollen socks, and Max was wearing a dark suit with a grey tie. Getting on for eighty, Wilf was twice Max's age. They were opposites in every way.

'I hear a copper has called at my farm,' Wilf explained, 'but he'll have a job to find me at home. I need to be out mending the fences before spring.' He looked at Max. 'I thought, seeing as you were here, I could tell you what I saw on Monday.'

'I'd be grateful,' Max said.

'Ah, so I thought.'

Jill guessed it would be a long conversation.

'Do you want coffee, Wilf?'

'Can't bear the stuff. I were on my way back to the farm for my breakfast and a brew.'

'Tea?' she offered.

'Ah, that'd be more like it.'

While she made Wilf his tea, he sat at her table, leaned back and prepared to tell his story.

'The young woman who was murdered,' Max

43

began, taking the lead, 'was Lauren Cole. Do you know her?'

'Lauren Cole? No, I don't know the name. Mind, I see a lot of people walking round here and I don't know most of the names.'

'She was twenty years old,' Max said, 'with long, blonde hair. Five feet five inches tall. On Monday, she was wearing dark blue jeans and a red jacket. She had a dog with her, a small white shaggy crossbreed called–'

'Charlie?' Wilf guessed.

'That's right. You *do* know her then?'

'I've seen her about,' Wilf said, 'but no, I can't say as I know her. I'd know the dog, though. You see, my farm has a right of way across it and people cut through there. She often did. Sometimes she'd say good morning, but that were all. I do remember hearing her call the dog Charlie, though.'

'You didn't see her on Monday morning?'

'No. Sometimes, though, people drive up and park on the waste ground. If they're in a rush, they'll do that. If they do, I won't see them.'

'Did you see anyone else on Monday morning?' Max persisted.

'As I were telling Jill,' Wilf explained, 'I had the farrier out to the horses on Monday so we were out in the yard all day. From there, you can see everyone who goes out on to the hill.'

'Did you see anyone on Monday morning?' Max asked again, and Jill smiled to herself. This conversation would go at Wilf's pace, not Max's. And that pace would be slow.

'I did.' He nodded solemnly. 'Lots of people

44

round here walk their dogs up there. First I saw the woman who's just moved into the terrace. You'd know her, Jill. About fifty, she is. She has a couple of dogs, both crossbreeds. The young one looks like it's got a lot of labrador in it. It's always carrying a ball in its mouth. She carries one of them plastic things that helps you throw a ball. It's a skittish young dog. Needs a bit of training if you ask me. The other dog's older. Black. Going grey. A bit of collie in that one. He's either going deaf, or he's just a little bugger. She's forever calling him because he's wandered off.'

Jill recognized the description.

'Denise Bent,' she said, putting a mug of steaming tea in front of Wilf. 'She and her husband, Eddie, moved in a couple of years ago.'

'Is it as long as that?' Wilf asked, scratching his head. 'I suppose it could be.'

'Did you notice anything unusual about her?' Max asked.

'No. She were having to shout to that black dog, as she often does. Her walk took her about the same time as usual. About forty minutes, I reckon. No, there were nothing unusual. In fact,' he added, 'it'd have been odd if I hadn't seen her. Every morning she takes them dogs the same way.'

'Anyone else?' Max asked.

'Oh, yes. Next, I saw a chap – don't know his name – but he walks up this way from Bacup. He has a little brown dog. What do you call them? Ah, yes, it's a border terrier. Nice little dog. Mind, that one has a tendency to wander as well. So I saw him. I didn't see him come back because he walks the loop, you see. Once he's out of sight, I wouldn't expect to see him till the next morning.'

Jill, too, knew the man with the little dog. Like Wilf, she didn't know his name, but she'd often exchanged the time of day with him.

Wilf might talk too much, but Max couldn't fault the man's powers of observation.

'Now,' Wilf went on, 'the next person I saw were Steve Carlisle. He walks his dog up there most mornings, too. He has a greyhound,' he added for Max's benefit, 'and it's the laziest creature you could meet. The dog'd far rather be curled up at home in front of the fire than be out walking. Still, walk he has to. Every morning. At this time of year, the dog'll be wearing a tartan jacket. Looks right bloody daft in it, too.'

He took a long swallow of tea and Jill could see Max mentally digesting names and details of these people.

'I didn't see Steve set off,' Wilf went on, enjoying his captive audience, 'only when he were coming back. And that were a bit unusual.'

'Oh?' Max was struggling to keep his patience.

'He were running,' Wilf said thoughtfully. 'Well, when I say running, he were *trying* to run. He were trotting a bit, then stopping to call his dog. That dog of his only has two speeds; slow and stopped. So the dog were ambling along behind him and Steve were running a bit, then stopping to shout at the dog, then trotting along a bit further.'

'And you say that was unusual?' Max said.

'Yes. I've never seen him run before. In fact, he always walks about in a bit of a dream. He's a clever bloke so I suppose he thinks a lot. But yes, that were unusual. I'll tell you summat else that

46

were unusual,' Wilf went on, warming to his theme. 'He weren't carrying nothing. Very often, when he's on his way home, he'll be carrying a plastic bag full of rubbish.'

'Rubbish?' Jill asked.

'Yes. He's always having a rant about the amount of rubbish folk leave lying around. I have to agree with him on that one, too. Folk chuck empty cans and bottles in the hedge instead of carrying them home.' He looked at Max, a half smile on his lips. 'Mind, I blame the police for that. They ban drinking in the towns and villages so people go out to the hills and drink. Bloody daft!'

'So he picks up rubbish?' Max asked, ignoring Wilf's last comment.

'He does. Very often he walks back home with a plastic bag filled with empty cans and bottles.'

'A public service,' Jill said, surprised.

'Yes, and if he's not carrying rubbish,' Wilf went on, 'he's got a sack full of wood. A year or so ago, he had one of them wood burning stoves put in. Like yours, Jill.'

'I know. I had a look at his before I had mine put in.'

'Ah, well, he often brings back wood from the spinney. I wouldn't accuse him of cutting the young trees down,' Wilf put in quickly, 'but he finds quite a bit of wood. It's free, you see.'

'You say he carries a sack full of wood?' Max said. 'Does he get small pieces? Or does he chop it up and carry it home like that?'

'I wouldn't know,' Wilf admitted. 'I suppose he chops it up. Presumably he carries a saw in the sack.'

47

Jill looked at Max and she knew exactly what he was thinking. *Or an axe.*

Max had conducted the morning briefing, updated his boss on progress, or lack of, and issued a press statement before he finally had time to pay number three Bank Street a visit.

Officers were almost finished at Lauren Cole's home, but hadn't found anything of interest. Her computer had been taken away and Max just hoped there was something useful on that.

Her flatmate, Jo, was standing in the doorway to Lauren's room, watching proceedings in a state of shock.

Everything had been taken out of Lauren's small wardrobe and was being put back. The mattress had been removed and was standing up against the wall. The small square of worn beige carpet had been pulled back.

'You don't think he'll be after me, do you?' was Jo's first question to Max.

'What makes you think that?'

'Nothing in particular.'

'I can't imagine so,' Max said, 'but, until we know a bit more about it, it might pay to be extra cautious.'

Most of the houses in Bank Street had been bought as investments and several, including number three, had been turned into flats. Max hoped the rents were suitably low.

Wallpaper that had probably been stuck on twenty years ago was giving up the fight and peeling away to reveal large damp patches. Carpets were threadbare. Furniture was barely serviceable.

'Is there any coffee going?' he asked her.

'Eh? Er, yeah, if you like.'

They left officers to finish in Lauren's room and went into the kitchen where Jo took a dirty mug from a pile in the sink, washed it, thoroughly he was relieved to see, and hunted through cupboards for a jar of instant.

She was probably about the same age as Lauren, but had dark, almost black hair. Reed thin and pale, she looked as if she, too, was familiar with drugs. She was wearing jeans that needed a good wash, a grey baggy sweater and a huge pair of black boots.

'So,' Max said, as they waited for the kettle to boil, 'what can you tell me about Lauren? Been friends long, have you?'

'No. That is, we're not. I mean we weren't friends at all really.' The kettle boiled and she filled it. 'Oh, sorry, I don't think there's no milk.'

'That's OK, I take it black. What do you mean, you weren't friends?'

'When I split up with the boyfriend, I needed a cheap place to live,' she explained. 'Lauren had put an ad in the local shop window.'

'When was that?'

'Six weeks ago. I was the first to see it and moved in that same day.'

'I see. So you didn't know her well?'

'Not really, no.'

'You got along OK though, did you?'

'I suppose so,' she said, 'but she was a bit stuck up. God knows why. I mean, living in a dump like this didn't give her much to shout about, did it? But she always thought she was better than everyone else. Reckoned her dad had loads of money. Always said he'd give her anything she wanted. I used to ask her what she was doing living here then, but she never gave me a proper answer.'

She hadn't lied about her father's wealth. As partner in the thriving Cole and Dawson company, he was more than comfortably off.

'She was on heroin, wasn't she?'

Jo chewed on a finger. 'Dunno about that.'

'What about her friends? Did you know any of them?' he asked, changing tack.

'No. She didn't bring any of them here.'

'Her father said she had a boyfriend. Did you know him?'

'No.' She looked genuinely puzzled.

'Someone called Ricky?'

'Oh, him.' She nodded. 'He didn't last long. She dumped him.'

'What was his surname?'

'No idea.'

'Do you know anything about him? Where he lived? If he worked? Who he hung out with?'

'I only saw him twice,' she said. 'Once, he came back here and spent the night on the sofa. The other time was after she dumped him. She wouldn't let him in and he started hammering on the door and shouting through the letterbox.'

'What was he shouting?'

'Called her a prick tease, if you must know. Accused her of using him. Still, that wouldn't surprise me. She did use people.'

'Can you give me a description of him?' Max asked, not holding out much hope.

She thought for a moment.

'Quite tall and dark. About the same age as me and Lauren, I suppose. No older than twenty-five at any rate. Bad teeth. In fact,' she added with a grin, 'I always reckoned a dentist did his hair and a barber did his teeth. Hair was all shaggy and half his teeth were missing.'

Not Ricky Marshall, surely. Marshall would fit that description and, if Max's memory served him correctly, and it usually did, he was currently on probation.

'Like I said,' Lauren went on, 'I only saw him twice. And the second time was when he was hammering on the door. I was watching him from the window and I thought he'd have the bloody door bashed in.'

'But he went away?'

'Yeah.'

'And you didn't hear anything about him after that?'

'No.'

'How long ago was that?'

'A couple of weeks.'

The flat was cold and damp. There was a clothes airer in the corner of the small kitchen and three pairs of wet jeans were draped over it. Without some heat in the room, they wouldn't be dry before the new year.

'There was someone else, too,' she remembered. 'Josh his name was, but I never saw him. At one time, when I first came here, he was texting or phoning her a dozen times a day. That soon stopped, though. Lauren went out and bought a new sim card for her phone so he wouldn't know her number.'

'What did she do with the old card?' Max asked.

'Binned it, I suppose.'

They'd found Lauren's phone in her car. She was on Pay As You Go and, with no contract, it would be almost impossible to get records from the old sim card.

'Why did he call so often?' Max asked.

'Dunno. They'd always argue, though, and more often than not, she'd cut him off.'

'And you don't know anything about him?'

'No. Sorry.'

'What did Lauren do with her time, Jo? Where did she go?'

'Dunno really. She walked her dog a lot. What's happened to him then? The dog, I mean?'

'He's being looked after at the kennels,' Max told her. 'Where did she walk him?'

'All over the place. The thing was spoilt rotten. He used to sleep on her bed and on the sofa. Sometimes, if I went to sit down, he'd growl at me. He was only a little thing, but he could be mean. He hated the postman, too. Every time he saw a postman, he went mad. He'd lie in wait and pounce when something came through the letterbox.'

Most dogs hated postmen. Quite right, too, really. Dogs thought it their duty to protect property and it must seem to them that postmen tried to break in on a daily basis.

'Charlie liked his walks,' Jo went on. 'You only had to change your shoes and he thought he was going for a walk. It was always easier to take him than put up with him running around and yapping. She could never tire him out though. She used to take him miles over the hills and he'd still be ready to go again five minutes later.'

Max knew all about that. He shared his home with three dogs and two of them would run all day every day.

'I heard she was on heroin. Is that right?' Max tried again.

'Dunno about that,' came the same response.

'Where might she have got it?'

'I wouldn't know.' Jo looked everywhere but at Max.

'Where do you get yours from, Jo?'

'Me? Oh, no, I've never touched the stuff.'

'But if you did, who would you get it from?'

'Dunno, do I?'

Max wasn't getting much of use from Jo. They needed to find Ricky and, if it wasn't Ricky Marshall, that was going to be tricky. Officers would have to ask after a man with bad teeth and a dodgy haircut. Still, at least they had a description of sorts. They didn't even have that for Josh.

He handed Jo a card.

'If you think of anything else, Jo, anything at all, will you call me?'

'Yeah.'

'Anything at all. If you remember anything about her friends, where she went, where her boyfriend, Ricky, hung out – anything at all, OK?'

'OK. What about the rent on this place? Can I get someone in to share?'

'You need to discuss that with the landlord.'

'Does he know? About Lauren I mean?'

'He does, yes.'

'I'll ring him up then and ask if I can put an ad

53

in the shop window.' With a plan in mind, she looked happier, more relaxed.

It was as if her flatmate had already been forgotten.

Chapter Five

The day wasn't going Jill's way. She should have been in court as an expert witness in Jason Lyle's case. Lyle had been stealing cars from the age of nine. Now, thirty years later, he'd stolen a BMW, driven it straight through a shop front in Harrington, stolen thousands of pounds worth of electrical equipment and, while speeding away from the scene, had caused a traffic accident in which a man died. His defence was planning a plea of diminished responsibility and it was Jill's job to convince the jury that he was simply an habitual criminal. At the last minute, however, after Jill had spent days preparing for it, Lyle changed his plea.

At least it gave her time to catch up on her other work and she had a fairly productive morning. At two o'clock, she was about to exchange her office for the canteen when her plans were thwarted yet again.

'It's me,' Max greeted her when she picked up her phone. 'I'm going out to Kelton to speak to Steve Carlisle. Can you spare an hour or so to come with me?'

'Steve? Why? He'll have heard the news and

he'd have been in touch if he'd seen anything.'

'Will you come with me?' Max asked again, ignoring that.

'Well, yes, I suppose so, but I don't see much point.'

'The point is that he was seen running from the scene.' Without waiting for a response, he said, 'My office in five minutes?'

'Right.'

Bang went lunch. She grabbed her coat and bag, left her office and went to the machine on the ground floor.

DS Fletcher had beaten her to it.

'No Mars bars,' he said in disbelief.

Jill, whose own lunch would have been a Mars bar, laughed at the expression on his face.

'I thought you were on a diet, Fletch.'

'Only at home.' He put coins in the machine and, after a great deal of deliberation, hit the button to send a Crunchie bar falling down the chute. 'I need an energy boost.'

'Me, too.'

Jill chose a Crunchie and a Twirl, put them in her bag and went to Max's office. He was ready to leave. He grabbed his jacket, checked his pocket for car keys and led the way out of building.

Someone had made a half-hearted effort to clear the car park of snow. What they'd actually done was pile it up against the walls where it sat attracting dirt.

As soon as they were in the car, Max turned the heater on full blast and, within a few moments, Jill felt a hint of warm air coming through.

'Tell me what you know about Carlisle,' he said

55

as he drove them out of the car park.

'He's lived in the village all his life,' Jill began. 'He's been married to Alison for around twenty years. They both worked in sales, him in the construction industry and Alison in cosmetics. Alison seems to be doing OK but Steve lost his job about a year ago. A recession always hits the building industry first.'

Max nodded at the truth of that.

'There are rumours in the village,' she went on, 'and I'll stress that they are only rumours, that he's started drinking a bit.'

Jill had thought those rumours unfounded, but she'd seen Steve a couple of mornings recently, and guessed he'd already had a drink.

'That's probably understandable,' she said. 'He's heading towards fifty, he's lost his job and, a year on, he still hasn't found another. It must get him down.'

'So his wife's the breadwinner?'

'I've no idea. She might be, although they seem pretty well off. He'd been with the same company for around twelve years though, so I expect he got a decent redundancy package.'

Jill thought for a moment and realized that, although she liked Steve, she'd never really taken to Alison. She didn't dislike the woman, but she couldn't warm to her.

'I imagine Alison is a good saleswoman,' she added. 'She's charming and very confident. Steve is less confident but, presumably, as he kept it so long, he was good at his job. If I was buying a used car, though, I'd buy from Steve rather than Alison.'

'Are they happily married?'

56

'As far as I know, yes.' Outwardly, they had the perfect relationship. What went on behind closed doors, of course, was anyone's guess. 'Yes, I'd say so. They go out as a couple. To the pub, restaurants, shopping, church and suchlike. They're quite religious, I gather, and go to the Catholic church in Harrington.'

The traffic lights changed to green and they were out of the town and heading over the moor to Kelton Bridge. On the brow of the snow-capped hill, the wind turbines were spinning. A couple of horses stood in the lee of a wall, smart blue jackets on their backs as protection from the wind.

'Where's Mason's Cottage?' Max asked as he drove into the village.

'Carry on past the church,' Jill said, 'and then take a right by the newsagent's.'

The main street was quiet today. With the weather so cold, people were staying indoors. Jill didn't blame them.

'It's along here?' Max asked.

'Yes. Just there.' She pointed to a large house at the end of the road. 'The one with the silver car outside.'

Max stopped the car outside Mason's Cottage where the perfectly smooth driveway had been cleared of snow. Jill supposed that, as he was at home all day, Steve liked to keep on top of jobs like that. At least the postman wouldn't be breaking an ankle and suing him. At Jill's cottage, people walking up her icy drive took their lives in their hands. But the Carlisles' drive was tarmac whereas hers was gravel.

'Is he expecting us?' she asked, and Max nodded.

'I phoned him.'

Steve must have been watching for them because he had the door open before they were halfway along the drive.

'Hello there,' he called from the doorway. 'Come in, quick, out of this awful wind.'

'Hello, Steve,' Jill said. 'Bitter, isn't it?'

'I've been out in the garden at the back trying to clear the path,' he explained, 'but my hands are so numb I can't feel what I'm doing.'

After they'd wiped their shoes on the mat, he led them through to the large sitting room where his greyhound was sprawled out on a leather armchair.

'Hello, Cally.' Jill gave the dog a stroke.

Cally stretched, climbed down from her chair, gave Jill's hand a lick, inspected Max, decided she couldn't be bothered with company, and went back to bed.

'It's a dog's life, isn't it?' Steve said, smiling fondly at the animal.

'It certainly is,' Max agreed.

'Sit down,' Steve said. 'Can I get you something to drink? Tea? Coffee?'

They declined, although Jill wouldn't have minded a coffee.

This morning, Steve didn't look as if he'd been hitting the bottle. In fact, he looked in good shape. He wasn't one of those to lose his job and then sit around feeling sorry for himself. He must keep himself fit. Tall and slim, with neatly cut brown hair, he was an attractive man.

58

The room, thanks to a stove that made Jill's look like something from a doll's house, was deliciously warm.

The house had been built around 1870, later than Jill's home, but instead of a small cottage this was an imposing dwelling. In this vast sitting room, the stonework had been exposed to two walls. The leather suite, glass and chrome coffee tables and cream carpet were too modern for Jill's taste, and out of character with the house, but the room could easily have featured in a glossy magazine. There were no books lying around and no CDs. No clutter at all, in fact.

'We're sorry to bother you, Mr Carlisle–' Max began, only to be cut off.

'Steve, please.'

'Steve,' Max said. 'I gather one of our officers has already spoken to you?'

'Yes, early this morning.'

'I just wondered if you'd remembered anything more about Monday morning.'

'No, I'm sorry. Only what I told him.'

'We know you took your dog for a walk–'

'I did,' Steve agreed. 'I walk that way most days. But no, I didn't see anyone or anything out of the ordinary. Had I known then what I know now, of course, I would have paid more attention. That poor young woman. Dreadful to think of something like that happening here. You hear of such things on the news, but you can't quite believe it when it happens on your own doorstep, can you?'

'You can't,' Jill agreed.

'Did you know Lauren Cole?' Max asked him.

'That's the poor woman's name, isn't it? It was

59

in the paper. No, I'm afraid I didn't know her.'

'You probably saw her walking her dog,' Jill said. 'She was twenty years old, five feet five with long blonde hair, and she had a small, white dog called Charlie.'

Steve shook his head. 'I can't think of anyone like that.'

Max had brought along a photo of Lauren, one that he'd got from the girl's father, and the same one that had been in the press. It had been taken about a year ago, but was the most recent the man owned. He showed it to Steve.

'No, I don't recognize her at all,' he said. 'Sorry.'

'Going back to Monday morning,' Max said, 'would you mind telling me exactly what you did? From the moment you left home to the moment you returned.'

'Of course. I left here at a few minutes after nine. I leave at the same time most mornings. I listen to the news headlines on the radio, you see.'

'And you heard them on Monday morning?' Max asked.

'I did. And then I walked down past the church before cutting along the track by Wilf Appleby's farm. I walked by the stream for a while and then turned round and headed for home.'

'Did you go into the spinney?' Max asked him.

'I didn't, no.'

'Up Flat Top Hill? By Clough's Shelter?'

'No.'

A phone rang, but Steve ignored it.

'The answer machine will get it,' he explained.

'Did you see Wilf that morning?' Jill asked him.

'Wilf? No.'

'He saw you,' Max said. 'Apparently, he and the farrier were in the yard at the farm.'

'Oh? No, I can't say I noticed them.'

'Yet you walked past his farm twice?'

'That's right, yes.' Steve smiled a little self-consciously. 'I enjoy walking, more than Cally does in fact, and I tend to daydream as I walk. It's very relaxing.'

'Relaxing,' Max murmured. 'Hm. The thing is, Wilf Appleby says he saw you running back on Monday morning. Would that be correct?'

'Running?' Steve looked from Max to Jill as if she might have the answer to this particular conundrum. Then his frown cleared. 'Ah, yes, that's right. I was. You know how you sometimes worry that you've left the house unlocked? I did that on Monday. I couldn't remember locking the door, you see, and it was really bugging me. That's why I decided to turn round and head for home. I couldn't settle. By the time I reached Wilf's farm, I'd managed to convince myself that burglars were helping themselves to anything they wanted.'

'So you ran home to check?' Max asked.

'Yes. And, as you might guess, all was safe and secure. It's just habit, isn't it, locking the door, I mean? It's such a subconscious act that you don't remember if you've done it or not.'

'I suppose it is,' Max agreed.

'The same thing happened the week before,' Steve went on. 'As I walked, I grew more and more convinced I'd forgotten to switch the cooker off. The hob, you know? I had visions of the house

61

burning to the ground. Of course, when I got back all was safe.' He smiled as he added, 'I seem to be having more senior moments than my fair share at the moment.'

'I have them all the time,' Jill said.

'I hear you sometimes collect tins and bottles while you're out walking?' Max said.

'I do. I suppose that sounds silly, but the amount of litter that people leave around really annoys me. It's not exactly difficult to take it home, is it? So yes, I sometimes take a couple of carrier bags and fill those up. Mind,' he added, 'when the council starts charging us by weight for our waste, I won't be doing it.'

'What else do you collect when you're out?' Max asked.

'Collect? Why nothing.' Again, his frown suddenly cleared. 'Ah yes, sometimes I bring a bit of wood back.' He nodded at the stove. 'This thing eats wood so, if I find some lying around, I bring it back. Usually, it's fallen branches, but you wouldn't believe what I find out there. Someone had dumped a small table and four chairs once. God knows why. It would have been easier to take it to the tip. But there, people seem to take pleasure in dumping stuff. I chopped them up and brought them home.'

'Chopped them up?' Max queried.

'I certainly did. I noticed them in the morning so, in the afternoon, I took a saw along and began bringing bits home. I couldn't have carried them in one go,' he explained.

'So you sometimes take a saw with you?' Max asked.

'I don't take it on the off chance.' Steve smiled at the idea. 'But if I see some wood lying around, I'll take it with me the next time I go out.'

'Can we see this saw?' Max asked.

'See it? Well, yes, of course you can. It's in the shed.' He got to his feet. 'You'll have to be careful how you walk, I'm afraid. As I said, I was trying to clear the path at the back.'

They followed Steve through a huge kitchen that gleamed with gadgets to the back door. What he called a garden, Jill would have called a field. It was huge. By the house was a wooden store filled with logs. At the far end was a shed. There was also a greenhouse.

'The shed is mainly a wood store,' Steve explained at they approached it. 'As I said, you wouldn't believe how much wood we get through.'

He took a small key from his pocket and undid the padlock. When he opened the doors, they saw, filling one side, a tall, neatly stacked pile of logs.

'There's my saw,' he said, pointing.

It was hanging on two hooks on the opposite side of the shed, along with three spades, a fork and various other garden tools.

Max picked up one of the logs.

'You didn't use a saw on this,' he said.

'Good Lord, no. Sadly, I don't find enough wood on my walks. I have to buy most of the wood. These logs came from the garden centre in Harrington. Two pounds a bag. Not bad value.'

To Jill, who'd just paid three pounds for a bag of logs, it was excellent value.

'Do they deliver?' she asked Steve.

'Yes, so long as it's twenty bags or more.'

63

As they walked back to the house, Jill made a mental note to put in an order. At least this visit hadn't been a complete waste of her time.

Chapter Six

Ruth Carlisle would soon be celebrating, if that was the right word, her seventy-seventh birthday. These days, her age came as something of a shock and she found it hard to understand how the years had vanished. Sometimes, when she looked in a mirror, she would be momentarily taken by surprise to see a grey-haired, wrinkled woman staring back at her, but other than that, she didn't give her age a second thought. Now, looking at her youngest son, she felt every one of those years hanging heavily. That in itself surprised her because it had always been Steve who made her laugh, who made her feel young.

'What's wrong?' she asked him.

'Nothing. What could be wrong?'

'If I knew that, I wouldn't be asking.'

'Really, I'm fine.'

He wasn't, she was convinced of that. She'd thought he looked distracted on Monday night. Last night, she'd been sure of it.

Steve always came to them for his evening meal when Alison was working away. It wasn't that he was incapable of cooking his own food, it was his way of keeping the family ties strong. As her other children had left the village, she was glad of that.

64

He always brought his dog, Cally, with him, too. The dog was no trouble, though. As Frank often said, the animal was too lazy to be a problem.

'Your dad will be here soon,' she said as she carried on peeling potatoes for their meal.

'Where is he?'

'Down on the allotments with Bill.'

'In this weather? What on earth are they doing?'

'They're supposed to be planning next year's flower show, but I expect they're just putting the world to rights. Him and Bill took off with their flasks and some sandwiches. They have that old heater in the shed so they'll be fine.'

Ruth had been glad to see him go. She'd had a heart attack last year and, although it had been a mild one, he'd rarely spent a whole day out of the house since. Ruth had told him not to fuss and worry, but he still liked to keep a close check on her. It was a bit much at times.

'Where's Alison this week?' she asked Steve.

'At a sales conference in Leeds.'

He picked up the evening paper where the photo of the dead girl almost filled the front page.

'Something like that gives everyone a shock, doesn't it?' she said, shuddering to think of what the poor girl's family must be going through. 'I can't believe it. I mean, a place like this.'

'It's dreadful,' Steve agreed.

He quietly thumbed through to the jobs pages and Ruth prayed that, today, there was something suitable for him.

Ruth had four children and loved them dearly. She didn't have a favourite, but she had to admit that Steve held a special place in her heart.

65

Her firstborn, Toby, had been a demanding baby. Then Amy had come along and Ruth had never known two children fight more. They'd quarrelled from morning till night. When Louise, more delicate, had followed, things had settled down a little. All the same, Ruth's hands had been full with the three of them and the last thing in the world she had wanted was another child.

Steve had been a mistake and she'd panicked when she'd known she was carrying him, quite convinced that four children would have her locked away in the madhouse. Yet, from the moment he'd been born, his sunny nature and smiling face had captivated her.

She'd thought there would be the obligatory tantrums when he was two or three, but no. Then she'd worried he would turn into the teenager from hell. Nothing could have been further from the truth. Steve hadn't caused a moment's anxiety all through his school years. He'd been average at his lessons, nothing more, but he'd been a laughing, happy boy who was always eager to please.

How things change. Looking at him now as he hunched over the newspaper, she tried to remember the last time she'd seen him happy. Not for the last ten years. Nor the last twenty come to that.

After school, instead of following the others to university, Steve had taken a job in a busy office. He'd been responsible for orders and deliveries, making sure bricks and timber were delivered on time. Then, because he soon knew the products inside out, and because he had a good way with people, he'd been invited to apply for a salesman's position. With an extra two thousand pounds a year and a company car on offer, he hadn't thought twice about it.

He'd kept that job until the company was taken over and several were made redundant. As far as Ruth remembered, he'd been out of work for less than a month and had walked straight into his last job. He'd seemed to enjoy it. A year ago, however, along with a lot of others in the industry, redundancy had claimed him again.

'Anything interesting?' she asked him as he turned the page.

'Nothing I'm qualified for,' he said. 'And I expect they'd take one look at me and decide I was too old.'

'Too old? At forty-seven? Nonsense!'

The back door opened and Frank came in. He took off his thick coat, hung it on the back of the door, and rubbed his hands together.

'They reckon more snow's on its way, but it feels too cold.' He gave Ruth a quick kiss. 'What do you know then, Steve?' he asked.

'Not a lot, Dad. You?'

'No more than that.'

'Steve reckons he's too old to get a decent job,' Ruth said. 'What nonsense is that?'

'You can retrain, can't you?' Frank suggested.

'As what?'

'I don't know. A plumber or a sparky. The country's crying out for good tradesmen.'

'Maybe. I don't know. I do know I'll have to do something soon, though. I can't live off Alison for the rest of my days.'

Ruth wondered if that's why he seemed so distracted. Maybe he and Alison had argued about money. They wouldn't be the first couple to do that.

There was little said as they sat at the table to eat. Steve, like his dad, preferred to concentrate on his food rather than make conversation. Today, though, he was pushing potatoes round his plate.

'Aren't you hungry?' Ruth asked him.

'Sorry, Mum, I had a big chunk of cake before I got here.'

She didn't believe him. While Frank spoke of the weather and plans he had for the allotment, Steve, slowly but surely, cleared his plate. Ruth knew the effort it had taken, though.

'I'll help with the washing-up, Mum, and then I'll be off,' he said, rising to his feet.

'Anything planned?'

'My computer's playing up. I updated some software and it hasn't been right since. I need to sort that out.'

Ruth had never owned a computer and never wanted to. She hadn't a clue how they worked or what anyone would want one for, but she guessed Steve was making an excuse to get away. Whether he admitted it or not, her son had things on his mind.

'It's a poor do when a man can't tell his mother what's bothering him,' she said, plunging her hands into the hot soapy water.

'There's nothing bothering me, Mum. Really, I'm fine.'

'And I'm a monkey's uncle,' she retorted.

He took a tea towel from the top drawer.

'There's nothing to worry about, Mum, I promise you.'

Ruth continued to worry.

Chapter Seven

It was almost nine o'clock that evening when Max picked up his jacket and left his office.

Paddy was manning the desk, a phone to his ear and half a sandwich in front of him. While he listened, he was doodling on a notepad.

'We'll send someone round tomorrow,' he promised as he ended the call.

'Busy?' Max asked him.

'Just the usual. You off to the Green Man then?'

'Nope, I'm off home.' Max frowned. 'Why? What's going on at the Green Man?'

'Sam's engagement celebration.'

Now Paddy mentioned it, Max could remember the invite. He could imagine the state his officers would be in when the morning rolled round, too. There always seemed to be something to celebrate. Last week, they'd been wetting Colin's baby's head and the Green Man hadn't closed till gone three.

For a brief moment, Max thought of joining them, but he dismissed the idea and trudged through the slush to his car. He needed to see if his sons still recognized him.

Then again, it was his job to motivate the team. They'd worked long frustrating hours lately, looking into the disappearance of Yasmin Smith and, now with Lauren Cole's murder on their doorstep, would be working a lot more. An hour spent with them might do everyone good.

Besides, his kids were happy enough and had a far better social life than he did. It wasn't too long till Christmas and, for the first time that Max could remember, he'd be spending almost a fortnight at home with them. With his kids and his dad.

He was trying not to think too much about his father's visit because he knew it would be difficult.

Max had got the phone call on 4 April, almost eight months ago now. He'd raced to the hospital and to his mother's bedside and had spent the next hour holding her hand and willing her to pull through.

Then he'd remembered other stroke victims he'd seen and heard about, and he'd known that she wouldn't want to 'pull through'. She would have needed to learn to speak and eat all over again. She would have hated it. They all would.

Eventually, he'd left his father at her bedside and stepped outside to speak to his brother.

'He blames himself,' Dave said.

Max knew that. Their father had left for a day trip to London to catch up with ex-colleagues. When he'd walked out of the door to catch the train, Margaret Trentham had been sitting at the kitchen table eating breakfast with the morning paper open beside her. When he'd returned shortly after ten that night, she'd still been there, the paper still open, her breakfast cold before her. She'd been slumped over the table unconscious for most of his fifteen-hour absence. She was sixty-seven years old.

Despite the odds, she lay in her hospital bed for three long days before Max got the next phone call.

'She's gone,' Dave had said simply.

Shrugging off his memories and putting all thoughts of his father's impending visit from his mind, Max headed towards the lights of the Green Man.

The best, and probably the only good thing about the pub was that it was close to head-quarters. And it was well-heated, Max decided as he stepped inside.

This evening, it was packed, mostly with cop-pers. Jill was standing at the bar chatting to DS Grace Warne, and Max fought his way over to them.

'I didn't expect to see you here, guv,' Grace said, her face flushed from heat, embarrassment or alcohol.

'I didn't expect to see most of the team here, either,' he replied, looking around him and won-dering who would be fit to drive in the morning.

'Yeah, well. Most have only dropped in for a quick one. I'll, um, go and remind them about the morning briefing.'

Grace left them and Max watched her for a few moments. He guessed her colleagues were being warned of his presence rather than reminded about the early briefing.

Jill was holding a glass of orange juice which meant she was driving. Trying out her four-by-four no doubt.

'Have you had any ideas?' he asked her, shouting above the din. 'I mean about the phone calls, about someone who might bear a grudge?'

'None. I honestly can't think of anyone, which is why I'm assuming it's kids.'

But kids didn't string up cats. Not unless they wanted to be psychopaths when they grew up.

'What about you?' she asked. 'Anything new come up?'

'Nothing.' And wasn't that the truth? 'What I can't understand is how anyone could be in Kelton Bridge, carrying a bloody axe of all things, without the whole damn village knowing about it.'

'A backpack? Lots of people walk in the hills. No one would think twice if they saw someone in walking gear. Or a four-by-four,' she added. 'Marvellous vehicles. You can fit everything in the back and get from A to B in no time.'

Max smiled at that. 'I take it you're still impressed with your purchase then?'

'I love it. I don't know why I didn't get one years ago.'

They were joined by Clive White and, immediately, Max sensed the tension in the air. Clive and Jill nodded at each other, and mumbled quick greetings. Much like two boxers might face each other in the ring.

Like everyone else, Clive looked as if he'd had a few drinks before Max arrived. That was his choice, though. Sadly. It grieved Max to think of good coppers idling away their time at home when they could be of use out in the field. And,

72

despite what Jill thought, Clive was a damn good copper.

'How long till you're back with us?' Max asked him.

'Not long I hope. You'll have to ask Jill,' he added, winking at her.

Max saw the way her lips tightened at that wink.

'You're up for review in six weeks,' she reminded him.

'Six weeks?' Max couldn't believe it. Hell's teeth, that was ridiculous. Clive was as fit as any of them. That was the trouble with this culture of counselling. Why people couldn't be allowed to get on with the job, he had no idea.

But he wasn't having another row with Jill about that. It was ridiculous, but unfortunately, it was her decision.

''Fraid so,' Clive said. 'And it can't pass quickly enough. I'm bored rigid. I've practically decorated the whole house.'

Clive was young and energetic, a keen, enthusiastic copper. He'd been tailing a stolen car that had mounted the pavement and killed a pedestrian. While Max acknowledged that it was a tragedy no one should have to witness, he couldn't understand that keeping Clive away from a job he loved was beneficial to anyone.

'Six weeks is nothing,' Jill was saying. 'And just think, you'll be at home for Christmas.'

'Oh, great.' Clive groaned with laughter. 'If there's one thing I hate, it's Christmas.'

'Me, too,' Max said. 'A total waste of time and money.'

'Bah humbug to both of you then,' Jill put in. 'I won't invite either of you to my Christmas party.'

'You having a party?' It was the first Max had heard about it.

'I might.'

The barmaid had finally noticed Max. 'A pint of Black Sheep, please. Jill? Clive?'

'I'll have a pint of the same, please,' Clive said.

Max supposed the bloke had nothing better to do than drink away the time. If they weren't careful he'd go from good copper to dypso.

'Jill?'

'No, thanks. I only came to say hello so I'll be off soon.'

As soon as Clive had his drink in his hand, he went off to catch up with his friends.

Jill gave Max a guarded look, no doubt daring him to comment on her decision to keep Clive away from the job. Max knew he should keep quiet, but–

'I really can't see the need to keep him off work for another six weeks. We're short of officers as it is.'

'I'm not arguing with you, Max. I believe he's unfit for work and that's that.'

'He seems all right to me.' And how anyone could decide one way or the other after showing him a few ink blobs, or whatever it was they did, Max had no idea.

'At least he seems more cheerful,' Jill agreed, watching Clive laughing with fellow officers on the far side of the room. 'Usually, I can't get two words out of him.'

Max was about to comment on that, but then

he spotted another familiar figure.

'Don't look now, and whatever you do don't make eye contact, but Adam Smith is sitting in the corner.'

'You and your shadow, eh?'

Max was halfway down his pint when Smith, swaying slightly, made his way to the bar to stand beside Max.

'You'll be busy looking for this girl's killer then.' His bloodshot eyes were sinking into his skull. The weight was falling off him. 'That's it, isn't it? My Yasmin has been forgotten. Case closed.'

'Not at all, Mr Smith. The case won't be closed until your daughter has been found. I give you my word on that.'

'Your word? What good's that, eh? You told me you'd find her. It's been four months now. Four months!'

'I know.' Max also knew that if one of his boys was missing, he'd be frantic, too. In fact, he'd be doing exactly what Adam Smith was doing, walking the streets day in, day out. 'Believe me, we're doing everything we can to find Yasmin.'

'No you're not. You're looking for the bloke who killed that girl. And what use was she to the world, that's what I want to know? My Yasmin has her whole future ahead of her. She's bright, clever. She'll make something of herself. Not that other girl. She was a drug addict, that's what it said in tonight's paper. Who cares if she lives or dies, eh?'

'We're doing all we can to find your daughter.' His heart went out to Smith though. He wondered if Smith, too, was wondering if the killer of

Lauren Cole had known his daughter. 'Can I buy you a drink?'

'No, you bloody well can't!' Smith spat on the ground at Max's feet. 'You enjoy your little party. I just hope you can damn well sleep at night because I can't!'

It didn't do to shout at senior officers in this place and a couple of PCs soon had Smith by the arm.

'Leave him,' Max said.

Smith freed himself from the officers' grasp and stormed out of the pub.

'He's right,' Max said when he and Jill were alone again. 'What right do I have to stand here drinking a pint when his daughter's missing?'

'Every right in the world,' she replied easily. 'Yes, it's awful for him and yes, we'd all be wrecks in the same situation, but you can only do your job, Max. And you can't do that twenty-four hours a day.' She looked at him. '*Are* you sleeping?'

'You should know.' But last night, she'd been asleep within seconds and Max had tossed and turned beside her. 'If you've forgotten, you can come back to my place and find out.'

'Ha.'

'OK, I'll come back to yours,' he suggested.

'I thought you were supposed to be with your kids tonight.'

'I am.' As much as the idea appealed, he couldn't spend another night at Jill's. 'And I will be soon. Come with me.'

'I can't. In any case, I want an early night.' She emptied her glass and put it on the bar. 'Be seeing you, Max.'

76

Max bought himself another pint, spent twenty minutes chatting to various people, then decided to leave them to it. And God help them if there was even a whiff of a hangover at the morning's briefing.

After trudging through freezing slush to his car, he began the drive home. He was turning into Bailey Street when he saw the unmistakable figure of Adam Smith heading towards the bridge over the canal. It was a common meeting place for drunks, druggies and prostitutes. Smith's head was turning from left to right, scanning every doorway, and his hands were deep in the pockets of a jacket that offered little resistance to the temperature.

Smith rarely slept and, by the look of him, rarely ate. He'd given up his job as a lorry driver and spent every minute of every day searching for his daughter.

Max wondered what he'd do if he got home to find that Harry or Ben was missing. It was every parent's nightmare and simply didn't bear thinking about.

Linda's last words to him had been, 'Take good care of my boys, Max.'

He could remember feeling the weight of that responsibility at Linda's funeral when he'd said a final goodbye to his wife.

His marriage had been over long before then, though. He and Linda had shared the same house, and the same bed, and would probably have stayed together for the sake of the boys, but it had been over. They'd both known it.

He only remembered two things from the

funeral. One was the sheer panic of trying to raise two boys on his own. The other had been the rain. It had been relentless as he and his sons had stood beside that sodden, miserable grave, oblivious to the dozens of mourners around them. Undertakers had fussed around with huge, black umbrellas but he and the boys had preferred the rain.

Max pushed the memories away and concentrated on the murder of Lauren Cole.

Motive. He needed to concentrate on motive. Why would anyone want her dead?

Max had an uneasy feeling about it all. Was the person who chose an axe as a murder weapon the same person who enjoyed stringing up cats?

He suddenly slapped the steering wheel.

Percy Jacobs!

Seven years ago, Bill Jacobs had been sentenced to life imprisonment for the vicious rape and murder of a teenager. Jill's profile had helped to bring about an arrest.

His brother, Percy, had always, despite hard evidence and a confession, protested Bill's innocence. If anyone bore Jill, or the force in general, a grudge, it was Percy Jacobs. And Max would bet his life that the grudge was weighing even heavier now that Bill had passed away. He'd died in prison two weeks ago.

Percy was a nasty piece of work, too. No better than his brother, he'd been detained at Her Majesty's pleasure for rape.

Perhaps it was time to pay him a visit.

Chapter Eight

When Jill arrived at headquarters the following morning, she went straight to the coffee machine. If she'd known Clive White would be standing there, a clipboard under his arm as he took a full plastic cup from the dispenser, she would have given it a miss.

'Hi, Jill. I wanted to buy you a drink last night, but you'd already left.'

'I was driving so I didn't stay long.'

'No hangover for you then?'

'Nope. I just need a coffee to warm me up a bit. Why? Are people feeling a bit the worse for wear after last night's session?'

'A few are. The boss won't be pleased.'

He certainly wouldn't.

'So what are you doing here, Clive?'

Her tone was sharper than she'd intended, but seeing him at every turn was beginning to annoy her.

'Don't worry, I'm not working.' He thrust the clipboard at her. 'You remember last year I organized the New Year Run? I'm doing it again this year.'

'Really?' And now she felt guilty, which was absurd. 'Good for you.'

But she felt guilty every time she saw him, as if she'd stolen a favourite toy from a child, and that was ludicrous. She should have more confidence in herself. She'd deemed him unfit to continue in his job, and that should be the end of it.

'Any chance of some sponsorship?' he asked. 'I'm raising funds for the hospice, the same as last year.'

'Yes, of course.'

She took the clipboard from him, signed her name and promised a more than generous donation if he completed the run. She was sure he would. He found it difficult to accept failure.

'So are you out training in this weather?' she asked.

'I'm trying to. It'll either get me very fit or kill me.'

She smiled at that. 'Rather you than me.'

'Jill–' He hugged the clipboard to him, and clutched his hot drink tightly. 'About the time–'

'Let's forget it, shall we?'

She knew exactly what he was referring to, and she really didn't want to talk about it.

'I just want to say sorry.' He shuffled his feet. 'I was horrified to be suspended from duty and I was angry. I shouldn't have taken it out on you, though, and I'm sorry about that.'

She'd known an apology was coming, but the fact that he sounded sincere surprised her.

They'd bumped into each other in the Green Man, the day she'd deemed him unfit to work. He'd lost his temper with her, calling her a power-crazed shrink among other things.

'Forget it, Clive. In the same situation, I would have been angry, too. But you did witness a terrible tragedy. Not only were you chasing a suspect, you had to try and save the life of an innocent bystander.'

And watch the young man die as they waited for the ambulance.

'Anyone would struggle to cope with that,' she went on, 'and I'm sure some time away from the job will do you good.'

'But that's just it. I'm not struggling. These things happen and I can accept that.'

In other words, he was pushing it from his mind and that wasn't healthy.

'You'll soon be back with us. And probably wishing you were still at home,' she added with a dry smile. 'It's manic here right now.'

'I can imagine. Trust me to be stuck at home when there's a good juicy murder, eh?'

The words sounded callous, but he wouldn't be the only officer thinking that way. Clive was ambitious. He was young, too. He would have seen this as a chance to shine in front of superior officers. To him, a murder investigation would represent promotion.

'There will be others, Clive.'

'Yeah. Anyway, I'm sorry about – well, you know. And thanks for the sponsorship. I'm hoping to beat last year's effort. I raised just over three grand then.'

'I remember. Good luck.'

'Thanks. And thanks for being so understanding. I'm really sorry.' He spotted a couple of officers heading towards the main reception. 'I spy more sponsorship. See you, Jill.'

'See you.'

As she waited for her plastic cup to fill, she watched him laughing with the two PCs. They wrote on his clipboard so she guessed he'd managed to get more sponsorship.

She carried her coffee to her office, and saw that a large note had been stuck to her desk. 'Marshall in rm 3. Give me a buzz when you're ready.'

Max would have to wait while she drank her coffee and checked her email.

She was pleased they'd found Ricky Marshall, but why interview room three? It was easily the coldest place in the building and competition was stiff for that particular accolade.

Fifteen minutes later, she phoned Max. 'You've found Ricky Marshall then? How did you manage that?'

'He's well known. Are you ready for a chat with him?'

'I can be.'

Jill kept a spare jumper in her office for emergencies such as this and, before going to meet Max, she put it on. She loathed being cold. It slowed her thought processes.

'Why,' she demanded of Max as they headed along the corridor towards it, 'is the room never used in the summer and yet seems to be first choice in winter?'

'The others have been painted,' he explained, 'and we can't subject people to fumes. Had I known we'd want you along, I'd have told you to wear your thermals.'

'Who says I'm not?'

She pushed open the door, saw Ricky Marshall and had to bite back a laugh. Lauren's flatmate Jo had said she thought Ricky had his teeth done by his barber and his hair done by his dentist. A more apt description of anyone it would be difficult to find.

She looked at Max and saw the same amusement in his eyes.

They sat opposite Marshall and went through the usual performance of switching on the equipment, informing him he was being recorded and introducing themselves.

It became clear that he enjoyed being under the spotlight. As he had several previous convictions for theft, he was well used to the procedure.

'When did you last see Lauren Cole?' Max asked him.

'I've already told you.'

'Then tell me again.'

'A couple of weeks ago.'

'Where?'

'Can't remember. Some pub or other, I expect.'

'OK, let's start at the beginning,' Jill suggested. 'Where did you first meet her? Can you manage to remember that?'

'Yeah. It was at the Commercial.'

Jill had never been inside, but she knew the place by reputation. It was an ugly, sprawling town centre pub where fights broke out on a regular basis. Drinks were cheap so it attracted a young crowd.

'When was that?' she asked him and he shrugged.

'About six weeks ago.'

'Tell us about it. She was there with friends, yes? You got talking?'

'No.' He had a sneering smile that made Jill long to slap him. 'She was there on her own. She wasn't bad looking, and there was nowt better in, so I went up to her.'

Nowt better in? Jill could have howled with laughter. He thought he was a gift to the female species. He believed he'd done Lauren Cole a favour.

'She was very attractive,' she corrected him, 'and you're trying to tell us that you were the best she could do? I find that hard to believe. Let's face it, Ricky, you haven't been well blessed in the looks department, have you?'

He didn't answer, just stared back at her, and Jill waited for the insult that she felt sure was coming. But either he couldn't think of anything suitable, or he couldn't be bothered.

'So, having gone to chat her up, did you wine her and dine her? Or is a quick shag in the bogs more your style?' Jill leaned back in her chair to wait for his answer. Often, when she reduced conversation to the opposition's level, they talked. Ricky was the exception; he didn't say a word.

'Lauren was a bit classy, wasn't she?' she pushed on. 'She came from a good family. So what was she doing with you? Did she fancy a bit of rough, Ricky?'

No answer.

'It didn't last long, though, did it? And you didn't get to have sex with her, did you?'

'I did!'

'Liar,' Jill scoffed.

'What do you know about it?'

'I know you didn't sleep with her. You called her a prick tease. You thought you were on a promise but she didn't deliver, did she?'

'So what?'

'So the fact that you were seen hammering on her door and calling her names makes you a suspect in a murder investigation,' Max informed him.

'You what?'

Gone was the cocky young man who enjoyed being the centre of attention. In his place was someone who was suddenly looking very nervous.

'Now, look, that's nowt to do with me. You know that. Aw, come on, that's bloody daft.'

'Is it?' Max asked. 'Why?'

Jill brought to mind photos of the dead girl. It had been a brutal killing, but swift. Someone had lifted that axe and brought it down right through her skull.

'Why the hell would I kill her?' Marshall asked urgently. 'I told you, I saw her a fortnight ago and that was it. I haven't seen her since.'

'You'd kill her for revenge,' Jill said. 'You thought you were guaranteed great sex and she didn't deliver. You thought you'd teach her a lesson.'

'Bollocks! Christ, she reckoned everyone fancied the tits off her. Maybe it was one of them did it to her.'

'Like who?' Max asked.

'Well, I don't know, do I? Everyone. She reckoned everyone she spoke to fancied her.'

'So you said. Give us an example, Ricky.'

'There was her landlord for a start. She reckoned he only called in to chat her up.'

Lauren's landlord was overweight, pushing sixty and, more important, gay. He'd be more likely to go for Marshall than Lauren.

'Who else?' Max asked.

'I don't know.'

'You're not doing very well, are you?' Jill said.

'Wait. There was another bloke she saw when she walked that dog of hers. He gave her the creeps, she said, but he fancied her, too.'

'Another bloke? That narrows it down a lot,' Max said.

'She sometimes saw him when she was taking the dog for a walk. She reckoned he was old, about fifty probably. Called him a dirty old man. Said he wore a funny grey hat, like his mum had knitted it for him.'

'Where did she see him?'

'I don't know.'

'Where did she walk her dog?' Jill asked.

'I don't know. I've told you, I don't know.'

'You must have some idea,' Max insisted.

'Sometimes she walked the dog through town. Sometimes she drove out to Kelton Bridge and walked the dog over the hills there.'

'So?'

'So where did she see this man?'

'I don't know,' Ricky said again. 'All I know is that he used to chat her up. Or so she said. And he had a dog.'

'What sort of dog?' Max wanted to know.

'I don't know. Christ, I wasn't interested. If I'd took an interest in every bloke she claimed fancied her, I'd have a bloody degree in it!'

'She loved that dog of hers,' Jill said, 'and the dog loved to go for walks. Now, given this big romance you had going with her, I'm surprised she didn't invite you along when she took Charlie out.'

'She did,' he boasted. 'I went three or four

86

times. We went into Burnley and walked round Towneley Park.'

'And you didn't see any men in grey hats?' Max asked.

'No. We saw no one. Oh yeah, once we saw a woman with two little yappy dogs. Lauren said hello to her.'

Jill couldn't understand what had attracted Lauren Cole to Marshall in the first place. Assuming she'd been looking for thrills and excitement, perhaps his lack of respect for authority had appealed. If she'd been after scintillating conversation, however, she must have been sorely disappointed.

'What about Josh?' Jill asked. 'Does the name ring a bell?'

'No.'

'Really? I'm surprised. He was always on the phone to her apparently,' Jill informed him. 'She must have mentioned him to you.'

'No.'

'Perhaps that's why she didn't want sex with you,' Jill said. 'Perhaps the lucky Josh was wearing her out.'

'Never heard of him.'

'You used to phone Lauren presumably?' Max asked.

'Course I did.'

'What number did you have for her?'

'You what?'

'Tell me Lauren's phone number.'

Marshall's phone was clipped to his belt and he switched it on.

'I've probably deleted it,' he muttered, scrolling

87

through a list of contacts. 'No, I haven't. There it is.'

He thrust his phone at Max.

'Thanks.'

Max, too, scrolled through the list of contacts.

'Tell you what,' he said pleasantly, 'we'll leave you alone for an hour or so and you can have a little think. Maybe you'll remember something else. Hey, I'll even get someone to bring you a cup of tea.'

'What about my phone?'

'You'll get it back. Later.'

Jill's feet were numb and she was more than happy to end the interview.

'What did you think?' Max asked when they were out of the room.

'I think he's an obnoxious little shit,' she said.

'Agreed.'

'But I don't think he knows anything more than he's told us. He doesn't seem bright enough to lie.'

'He doesn't seem bright enough to breathe. Still, it'll do him good to sit in there and freeze. I'll get this phone looked at and send someone out to Towneley Park with Lauren's photo.'

'In that case, I'll go back to my nice warm office.'

'Is it warm?'

'It is now I've pinched a heater from CID.'

Bellingham's Turf Accountant Limited was Kelton Bridge's most recent acquisition and Jill loved it. It was different to any other book-maker's she'd ever been inside. For one thing, it was clean. Bert and his wife Stella had recently sold a thriving business in Cornwall and moved to the village to retire. It was Bert who couldn't idle away his days and Stella who was responsible for the two vases of fresh scented flowers and the tasteful Christmas decorations, something Jill had never seen in a bookie's before.

Over the years, she'd been in some disreputable bookmaker's, the worst in Manchester where the owner hadn't seemed to care that his dog, a Rottweiler, kept its teeth permanently bared. Here the 'bookie's dog' was a Yorkshire terrier called Minty who had a yellow ribbon in her hair and a welcome for everyone.

Three large television screens above the counter were loud enough to be heard, but not too intrusive and half a dozen people were watching them. Jill exchanged pleasantries with them, but she knew they were humouring her. As far as they were concerned, a female couldn't be expected to know one end of a horse from another.

To take her mind off crank callers last night, she'd studied form, chosen six promising horses and called in on her way to headquarters this morning to place her bets. She had an account with William Hill, but phoning bets through wasn't so much fun. This way, she could collect her winnings in person.

From the age of about five, when she'd hung about outside the bookie's in Liverpool, waiting for her dad to place his bets or watch an important race, she'd been fascinated by the places. People coming out of the door, letting clouds of smoke out with them, had either been in high spirits, sometimes happy enough to give her a coin for sweets, or in foul moods and inventing stories for their wives as to where that week's wages had gone.

Her mother had been horrified to learn that Jill had been within a hundred yards of a book-maker's.

'She hasn't been inside,' her dad had protested.

'She's been close enough. What sort of example is that to set the girl? Don't you dare take her anywhere near those places again!'

In future, when Jill had been hanging around waiting for her dad, peering in through the smoke-grimed windows, they'd kept it as their own secret. Then, when she'd been a few years older, probably about eleven, her dad had given her a couple of pounds and she'd known the thrill of choosing a horse and willing it to romp to the finishing post.

'I'm surprised you're not snowed in along the lane,' Bert greeted her.

'Some of us have sensible vehicles for the job,' she replied with a smug smile.

'Roll on summer, I say,' he muttered. 'You know where you are then. You know it'll be raining from morning till night.'

'Well, yes.' She laughed at that.

'You'll be here to collect your winnings then,' Bert guessed, shaking his head. 'I keep telling you, you're not from these shores. You've got the luck of the Irish.'

'It's not luck, Bert. It's sheer skill.'

As he counted out her money, over three hundred pounds, Jill wondered why cash from a bookie was so much more exciting than a salary.

She was leaving at the same time as Tom Canter and they stood in the doorway for a few minutes chatting about the weather and the day's racing.

'I don't suppose they've found the bloke who murdered that poor girl yet?' Tom said as they walked beneath the streetlights towards Jill's car.

'Not yet, no.'

'What a bloody terrible thing to happen. And her only twenty. There's some wrong buggers in this world and that's a fact.'

'You're right there, Tom.'

'Her photo were in this evening's paper,' he went on, 'and do you know, I'm sure I've seen her about. Can't think where though.'

'It's possible. She used to walk her dog up the hill quite a lot. A small white dog she had. Perhaps you saw her there.'

'I might have.'

Tom had farmed in Kelton Bridge all his life. He was in his late seventies, a forthright man who didn't suffer fools gladly and who believed in speaking his mind. Yet now, he looked uncertain.

'It annoys me when I can't remember stuff, but yes, I'm sure I've seen her before.'

'If you remember, Tom, will you let me know? Or call the police about it?'

'I will. Yes, of course I will. I expect they'll be getting round to calling on me soon. I hear they're speaking to everyone in the village. They haven't got to me yet, but I'm so far off the beaten track, they might not bother.'

He could be right. Tom lived a couple of miles out of the village, and while his Land Rover might get through to his farm easily enough, the patrol cars would struggle.

'I see Clough's Shelter is awash with floral tributes,' Tom said. 'I've never seen the point in that. They'll just rot in the snow.'

'People like to express their sympathy. It makes them feel better.'

'Oh, I know that. But it's all a bit public for my liking. A simple note to her family would be better in my view.'

Jill knew exactly what he meant. She also knew that many of the tributes at the shelter had been left by people who hadn't known Lauren or her family.

'It's a funny old world,' Tom said. 'Ah, well, be seeing you, Jill. And if I remember where I saw that young girl, I'll let you know.'

Chapter Nine

Max was surprised to see DS Fletcher still at his desk at eight o'clock that evening.

'Haven't you got a home to go to, Fletch?'

Fletch, his mouth too full of bacon sandwich to allow speech, made the sign of the cross, as if he was warding off vampires.

'Ah.' Max understood immediately. 'The mother-in-law?'

Nodding, Fletch swallowed his food. 'Till after Christmas. I'll be volunteering for any overtime going.'

Max had been unfortunate enough to meet

Fletch's mother-in-law. She'd had high hopes for her daughter, hopes that featured neurosurgeons and rocket scientists. She'd never recovered from watching her daughter marry a copper and she made sure Fletch knew that.

'I'm about to do a spot of unpaid overtime myself,' Max told him. 'Strictly off the record.'

'Oh?'

Max perched on a small gap on the edge of Fletch's cluttered desk. 'You remember Bill Jacobs, don't you?'

'I certainly do. Vicious rapist. Killer. Died a couple of weeks back.'

'That's him. How about his brother? Remember him?'

'I'm not likely to forget. The toerag broke one of my ribs.' Grunting at the remembered injustice, Fletch took another bite of his sandwich.

'So he did. I'd forgotten that.'

When Bill had appeared in court, his brother Percy had mounted a vigil outside the building. Fletch had arrested him, and suffered a broken rib for his trouble.

'It's Percy I'm off to visit,' Max said. 'Fancy coming along?'

'Count me in.' Fletch swallowed the last of his sandwich, brushed crumbs from trousers to floor, and got to his feet. 'What do you want with him?' he asked, grabbing his jacket.

'Jill's had some nuisance phone calls,' Max explained as they headed for the car park. 'A cat was hanged by her front door, too.'

'What?'

'Not one of hers, thank God. A stray she'd been

93

looking after.'

'She hasn't mentioned anything.'

'She's trying to convince herself it's just kids messing around. But kids don't hang cats. Or most kids don't. Besides,' he added, taking his car keys from his pocket, 'since she's done this Thai boxing thing, she thinks she can take on the world.'

Fletch grinned. 'I heard about that. What exactly is Thai boxing anyway?'

'Bloody ridiculous. I gather it's like normal boxing, but instead of just fists, you can use hands, shins, elbows and knees.'

'I bet they can scream and bite at the same time. Bloody hell, women have been doing that for years,' Fletch scoffed, and Max supposed he had a point.

They got in the car, and Max turned the heater on full.

'She looks good on it though,' Fletch said as he fastened his seat belt.

She did. Her body was looking very toned which, according to Jill, was the main purpose of the exercise. The self-defence aspect was simply a bonus.

'She has to do something to counteract all the junk food she eats. Woman can only live on Mars bars alone for so long, Fletch. Her diet's worse than yours.'

'It probably is actually,' he agreed.

There were roadworks a couple of hundred yards from headquarters and, even at this time, there was a queue waiting for the temporary lights to change to green. During the day, half a dozen men leaned on the barriers and stared at an impressive hole they'd made. At this time of night, there was no one in sight.

'So you reckon Percy Jacobs has been hanging cats?' Fletch asked.

'I don't know. I'm trying to think of someone who might bear Jill a grudge, and his opinion of anyone connected with the force is pretty low. Despite everything, he always maintained that brother of his was innocent. Now that Bill's dead, maybe he's out for revenge.'

'What's he been up to lately?'

'Nothing that we know about. Mr Law Abiding.'

'Sick pervo,' Fletch muttered.

It took less than fifteen minutes to get to the place Percy Jacobs called home. It was a concrete block of flats on the southern side of Harrington. The residents' car park could have passed for a scrap yard. Rusting heaps of all descriptions were abandoned there.

Half a dozen youths were messing around looking for trouble. They'd have no problem finding it.

Max got out of the car and approached them.

'I'll give you a fiver if my car's still here, untouched, when I come out.'

'Make it a tenner,' one suggested.

'A fiver or a belt round the ear. Your choice.'

'OK,' he agreed, somewhat grudgingly.

With the car as safe as it could be, Max and Fletch crossed the car park to the entrance lobby, trying not to inhale once they reached the stairwell. A hand-penned note taped over the button for the lift read: *Not working*. It looked as if it

95

hadn't worked for a decade.

'He's on the fifth floor,' Max said, and Fletch groaned.

Once away from the lobby, the stench of urine wasn't so bad and the artist with the spray can telling them that Daz was a great shag and Maria had big tits hadn't bothered to go further than the third floor.

'Number fifty-seven,' Max said as, breathless, they arrived on the fifth floor.

The door's flaking paint was blue. A small, square pane of glass was cracked. The handle was loose.

'How the other half live, eh?' Fletch said.

Max hammered on the door.

A television could be heard blaring out – an advertisement for washing powder which would go right over Jacobs' head – so Max knocked again, harder this time.

Eventually, a shuffling sound was heard and a muttered, 'Hold your horses, can't you?'

The door opened five inches, enough for Max to get his foot in the gap, and Percy was peering out at them.

Recognition was almost instant. 'It's you, is it? I thought there was a strong smell of bacon round here.'

It was a couple of years since Max had seen Jacobs, but he hadn't improved with age. A grubby sweatshirt was stretched over his belly and his bald head was covered with beads of sweat. A gold hoop earring dangled from one ear and he wore a thick gold chain around his neck. He was wearing black, baggy tracksuit bottoms and black socks.

'There's a strong smell, Percy, but it's not bacon,' Max told him. 'Mind if we come in for a word?'

'Yeah, I do mind. Got a warrant, have you?'

'Don't need one.' Max put his weight behind the door and, as Percy stepped back, Max almost landed on top of him. 'This is a social call,' he explained when they'd both recovered.

'You can't come barging in here!'

'That's where you're wrong, Percy. We're off duty so we can do exactly as we like.'

Without waiting for an invite, Max and Fletch walked into the sitting room. A remote control sat on the sofa, but it was so dirty that Max switched off the television at the socket.

'That's better. We can hear ourselves think now.'

The place was a mess. An overflowing ashtray and a couple of well-read porn mags shared the low coffee table with empty beer cans.

'Cleaner's day off is it, Percy?' Max asked him.

'I don't clean up for pigs like you. Tell me what you want and then bugger off.'

'What I want,' Max said, 'is to know the last time you visited Kelton Bridge.'

'Eh?' Percy looked genuinely surprised. 'What the bleeding 'ell would I go there for? A game of friggin' bowls?'

'You tell me.'

'You what?'

'Tell me the last time you visited Kelton Bridge,' Max insisted.

So far, Fletch hadn't said a word. He was standing in the centre of the room, arms folded across his chest as if he had to keep them that way to

97

stop them flying out and punching Jacobs in the mouth. Max knew how he felt.

'Can't remember,' Jacobs said.

'Try,' Max suggested.

'Perhaps we could refresh your memory,' Fletch said pleasantly, and Max noticed how he rubbed his mended rib.

'I've not been there for years,' Jacobs said. 'Why the hell would I? There's nowt there for me. Nowt there for anyone.'

'So what have you been doing with yourself lately?' Max asked.

'Grieving if you must know.'

'Ah yes, poor Bill. That was a surprise, wasn't it? I always thought that only the good died young. What was he? Fifty?'

'Forty-nine. And you can say what you like about him. I know what I know.'

'And we know what the evidence showed,' Fletch said. 'Not to mention the fact that he confessed.'

'Yeah, when you buggers had beaten it out of him.'

'It was all recorded, Percy,' Max reminded him. 'Anyway, that's old news. I'm more interested in your current activities. I especially want to know when you were last in Kelton Bridge.'

'I've told you–' His expression changed. 'Hey, that bird who got done in was found there.'

'As bright as ever, Percy. What do you know about that?'

'Only what I heard on the telly. Here, you're not thinking I had anything to do with that, are you? Christ, I never even heard of her.' His top

98

lip was covered in sweat and he wiped it away with his arm. 'You can't fit that one on me. I know you bloody lot. You'd beat a confession out of any bugger you fancied.'

Max wandered to the window and peered through the filthy glass to the dimly lit car park below. His car was still there. It still had four wheels, too.

He turned round, and was about to ask Percy about Jill, when a fat ginger cat ambled into the room.

Percy picked it up and the animal purred like a vacuum cleaner.

'Like animals, do you?' Fletch asked, taking the words out of Max's mouth.

'Better than people.'

'A friend of mine has three cats,' Max said, scuffing the dingy carpet with his foot. 'She did have four, but one was murdered.'

'Murdered? A cat?'

'Yup. It was hanged.'

'What sort of sick bastard would do that?'

'The same sort of sick bastard who'd rape young women, I suppose.'

Percy, the cat tight in his arms, stepped forward until he was inches from Max's face.

'It wasn't rape. She was asking for it.'

'Begging for your body, Percy? Then crying rape? Ending up in A&E? I don't think so.'

'Bitch!'

'Do you remember Jill Kennedy?' Max asked.

'I remember her. Smells of pig, like you lot. She was on the telly the other night. Full of herself.'

Jill had been on a programme to promote the

self-help books she wrote.

'I didn't know that,' Max lied. 'What was she doing on the telly?'

'Saying how great she was. Saying everyone should buy her books.'

'You watching book programmes, Percy? I wouldn't have thought that was quite your thing.'

'There was nowt else on.'

'Have you seen her lately?'

'Who? That Kennedy woman? No.'

Percy was still stroking the cat. It was a well-fed animal and more than content to lie in Percy's arms.

'Where were you at the weekend?' Fletch asked him.

'Clitheroe.'

'Doing what?'

'Camping. I have a tent and go there a lot, mostly weekends.'

'At this time of year?' Max scoffed.

'Any time of year.'

'What do you do with your cat?'

He looked at Max as if he were raving. 'Take her with me, of course. What do you think I do with her?'

Max wasn't a cat person. Dogs, yes. Cats, no. He couldn't see the sense in them. All they did was bring dead things into the house. He very much doubted, however, that anyone daft enough to take a cat camping for the weekend would hang one as an act of revenge.

'Any witnesses?' he asked Percy.

'Plenty. They all know me there. And they've got cameras on the gates. The bloody tents would go walkabout if they didn't.'

'Have you got the address for this campsite?' Fletch asked.

'I've got their leaflet.' Still holding the cat, he went to the kitchen and came back with a leaflet giving prices and details of the facilities for the campsite.

'We'll get it checked,' Fletch told him, adding a grim, 'and if we find out you've been telling porkies, Jacobs, I'll be back in person to remind you about that busted rib you gave me, OK?'

'Yes, well...'

They left Percy and his cat, and made the long descent to the car park.

'I don't think he's your man,' Fletch said.

'Me neither. Pity.'

So who the hell was hanging cats? And why?

'You said a tenner,' the young lad told him when they reached Max's car.

'I said a fiver or a belt round the ear. So, which will it be?'

The lad stuck his hand out and Max put a five-pound note in it.

'You a copper?' the lad asked.

'I am. So watch it.'

'Thought I could smell pig,' he muttered.

'And I think I can smell illegal substances,' Max retorted. 'Any ideas?'

'Nope.' The kid shuffled off.

'What a place,' Fletch muttered once they were in the car.

It was the sort of place that made Max shudder. He always experienced a sense of there but for the Grace of God. Birth was a lottery. You could either be born to decent, hard-working parents, or you could be born into a hell-hole like this. If it was the latter, your fate was sealed.

'Even the mother-in-law should look appealing now,' he said, and Fletch groaned.

'I've been put on a diet, too,' he complained, but then, brightening, added, 'Still, the morning briefing's nice and early. I'll stop for a decent breakfast on my way in.'

Mention of the briefing brought with it a reminder of just how little they'd come up with. The identity of Lauren Cole's killer remained a complete mystery.

The whereabouts of Yasmin Smith was another puzzle. Max hoped to God that, while her father was tramping the streets, searching every dark corner, she wasn't lying in the snow with an axe in her head.

Chapter Ten

When Jill's bedside phone rang out, she was instantly awake. The clock was reading 2.14 a.m. No prizes for guessing who was calling then.

She grabbed the instrument, all set to tell her caller that middle-of-the-night chats weren't an option.

'So you've sent your boyfriend running to Percy Jacobs?' the voice said. 'A waste of time, sweetheart. I'm out to get you.' The connection was cut mid-laugh.

Even if she'd been given the opportunity to speak, Jill couldn't have come up with anything suitable. She was too taken aback.

Percy Jacobs? The name sounded familiar but she couldn't place it.

She was about to settle down again when it clicked into place. Percy Jacobs was brother to Bill Jacobs, a vicious killer, a man she'd helped the police bring to justice. From what she remembered, Percy wasn't much better. He'd spent time behind bars for something, she was sure of it.

Had Max really visited Jacobs? Surely not. He would have told her. More important, if he had, how did her crank caller know about it?

She wasn't the only one to resent early morning phone calls. Sam had been sleeping peacefully on her bed. Now, he was restless and pawing at the cover.

Jill got out of bed, put on a shirt and went downstairs. Rabble was curled up on the kitchen chair and didn't even look up. Tojo was nudging the cat flap and trying to figure out why it wasn't opening.

This was madness. She shouldn't be deprived of sleep, and her cats shouldn't be confined to the cottage just because some tosser wanted to play games with her.

She paced around her kitchen, anger mounting with every step. Three o'clock came and went. Then four o'clock.

Banishing all thoughts of going back to bed, she showered, dressed and then, only when she could supervise them, let out the cats. Breakfast consisted of a strong coffee and four chocolate biscuits which she ate while sitting in the chair by the window. It gave her a chance to watch the cats playing in the snow. It was still thick, offering a scene from a Christmas card, but it was expected to thaw later.

With the cats locked in again, she promised to return at lunchtime and then set off for headquarters.

She was there soon after seven o'clock and realized there were advantages to that, the main one being that the car park was almost empty and she could grab a space at the back. That way, she didn't run the risk of getting blocked in.

Guessing Max would be in early, she went straight to his office. He was staring at his computer, tapping a pen against his teeth.

'Percy Jacobs,' she said, getting straight to the point.

'Good morning, my love. Wonderful to see you, too.'

'Percy Jacobs,' she said again. 'What's going on, Max?'

'Fletch wasn't supposed to tell you.'

'He didn't. My friendly, early morning caller told me.'

'He did what?' The smile had gone. 'I had a chat with Jacobs, that's all. Fletch came with me, but he knew it was strictly off the record. So how the hell...? Either we were followed by your man or Jacobs tipped him off.'

Both options were unsettling to say the least.

'What did he say?' Max asked.

'He said, "So you've sent your boyfriend run-

104

ning to Percy Jacobs." He said it was a waste of time because he was out to get me.'

'Who would know we were a couple?' Max mused, the pen tapping against his teeth again. He didn't wait for an answer. 'I don't like this, Jill. Why not spend the weekend at our place?'

She shrugged that off. 'I can take care of myself.'

'You can't even keep a door locked!' he retorted. 'And don't think a few boxing lessons will protect you from a psychopath with an axe.'

'My caller isn't the same person who killed Lauren Cole. He's far too much of a coward. And even if he is, he left his axe at the scene. He's unlikely to have a supply of the damn things.'

Jill wasn't worried exactly, but she had been a lot happier when she could dismiss the calls as the actions of children having a laugh. That was impossible now.

Max's phone rang and he snapped his name into it. He listened to his caller then, on a sigh, said, 'OK, thanks, show her in.'

As he was expecting company, Jill turned for the door.

'I could do with some moral support if you feel like hanging around for a few minutes,' he said. 'Vivienne Smith,' he added as explanation.

Before she had chance to agree or decline, a knock on the door preceded Mrs Smith's arrival. Jill, who had only seen her once before, was shocked by her appearance. Just as the weight had dropped off Adam Smith, so it had from his wife. She was shapeless, like a stick, whereas before she'd been curvy and attractive.

'You remember Jill Kennedy, don't you?'

Vivienne Smith nodded.

'Please, sit down, Mrs Smith.'

She sat, stiff and erect, a black leather handbag clasped tight on her lap.

'What can I do for you?' Max asked.

Jill heard the awkwardness in his voice. They all knew what he could do for her; find Yasmin. But that was too much to ask of anyone. Yasmin had left home for school one morning and vanished. She'd been last seen on CCTV waiting for the bus. A lot of people claimed to have seen her since, but no firm leads had come from those sightings.

'I'm sorry to bother you,' she said quietly, 'especially at this early hour, but I haven't been able to sleep. I want to know if you think the person who killed Lauren Cole has killed my Yasmin.' Her unwavering gaze demanded the truth.

'There's nothing to suggest that,' Max replied.

'But what do *you* think?' she insisted. 'What's *your* feeling?'

'I truly believe it's highly unlikely,' Max said.

'The profiles of the girls are very different, Mrs Smith,' Jill said gently. 'Lauren was twenty whereas Yasmin is only fifteen. Those five years are vital. The difference between twenty and twenty-five is nothing. The difference between fifteen, a schoolgirl, and twenty, a grown woman, is vast. The girls are totally different, too. Lauren was involved with...' she hesitated, trying to choose the right words – 'what parents would call a bad crowd, I suppose. She was taking drugs. Yasmin, as far as any of us are aware, has no such problems. She's a happy girl who enjoys school and wants to do well.'

'I see,' Vivienne Smith said at last. 'Tell me, was Lauren Cole – raped?'

'No,' Max said immediately.

She looked at Max for a long time.

'What would you do if your child was missing?' she asked him.

Jill's heart went out to the poor woman. Many years ago, one of Jill's cats had gone missing. She'd hunted everywhere, checked with all neighbours and asked them to look in sheds and garages. She'd put notices in local shops, on telegraph poles, in the vet's surgery – everywhere she could think of. Yet still she'd thought there must be more she could be doing. Every waking moment was spent wondering what she hadn't done and believing she'd failed her pet. After all that, the cat had wandered through the back door as if nothing had happened. Jill never did know where it had spent that fortnight. She couldn't even begin to imagine the heartache of having a child lost in the world.

'I would do all in my power to find that child,' Max said carefully. 'And believe me, Mrs Smith, we are doing all we can. We're following up every new lead, every possible sighting. We're keeping details in the media.'

'They've lost interest now, haven't they?' She spoke without emotion. 'They're just waiting for a body to be found.'

The awful thing was that she was right.

'What I wouldn't do,' Max went on, ignoring that, 'was give up hope. I would never give up hope. Never.'

'I won't do that,' she said. 'Adam won't either.' At mention of her husband's name, she flushed slightly. 'I'm sorry Adam's being a bit difficult at the moment, but it's so hard for him. He has to be doing something, you see. To look at him, you'd think it was killing him, but if you saw him at home, trying to sit still for five minutes, you'd know it was for the best. But I'm sorry he's behaving as he is. He doesn't blame you, he knows you're doing all you can. It's just very hard for him.'

'I understand,' Max assured her.

She rose to her feet.

'Thank you for your time. I'm sorry to have bothered you, especially at this hour.'

'You can call me anytime, you know that,' Max reminded her. 'And as soon as we hear anything, you'll be the first to know.'

'Thank you.' She nodded at them both, a despairing pain in her eyes as if they couldn't be expected to understand what she was going through. And she was right, they couldn't. 'Goodbye, both.'

When the door closed behind her, it was as if Vivienne Smith had left a coldness behind her.

'What *do* you think happened to Yasmin?' Jill asked Max.

'I think she met up with someone she found on the internet. She was – *is* – a naive, trusting, outgoing girl. We know she used chat rooms from her home computer. But all that seemed to stop about a year or more ago.'

'You think she was using another computer?'

Max nodded. 'But we've checked everywhere we can – the library, local internet cafes–' He sighed.

108

'If she'd had the chance, though, she would have let her parents know she was safe. She was – *is*,' he corrected himself again, 'that kind of girl.'

'God, what a bloody depressing job this is.'

His look was sharp. 'Watch it or we'll have to deem *you* unfit for the job.'

She smiled at that.

'Clive's made his peace,' she told him. 'Mind you, I suspect that was probably only because he wanted sponsorship from me. Still, at least he's not looking daggers every time he sees me so that's an improvement. It's worth the money for that alone.'

'He's a good copper. We could do with him right now.'

'No one's said he isn't a good copper. At the moment, he needs a rest from it, that's all.' She wasn't getting drawn on that one. 'Right, I have work to do...'

Jill was glad to get home to the peace of her cottage that night. Her day had been no better or worse than usual, but she knew that witnessing the pain on Vivienne Smith's face and then looking at photos of a brutal killing wasn't particularly healthy. Still, it was Friday night and she didn't have to think about work until Monday.

When the cats had been fed and logs were crackling cheerfully in the stove, she curled up on the sofa, picked up the phone and called Max's mother-in-law.

'Kate, it's been ages. How are you?'

'What a lovely surprise, Jill. I'm good, thanks. Well, I'm in a bit of a mess wondering what to pack, but I'm good apart from that. What about you?'

'I'm fine. But what do you mean? Pack for what?'

There was a brief pause.

'Hasn't Max told you?'

Jill wondered how many times she'd been asked that particular question. As far as the job went, Max was judged to have marvellous communication skills. Away from the job, he was hopeless.

'Max tell me anything?' she scoffed. 'That'll be the day.'

'I'm spending Christmas in the States with Carol.'

'Oh, my!' Jill couldn't believe that Max hadn't mentioned it. He really was the limit. 'That's wonderful. How exciting. It's ages since you've seen her.'

'I know, and I can't wait.'

'What about Harry and Ben? Is Judy taking over?' On the rare occasions Kate wasn't available, Judy, long-time family friend, volunteered to move in and take over Kate's role of spoiling Max and his sons.

'Until Christmas Eve, yes. That's if I ever get packed. I've no idea what to pack. I don't suppose you fancy a day round the shops, do you, Jill?'

'I'd love one. Tomorrow any good to you? We could hit the Trafford Centre.'

'Really? Yes, that suits me.'

Usually, Jill wasn't a fan of shopping, but she knew she'd have a good time with Kate. It was months since they'd spent the day together, too.

They chatted for almost an hour, mainly about

110

Kate's forthcoming visit to her daughter, and Jill still couldn't believe that Max hadn't mentioned it.

She made a mental note to make sure her gift for Kate was small enough to go in a suitcase.

When she finished the call, she hit the button for her parents' number.

'Hello?'

'Hi, Mum!'

'Well, good God. Who are you? No, don't tell me. Your voice sounds familiar, but it's been such a long time—'

'Ha, ha. Very funny. I was going to ask how you are but I can tell you're in fine fettle.'

'It's just as well I am,' her mum retorted. 'So what have you been up to? Planning a wedding? Realizing it's high time you had kids? Making an honest man of Max? Giving those poor boys a mother?'

Jill, well used to her mother's preoccupation with marrying her off, simply laughed.

'I've been working, Mum.'

'Well, who'd have thought it?'

'My, you're hot with the sarcasm tonight. No gossip for me?'

'Not really. Oh my God, yes. Have you spoken to Prue?

'Not since Monday, no. Why?'

'She only walked into a door. Can you believe that? You know how these battered women always claim they've walked into doors? Well, that's exactly what Prue did. It's a good job I saw her do it, otherwise I'd have thought that lovely man of hers was knocking her about.' Her mother

111

cackled with laughter. 'Anyway, you won't believe this, but she's got a black eye. I never thought it was possible, did you?'

Smiling, Jill thought of the whirlwind that was her sister. 'With Prue, anything is possible.'

'That's true enough.'

'How's Dad?'

'The bane of my bloody life as usual. How's Max?'

The bane of my bloody life, Jill thought.

'He's fine. Busy, but fine. But guess what, Kate's spending Christmas in the States. I'm quite envious.'

'Good for her. Not that I should want to. All that foreign food would put me off.'

'Foreign food?' Jill spluttered with laughter. 'It's not– Oh, hang on a minute, Mum, there's someone at the door.'

Why she had such a start every time her doorbell rang, she had no idea. It was unlikely that her late-night caller would ring the doorbell if he was coming to get her.

'Your door's locked,' Max said with some surprise.

'I know. I have this burly copper who keeps reminding me about security.'

'Burly, eh?'

'You do have a key, you know,' she reminded him.

'I do, and I know exactly where it is. I'll put it on my key ring,' he promised.

He'd obviously been home because the suit he'd worn all day had been replaced with a claret and blue Burnley FC T-shirt.

112

'I'm on the phone,' she said. 'And by now, the whole of Liverpool will know that I have a man in my home.'

'Ah. And how is your mum?'

'On top form.'

Jill picked up the receiver.

'Mum, I'll have to go.'

'Was that Max I heard?'

'It was. It's work. I need to go, OK? I'll give you a ring tomorrow night. Or Sunday.'

She returned the phone to its cradle and breathed a small sigh of relief that she'd escaped the usual marriage lecture.

'It's not work,' Max told her. 'The kids are out ten-pin bowling so I thought I'd come and pester you for an hour before I go and pick them up.'

It was unlike him not to be at headquarters. With a murder case not yet a week old, he'd be working every spare moment.

'Are you working tomorrow?' she asked him.

'I'll be in for the morning, but come hell or high water I'll be at Turf Moor in the afternoon. Hey, I might be able to get you a ticket.'

She pulled a face. 'It'll be a sad day when I have nothing better to do than watch grown men kick a ball about.'

'No soul, that's your trouble.'

She smiled at that.

'I expect I'll be working after the game,' he went on. 'We're not making what you'd call progress, are we?'

'You're finding out more and more about the victim,' she pointed out.

Little of it was good. Lauren Cole hadn't been

113

popular. She'd treated her dog well but had had little regard for anyone or anything else. The boyfriend, Ricky, wasn't alone in calling her a tease. A pretty young woman, she had no trouble attracting members of the opposite sex. She loved the sense of power, loved stringing them along and then dropping them. To outsiders, she gave every indication of being a hard-nosed uncaring bitch. In Jill's view, she'd been desperately lonely, a girl who'd craved love...

But it was Friday night and Jill didn't want to talk about work.

'I'm out tomorrow anyway,' she told him. 'Kate and I are hitting the shops. I had no idea she was going to the States for Christmas. How come you didn't mention it?'

'Forgot. Sorry.'

Jill often thought that, one day, Max's mother-in-law would pack her cases and leave them to it. Kate had the granny flat in Max's home, which meant she could see her grandchildren whenever she liked, but few women would tolerate being general dogsbody to Max. Kate walked the dogs when no one was available, she ferried her grandchildren about, she organized Christmas and birthday celebrations. But Kate thrived on it. Or she had until now.

'Anyway, I'm trying not to think about it.' Max added. 'No Kate and a visit from my dad. When your luck's out, your luck's really out. But Christmas is ages away yet.'

'A whole fortnight,' she agreed with a wry smile. 'Still, good for Kate. It's high time she visited Carol. And a break away from home will

114

do your dad good, too.'

Max grimaced at that. 'It's the rest of us I'm worried about.'

'He'll be fine.'

It was a lot for the man to adjust to, that was all. He'd always been a fiercely independent, out-going, opinionated type. Like Max really. It seemed, though, that he could only be that way with his wife standing at his side. Without her, he was floundering.

'Fancy going for a pint?' Max asked.

'Why not?'

Max would go over and over every minute detail of each case he worked on. Give him a personal problem, though, like a father who wasn't coping as a widower, and he had a talent for pushing it from his mind.

Crime she supposed was easier for him. Most of the time, it was black and white. At least, he saw it that way. A crime was committed and it was his job to find the perpetrator. Simple. When it came to more personal problems, life became a very grey area. He didn't handle it well.

The Weaver's Retreat was only a short walk from Jill's cottage and it was a pleasant enough evening. Snow still lay on the footpaths and road-sides, but it was freezing hard and crunched satisfyingly underfoot.

'These scientists need to pay Kelton a visit,' Max said as he pushed open the door. 'If the planet *is* warming up, it's probably all down to Ian.'

The warmth that hit them was wonderful thanks to the landlord's obsession with his fires. Both were blazing merrily. Radiators were too

115

hot to touch.

'Don't knock it,' Jill said, shrugging out of her coat and going to hang it on the peg.

While Max got their drinks, Jill looked around the crowded pub and was pleased to see she knew most of the customers.

At the far end of the room several of the older residents were putting the world to rights over a heated game of dominoes.

'Tom!' Ian shouted across to one of them.

Tom Canter looked up from his game, saw Jill, and shouted out, 'Give me two minutes.'

'What's that about?' Jill asked Ian.

'No idea. Tom was asking if you'd been in, that was all.' He handed Max his change. 'Mind you, it must be important if he's going to interrupt his game of dominoes.'

The game lasted another ten minutes but then Tom left his friends and, pint in hand, came over to Jill and Max.

'I said I'd let you know when I remembered where I'd seen that girl before, the one that were murdered,' Tom said.

'And have you?' she asked him.

The door burst open, letting in a blast of cold air as well as Steve and Alison Carlisle.

'The men driving the gritting lorries will be making some money if this weather keeps up,' Alison greeted them, rubbing her hands together. 'Hello, Jill, Tom.' She looked at Max. 'You'll be?'

'Max Trentham,' Max introduced himself.

'The policeman?'

'That's me.'

'What's anyone having to drink?' Steve asked.

'Steve,' Tom said, somewhat impatiently, 'I were just telling Jill and Max here that they should speak to you about that young girl who were killed.'

'Me? Why would they want to do that?'

'Well...' Tom's frown deepened. 'Because you're someone who knew her.'

'What are you talking about, Tom? I never knew her.'

'Shall we get drinks?' Alison said. 'What's anyone having? Tom?'

'Not for me, thanks. I've just got one.'

'We have, too. Thanks, Alison.'

Jill was far more interested in what Tom was talking about, and Max, she could see, was equally keen to return the conversation to Lauren Cole.

'You were saying, Tom?' she asked as Alison stood at the bar to order drinks.

'Just that Steve knew that girl. I saw you with her,' Tom told him.

'You couldn't have,' Steve said, shaking his head. 'I've never seen her.'

'Bugger me,' Tom said, scratching his head. 'I could have sworn it were you. I'd have staked my life on it.'

'Sorry, but it wasn't.'

'I can't help you then,' Tom told Jill. 'It's just that I were out in the field seeing to my sheep–'

'Sheep?' she said. 'I thought you'd retired.'

'Oh, I have really. I've only got the two small fields now. But I thought I'd get a dozen sheep. Otherwise I had nothing to do with my time. In any case, the dog were bored without sheep to work.'

Jill supposed she shouldn't have been sur-prised. Farming was in Tom's blood. For gener-ations, the Canters had been farming that land. It must break his heart to know that his sons had no interest in it whatsoever.

'Anyway, that's when I saw the girl,' Tom went on. 'The girl who's dead. She were climbing over the fence at the bottom field. I watched her for a minute because she had a white dog with her and, whereas most dogs would have scrambled underneath it, she had to lift him over the fence.'

'Are you sure it was her?' Max asked him.

'Positive.' He looked at Steve. 'Well, I *were* sure.'

'When was this?' Max asked.

'A couple of weeks ago. Let me think, it would have been the Monday morning. So yes, a week before she were killed.'

'When she'd climbed over the fence and lifted the dog over, what then?' Jill asked him.

'Well, that's just it.' Again Tom scratched his head. 'I saw, or *thought* I saw, Steve here with that greyhound of his. He shouted to the girl–'

'Shouted what?' Max butted in.

'Just hello. Then he ran to catch her up. Bugger me,' Tom said again. 'I must be going senile. Are you sure it weren't you, Steve?'

'Of course I'm sure.' Steve was smiling indulg-ently at the old man. 'Had you been on the homemade wine, Tom?'

'No.' Tom supped at his pint. 'In that case, Jill, I can't help you. Sorry.'

Tom, still wearing a mystified expression, returned to his pals and his dominoes.

'How strange,' Steve said. 'I walk out that way

a lot, as you know, but I've never seen anyone else with a greyhound. It's unlike Tom to get confused too.'

Alison rejoined them, a glass of white wine in her hand and a pint of Guinness which she handed to Steve.

'Here's to Friday nights,' she said, raising her glass in a toast. 'I've had the week from hell and I am so glad it's over.'

'You've been away, haven't you?' Jill asked.

'Sales conference,' she said, nodding. 'I've been stuck in Leeds all week. Years back, a sales conference was fun. We'd have parties every night. Now, we spend every minute tied to our laptops deciding how we're going to improve on sales for the coming year. This year has been particularly bad figures-wise, so we all need to come up with some pretty drastic ideas. Still, it's the weekend now and I'm forgetting all about work until Monday morning.'

'Anything planned for the weekend?' Jill asked her.

'Not a thing,' she said with satisfaction. 'I quite fancy going somewhere on Sunday. What about you, darling?' she asked Steve. 'After church, we could drive up into the Yorkshire Dales.'

'Sounds good to me,' he agreed.

'That's settled then. Having said that, if we get more snow, as they say we will, we won't be able to get out of Kelton never mind Lancashire...'

They chatted for another half hour, until Max had to leave. Jill walked back to her cottage with him.

'You think Tom Canter is going senile?' he

asked her.

'No. I think he was merely mistaken.'

'Odd, though, don't you think? On the day of the murder, Steve Carlisle was seen running away from the area. He carries a saw, so he says, to chop wood. How do we know he didn't carry an axe? And now Tom Canter swears blind he saw him talking to Lauren Cole. Very, very odd.'

'Tom was obviously mistaken,' Jill said. 'Steve wouldn't lie. As for carrying a saw – well, so what? He takes a bit of free wood home now and again. That's not a crime. And he told you why he was running.'

'How well do you know him?'

'Well enough to know that he wouldn't go out and bury an axe in Lauren Cole's head.'

Chapter Eleven

On Sunday morning, Max decided to pay Percy Jacobs another visit.

As he drove through the town, he wondered if the Carlisles had managed their trip to the York-shire Dales. The sun was shining, most of the snow had thawed over the weekend, leaving the roads clear, so it was the perfect day for an excursion.

He parked his car outside Jacobs' block of flats. In daylight, the area looked even more run down. Today it was deserted.

The lift, unsurprisingly, still wasn't working so Max climbed the stairs to the fifth floor.

As he knocked on the door, he hoped Jacobs hadn't gone on one of his camping trips. He was in luck; Percy opened it almost immediately.

'Christ, I'm bloody popular with you lot!'

'What do you mean by that?' Max asked curiously.

'Like bloody buses you lot are. There's never a copper in sight when you need one. When you don't, they're crawling all over the place.'

Max walked inside and Jacobs didn't attempt to stop him.

'Do I take it you've been visited by police officers?' Max asked him.

'Yes. Straight after you.'

The room was stifling. Radiators were hot and the gas fire was turned to full. Jacobs might be allergic to work, but he could presumably afford huge gas bills. Today, he was sweating in a faded red T-shirt.

'Tell me about it,' Max said.

'About two minutes after you and that sergeant left,' Jacobs explained, 'I had another copper banging on my door.'

'What was his name?'

'Dunno. I didn't ask and, if he told me, I've forgotten.'

'Uniform or plain clothes?'

'Uniform. Here, what is all this?'

Max wished he knew.

'What did he want, Percy?'

'The same as you.' Jacobs looked at Max as if he should personally be held responsible for the hopeless inefficiency of the UK's police force. 'When I said you'd already been poking around, he said I was to tell him exactly what I'd told you. Christ, you lot are bloody crap. Talk about the left hand not knowing what the right's doing.'

It would be easy enough to find out who had knocked on Jacobs' door. That was assuming anyone from the force *had* knocked on it, and Max didn't believe it for a moment. It was far more likely that someone was impersonating a police officer.

'What did he look like?' Max asked.

'I dunno. Young. Average build.'

'Marked car?'

'Dunno. I didn't look. Anyway, it was pitch bloody dark outside.'

'So what did you tell him?'

'The same as I told you and that other bugger. That I hadn't been anywhere near Kelton Bridge, and that anyone who kills a cat should be hung, drawn and bloody quartered.'

At mention of the word cat, Jacobs' pet ambled into the room, its tail held high. Jacobs scooped it up and the cat's body vibrated as it purred.

'OK, Percy, that'll be all for the time being. But if anyone else comes calling, I'll be extremely pissed off if you don't let me know. Got that?'

Max left the building with a growing sense of unease. There might be a logical explanation, but he doubted it. It was too coincidental that this so-called copper had called on Jacobs two minutes after he and Fletch left. Someone must have followed them to Jacobs' flat, and that someone was impersonating a police officer. People like that were the lowest of the low because a copper's uniform gave anyone carte blanche to do exactly as they pleased.

After leaving Jacobs, Max drove out to Kelton Bridge, but there was no sign of Jill or her four-by-four so he decided to pay Tom Canter a visit.

Max only had a vague idea of where the farm was and getting to it was like solving the puzzle of the Rubik Cube. Roads – lanes really – that should have headed out to the farm, stopped abruptly for no reason that Max could fathom.

After turning round twice and driving back to the village, he eventually saw a track leading down to what had to be Brinks Farm. It was narrow, and potholes a foot deep threatened to break his car's suspension.

He eventually found himself in a large concreted yard where a black and white border collie raced out to meet him. There were a couple of geese in the yard too and, if the dog was friendly, the birds weren't. They hissed at Max with their wings at full stretch.

'They won't harm you,' a voice called out.

Max turned to see Tom Canter coming out of a barn, his wellington boots caked in something Max preferred not to think about.

'Oh, hello,' Tom said, recognizing him. 'It's Max, isn't it?'

'That's right. I was wondering if I might have a chat with you about Lauren Cole, the young woman who was murdered.'

'Of course, although there's nothing I can tell you.' He nodded at the house. 'Let's go inside. I'm finished here for the moment.'

Max followed him, through a porch filled with

123

enough outdoor coats and pairs of wellington boots to cater for everyone in the village, to a large, equally cluttered, but warm kitchen. A towel had been hanging from the Rayburn's rail and the collie pulled that to the floor and curled up on it, making sure he had the warmest spot in the house.

'Sit yourself down, lad,' Tom said. 'The kettle's on. Will you have a cup of tea with me?'

'That would be more than welcome. Thank you, Mr Canter.'

'Call me Tom or I'll think you're talking about my dad. And he's long gone.'

The farmhouse was big, at least four or five bedrooms, Max guessed. From what Jill had told him though, Tom lived alone. His wife had died several years ago and his sons were living in London.

'You live alone, don't you, Tom?'

He was warming an ancient teapot shaped like a house, but he stopped. 'I do. I have for more than ten years now. Well, apart from Jack,' he added, nodding at the dog. 'And the geese, of course. Sheep, too.'

Max supposed it must be hard, having farmed all your life, to cope without animals.

'I'll get some more chickens, too,' Tom said. 'In the spring, that'll be. And probably a few more sheep.'

'That'll keep you busy.'

'It will,' he agreed. 'My lads, both of them, reckon I should sell up and buy myself a bungalow in the village. What the hell would I do in a bungalow, eh? I was born in this house. I might not have much land left, but I know and love every inch of it. I know where the birds make their nests, I know where the best of the blackberries grow, I know where the fox raises her young – a bungalow,' he muttered with disgust.

'Of course,' he went on, 'they only want me to sell up because they reckon it would be more money for them. Oh dear, that sounds bad, doesn't it? I don't mean it like that. They're good boys. It's just that it'll grieve them when I go and the taxman has some of my money. It's no good though, I can't see myself in a little box in the village.'

'I can't say I blame you,' Max said, understanding perfectly. 'Although there would be less to heat and clean in a smaller place.'

Tom smiled at that.

'There would, lad,' he agreed, 'but I can get this kitchen warm enough for me. As for cleaning, the dust moves itself around without any interference from me.'

'I'm sure it does,' Max agreed, amused.

The tea was made, and a bottle of milk and a bag of sugar were put on the table.

'Tell me,' Max began, 'what made you so sure you'd seen Steve Carlisle talking to Lauren Cole.'

'My, that were funny, weren't it?' Tom said, shaking his head in puzzlement. 'I'd have staked my life on it being Steve.'

'But why?'

'Because it looked like him. From the lazy dog strolling several yards behind him, to the coat he were wearing. The dog, I mean. It wears a tartan coat all winter. I mean, I know my eyesight's not what it were fifty years ago, but I'd have sworn it were Steve.'

'And now?' Max asked.

'Now what?'

'Now you don't think it was?'

'Course I don't. If Steve says it weren't him, it weren't him, were it?'

Max looked at him for a few moments until surprise registered on Tom's face.

'You think he might have been lying?' Tom smiled at that. 'No, Steve's no liar. Why the hell would he lie?'

Off the top of his head, Max could think of a dozen reasons.

'He's a regular churchgoer, you know,' Tom went on. 'Not so many of those about these days.'

'So I believe.'

'Catholic,' Tom added with a wink, 'but you can't hold that against a bloke, can you?'

Tom, having put three sugars in his tea, was still stirring.

'It said on the telly that the dead girl came from Harrington,' he said thoughtfully.

'That's right.'

'Then perhaps the bloke I saw, the one with the greyhound, came from there too. I don't know of anyone other than Steve who has one round here. But if it were someone from Harrington...' He shrugged.

'It's possible,' Max agreed.

'One thing's certain,' Tom said with absolute conviction, 'it weren't Steve. He wouldn't lie. He'd have no need to, would he?'

Max decided to pass on that one.

'What was he wearing, this man you saw?' he

126

asked instead.

'A black coat like Steve wears, black trousers and a grey hat.'

'A grey hat? Are you sure?'

'Quite sure. Perhaps that's why I thought it were Steve. When winter arrives, the dog wears its tartan coat and Steve wears that grey hat of his.'

What had Ricky said? That the man who met up with Lauren, the man who'd given her the creeps, wore a funny grey hat, like his mum had knitted it for him.

'His hat,' Max said, 'does it look hand-knitted? A hat like that?'

'That's the sort,' Tom replied. 'Not that I can imagine Alison knitting it. Women don't knit these days, do they? They don't darn socks or mend sheets. We live in a wasteful society and that's a fact.'

'We do.'

Talk turned from the old days, when life had been simpler, to the recent spell of cold weather.

By the time he left the warmth of Tom's kitchen, Max was convinced that Steve Carlisle was lying.

There were far too many coincidences. Why had Carlisle been running that morning? Because he thought he'd forgotten to lock the door? Max found that doubtful. If he often took a saw on his wood-gathering trips, would it be surprising if sometimes he took an axe? No, it wouldn't. And this man with the grey knitted hat? How many men with greyhounds walked these hills wearing a grey knitted hat? Max would bet a lot on there being only one.

127

Chapter Twelve

Jill drove to headquarters on Monday morning through a world that was frozen solid. Most of the snow had thawed over the weekend, but last night, the sky had cleared and the temperature had plummeted. Icy roads were being held responsible for several accidents in the area.

When she walked into the building, Paddy, who was just about to pick up the phone, shouted across to her.

'Max wants to see you ASAP, Jill. He's been trying to get hold of you.'

'Oh?' She dug into her handbag and found her phone. The battery had died. 'What about, Paddy? Did he say?'

'At a guess, I'd say it was to do with the bloke who's been arrested for Lauren Cole's murder. He comes from your village, doesn't he?'

'An arrest's been made?'

'Yeah.' He sorted through papers on his desk until he had the name. 'A bloke called Carlisle.'

'You're kidding me. Right, thanks, Paddy. I'll find him...'

She went to her office, plugged in her phone charger and rang Max. Five minutes later, he burst into her office wearing a face like thunder.

'What the hell's going on, Max?'

'Your chum, Steve Carlisle, that's what. He's lying. I want you to step in.'

Jill had hoped for a calm, leisurely start to the week. There was no chance of that now.

'What's all this about?' she asked. 'Steve's already told us everything he knows.'

'Has he hell! A week ago today, when Lauren Cole was murdered, he was seen running from the scene.'

'He was seen running *home*,' she corrected him. 'He's already explained that.'

'And given how clever everyone says he is, you'd think he'd have come up with a better story.'

'But it means nothing.'

'Tom Canter saw him talking to her.'

'No,' she said patiently. 'Tom saw someone who looked like him talking to her. As Steve said, Tom was clearly mistaken.'

'OK,' Max replied. 'Tom Canter saw someone who looked like him, someone who has a greyhound just as he does, someone wearing a grey hat—'

'A what?'

Jill remembered Ricky Marshall mentioning a grey hat. He'd said Lauren had spoken of a man with a grey hat who gave her the creeps.

'Exactly,' Max said with satisfaction as he spotted her puzzled frown. 'Your friend is lying. Let's see if he'll talk to you, shall we?'

He was wrong, surely. Steve wouldn't lie to them.

'OK,' she agreed, keen to get to the bottom of this.

Max strode off in his usual hurried fashion and Jill followed at her own slower pace. She needed the extra few seconds to think about Steve and how well she actually knew him. Although they'd met five years ago, she supposed they were little more than acquaintances. Yet she trusted him. She'd always considered him an honest, open person. He certainly wasn't a killer.

Phil Meredith was under pressure to keep crime in the area to a minimum so Max was under equal pressure to find Lauren Cole's killer. That man wasn't Steve Carlisle, though.

Max held the door open for her and Jill entered the room. Steve had been sitting with his head in his hands, staring at the desk in complete bewilderment, but a spark of hope flared as he recognized her.

'Hello, Steve,' she said. 'Let's get this sorted out quickly, shall we? You'll want to go home.'

She sat opposite him and, while Max set up the machines, she studied Steve. He looked nervous, but she supposed that was understandable. The mere sighting of a police car can make the safest and most law abiding driver anxious. Few people ended up being questioned by police and it could be a frightening experience.

'Lauren Cole,' Max began. 'Tell me how you came to be talking to her.'

'I've told you. I've never seen the girl.'

'You're lying. You were seen with her.'

'A case of mistaken identity, I swear it.'

Interview room three was as cold as ever yet Steve, wearing only a shirt, was sweating. His skin, usually tanned and healthy from the time he spent in the fresh air, was pale.

'Steve, you've nothing to fear from telling the

truth,' Jill assured him. 'Knowing the young woman doesn't make you a suspect.'

'I've never seen her.' His voice was little more than a whisper.

'Right,' Max said, and Jill could tell he was struggling to keep a rein on his temper. 'One, we hear that, a week ago today, you were running away from the area in which Lauren Cole was murdered.'

'I've told you, I was worried that I hadn't locked the house.'

'Two,' Max went on, ignoring him, 'we hear that the young woman spoke of a man fitting your description talking to her when she walked her dog in the area.'

'It wasn't me.'

'Three, someone else sees a man fitting your description in conversation with the girl. It was a good description, too. A man of your height and build wearing a grey knitted hat and a black coat. You were able to show us these items of clothing. This person was even accompanied by a grey-hound wearing a tartan jacket.'

'Yes, but it wasn't me.'

'You have to admit that it's all very coincidental. I don't know about you,' Max said, 'but I find it hard to believe that two greyhounds are taken for walks in that area wearing identical tartan jackets. I find it even more difficult to believe that their owners wear identical grey hats.'

Max had to be right. Whether she liked it or not, Jill had to accept that Steve was lying. But why?

'Steve,' she began, 'you need to tell us the truth.

131

You have to tell us how you knew Lauren Cole. You also need to explain why you've lied about knowing her. You are lying, aren't you?'

Steve simply stared at an invisible spot on the wall.

'There's no crime,' she pointed out, 'in meeting up with a fellow dog walker, even a young, attractive dog walker, and striking up a conversation.'

'I realize that.'

'It only becomes a crime when you attack that woman,' Max reminded him.

He didn't have anything to say to that.

'Why did you wipe the murder weapon clean?' Max asked.

Steve didn't say anything, but he was visibly shaking now.

Ricky Marshall had claimed that Steve, or a man fitting his description, had occasionally met up with Lauren. He'd claimed that Lauren said the man gave her the creeps. Why? Because he made it clear he found her attractive? Because he was old enough to be her father?

As far as Jill knew, Steve was happily married. As far as she knew. What exactly went on behind the closed doors of Mason's Cottage? Was the marriage as solid as everyone in Kelton Bridge believed?

Steve had lost his job twelve months ago. How had that affected him? Did he feel useless, depressed, on the scrap heap? How did Alison feel about it? Did she treat him differently? Did she see him as worthless?

'Does Alison know you're here?' she asked him, and he nodded.

132

'How does she feel about that?'

He shrugged as answer.

'Angry?' she suggested. 'Shocked? Upset?'

'Shocked,' he said at last. 'Of course she's shocked. It's every person's nightmare, isn't it? You hear about innocent people being dragged off by the police but you never expect it to happen to you or to a member of your family.'

It was the longest speech he'd made since Jill had come into the room, but it sounded false and rehearsed.

'Few people are dragged off by the police, as you put it, when they're completely innocent,' she said.

'I'm sure I'm not the first. I don't suppose I'll be the last, either.'

He was becoming less anxious and more antagonistic.

'Was it Lauren who approached you?' Jill asked.

As he didn't comment, she went on, 'I suppose that makes sense. Perhaps she saw you as someone who might lend her money. We know she had financial problems.'

Still no answer.

'She was also taking drugs. Well, we think she was. She may have been clean for a few days, we don't know. But drugs, money – we believe she was quite desperate.'

A tap on the door forced her to break off. It was Fletch. He needed a word with Max.

It didn't take long and, seconds later, Max was sitting next to Jill again. And he looked furious.

'Right,' he said, 'the axe you own, Mr Carlisle. Where is it?'

133

'Who says I've got an axe?'

'Your wife. Where is it? We've searched your property but we can't find it.'

'That's because I don't have one.'

'You don't have one because you left it at the crime scene, didn't you?' Max banged his fist on the table. 'You killed Lauren Cole with that axe. You then wiped any fingerprints from it and ran home to play the out-of-work husband and neighbourly villager.'

'No!'

'Yes!'

Steve dropped his head on the table and began sobbing. He shook his head in denial as he wept.

'Tell us the truth, Steve,' Jill snapped. 'Tell us how you knew Lauren Cole.'

She was trying to remain calm, but it was difficult. She felt betrayed. While she'd been trying to convince Max of his innocence, Steve had been lying to her. It wouldn't take much for her to walk out and leave him to Max's anger.

Steve was drying his eyes.

'OK.' He took a deep breath. 'Yes. Yes, I knew her. A couple of months ago, I met up with her when I was out walking with Cally.'

Jill leaned back in her chair. Max did likewise, but she could tell he was struggling to remain silent. Silence was the only way to go, though. It encouraged people to talk.

'She had a dog called Charlie,' Steve went on, his voice breaking slightly. 'You get to know the dog walkers. You walk the same route for a few yards perhaps, you talk about the weather and about your dogs, and then you go your separate ways.'

He took a handkerchief from his pocket and blew his nose.

Jill was aware of Max fidgeting beside her. His left foot was tapping soundlessly, a sure sign of his irritation. She felt the same.

'That's what happened,' Steve continued. 'Our dogs played around for a couple of minutes and then I headed for home, back through the spinney, and she carried on up the hill. We talked about our dogs and the weather. Nothing more. I didn't even know her name until I saw it in the paper.'

He twisted his handkerchief round his fingers.

'So yes, perhaps Tom Canter did see me with her. My dog, my coat, my hat. But no one saw me with her the day she was killed. I didn't see her. I swear to you.'

He was still sweating profusely and he looked such a sickly shade of green that Jill expected him to vomit at any moment.

'Then why lie about knowing her?' Max asked.

'Because it looks bad.' Steve looked up at Jill, his eyes moist. 'I'm sorry I lied, but it does look bad, doesn't it?'

'It does,' Max assured him.

Steve buried his face in his hands and began to weep again.

Jill was about to speak when Max looked at the clock, snapped out, 'Interview suspended at eleven-fourteen,' and stood up, ready to leave the room.

Jill, taken by surprise, joined him.

'We'll get you a cup of tea and a sandwich sent in,' she promised Steve. She didn't add 'and think yourself lucky'.

Max was already halfway along the corridor and she ran to catch him up.

'What are you doing?' she demanded.

'Taking myself away from him before I deck him. Why do people insist on lying to me? Hm?'

'To piss you off?' she suggested. 'To make your job more difficult? To give you a coronary? Or maybe,' she added, 'and this is a long shot, they lie because they're scared to death that the truth will have them banged up on a murder charge.'

'We'll give him half an hour to calm down. Correction, we'll give *me* half an hour to calm down. Then we'll go to town on him.'

'In what way?'

'You didn't believe any of that crap, did you?'

'Yes. I think I probably did.'

She no longer knew what to believe. She was annoyed with Steve, though. Bloody annoyed.

'Come on, Jill. Just because he's a neighbour of yours, a friend even, doesn't necessarily mean he has to be telling the truth. Even people from Kelton Bridge tell porkies.'

'For some reason, he lied,' she agreed. 'He's no killer though.'

'How the hell do you figure that one out?'

'Trust me, Max, he's not your man.'

'So someone else was seen in the area? Someone else who wears a black coat and a grey knitted hat? Someone else who owns a greyhound that models tartan jackets? Someone else who just happens to carry an axe around with them? Get real!'

Put like that, Jill knew he had a point.

'I know he's a friend, Jill, and I sympathize, but, like it or not, he's our man!'

Jill decided to take the afternoon off. Thanks in part to Jason Lyle changing his plea, giving her time to catch up on her workload, she had more time on her hands than was usual.

She'd spent another hour in that interview room with Max and Steve, but Steve was sticking to his story, and Max was still convinced the man was guilty of murder.

Glad to be away from it, she drove out to Kelton Bridge. She gave her cats a brief taste of freedom and then walked through the village towards Mason's Cottage.

She met several people she knew and stopped for a quick chat with each one. The villagers didn't take to newcomers easily and she felt privileged to be part of such a close-knit community. Gossip was always rife, and it was impossible to do anything without everyone knowing about it, but, should a crisis occur and help be needed, there was nowhere she would rather live.

The village was even more picturesque than usual with shops decorated for Christmas and lights twinkling on small trees fixed to the buildings.

She was away from the shops when she heard a voice raised in anger. She couldn't see the owner yet, but it was a voice she recognized.

'Hello, Pat,' she said, when the woman and her son came into view. 'Hi, Jimmy. No school today?'

'The little devil's been suspended until after Christmas,' Pat said, her face red from either cold or anger. 'I was summoned to explain why he was either late or absent. Well! I knew nothing about it. Little devil.'

'That's not like you, Jimmy.'

At fourteen, the boy usually had plenty to say for himself. Now, he simply shrugged and shuffled his feet.

Jill could see something was bothering him, but it wasn't her place to pry.

Head down, Jimmy walked on ahead.

'I blame his dad,' Pat said, watching him go. 'He spoils him rotten. Of course, it's easy to throw money around when you're an absent father. Last weekend, he bought him an iPhone. I ask you.'

'An early Christmas present?'

'No. I shudder to think what he'll buy him for Christmas. A Ferrari probably.'

'Let's hope so,' Jill teased. 'We can take turns driving it.'

Pat laughed at that.

'True enough,' she agreed. 'Anyway, enough of my moans. How are you, Jill?'

'I'm good, thanks. Is Jimmy OK? Nothing bothering him?'

'I don't think so.' Pat sighed. 'I suppose he misses his dad. But he's missed him for almost three years now and he's never been any trouble before. But you know what they say, it'll all come out in the wash.'

'I'm sure it will.'

'If ever you think of having kids, Jill, take my advice. Don't. Not unless you want grey hair and sleepless nights.'

'You wouldn't be without him.'

'Yes, but I'm crazy. And talking of crazy, I'll be having the usual party on Boxing Day. I'll drop

138

an invitation through your letterbox.'

'Aw, thanks, Pat. I'll look forward to it.'

As she walked on, Jill marvelled, not for the first time, that she and Pat were the same age. And there was Pat with a fourteen-year-old son. Still, there was no point thinking about that...

There were two cars parked on the drive at Mason's Cottage. One belonged to Alison, but Jill didn't recognize the other. Presumably, Steve's was in the garage.

Alison opened the door and, surprisingly, she was looking immaculate, right down to sparkling acrylic fingernails.

'Jill, what a surprise. Come in.'

It didn't seem a particularly pleasant surprise.

'Thanks. I'm sorry to bother you, Alison, but I wondered if we could have a chat.'

'Of course.'

They went into the sitting room where a man, a stranger to Jill, was standing with his back to the window.

'This is Mark Radley,' Alison explained. 'What with all that's going on – Steve, you know – I've taken a couple of days off work. I can't think straight so it's a waste of time me trying to do anything. Mark's called in to pick up my files. He'll look after my customers for a couple of days.' She ran agitated fingers through her hair. 'Sorry. Mark, meet Jill Kennedy. She's a–'

'Forensic psychologist,' Jill helped her out.

Mark shook hands with Jill, joked about having to do the work of two people and then made himself at home in the armchair nearest the radiator.

He certainly seemed comfortable and at ease in

139

his colleague's home. He was early forties, she estimated. Dark haired, he was wearing a smart suit, silk tie and quality shoes.

'So you work with the police?' he said. 'You'll know what's going on then. They don't seriously think Steve had anything to do with the murder of that woman, do they?'

'It's crazy,' Alison said. 'Just crazy. That's the only word for it.'

The wood-burning stove looked forlorn. The room was warm, though, so the radiators were working well. Perhaps the stove was Steve's domain.

Alison was wearing black trousers and a striped black and white shirt. A black jacket was hanging on the back of a chair. Beneath the perfectly made-up face, she looked as most women would look if their husbands had been arrested – very frightened.

'Is Steve all right?' she asked Jill. 'They won't let me see him.'

'He's fine.'

He wasn't, but there was no point upsetting Alison. Besides, she had no intention of discussing Steve's mental state with a stranger present.

'Would it be better if I came back another time?' Jill asked.

'No, no it's OK. Mark knows everything. You can talk in front of him.'

Mark smiled at that. 'The soul of discretion, that's me.'

'He's being a great help to me,' Alison said. 'Sorry, Jill, sit down.'

Jill sat on the sofa and wondered where to begin.

140

'Has Steve seemed OK lately, Alison?' she asked. 'Has anything been bothering him? Has he been acting strangely?'

Alison looked to Mark before answering.

'It's difficult to say. Ever since he lost his job, he's been – different. But that's a year ago now. I don't know why he's finding it so difficult to find another, but...' Her voice trailed away.

'The young woman who was murdered, Lauren Cole, did he ever mention her to you?'

Again Alison looked at Mark before answering. 'Sort of.'

What the hell did that mean, Jill wondered. Either he'd mentioned her or he hadn't.

'What did he say?' she asked.

'Well, not a lot really. When I came home in the evening, I'd ask about his day. He'd tell me what he'd done and who he'd spoken to. Some days, he didn't speak to a soul. Other days, he'd tell me who he'd seen in the shop or the post office, or when he was out with Cally.'

'And he mentioned chatting to Lauren Cole?'

'Not by name, no. He just said he'd met a woman who had a white dog. That's how he described her. The woman with the white dog. He said the dog's name was Charlie, but he never mentioned the woman's name.'

'How often did he meet her?'

'I've no idea. He mentioned her to me twice.' She looked at Mark, then returned her attention to Jill. 'Last week, as I told you on Friday night, I'd had a hell of a week. You were at the sales conference, weren't you, Mark? It was really intense, wasn't it? As soon as I got home, I wanted to go

141

to the pub and relax. Steve wasn't keen, and I couldn't think why.'

'Did you ask him?'

'No. I needed a drink and I thought it would relax us both. Then, when we were in the pub, Tom Canter said he'd seen Steve talking to the woman who'd been killed.' She rubbed her hands together as if trying to warm them. 'I didn't realize that the dead woman was the one who had the white dog.'

She stood up, took a couple of paces and then sat down again.

'And now,' she went on, 'the police have been looking for that axe Steve uses to chop up his blasted wood. For God's sake, who the hell carries an axe around with them? How stupid can you get? No wonder the police have got him locked up.'

'But he doesn't carry it around, does he?' Jill asked. 'The way I understood it, if he was out walking and spotted some wood, either a fallen branch or wood that someone had dumped, he took his axe or a saw out to chop it up and bring it home.'

'Well, yes, but all the same, it seems like a damn stupid thing to do.'

It did now, but hindsight was a wonderful thing.

'Where's Cally?' Jill asked, realizing the dog wasn't on her chair.

'In the kitchen,' Alison answered vaguely. 'She keeps whining and looking for Steve. I can't be doing with that.'

'Calm down, Alison,' Mark said. 'There's no point worrying, is there? I'm sure this mess will soon be sorted out.'

'Yes.' She gave him a grateful smile. 'Of course it will. It will, won't it, Jill?'

'Let's hope so.'

'And why did Steve deny knowing the woman?' she demanded of Jill. 'How stupid was that? It makes him look guilty, doesn't it?'

If one thing was becoming clear to Jill it was that Alison didn't know anything that could help Steve. She was too busy blaming him for the mess she found herself in. If Steve hadn't carried that axe, if he hadn't denied speaking to Lauren Cole...

'I'll leave you to discuss work,' Jill said, smiling as she stood up. 'If I hear anything, I'll let you know. Meanwhile, I know it's difficult, but try not to worry too much.'

Jill had left her car at her cottage. Now, as she walked back through the village, she was glad she had. It gave her time to think and uppermost in her thoughts was the fact that nothing had seemed right back there.

Then again, nothing *was* right. Alison's husband was facing a murder charge.

Chapter Thirteen

At the bottom of Ruth Carlisle's garden, a gnome was perched on a toadstool in what was left of the snow, his eyes bright with mischief. It had been sitting there for almost forty years. She would never forget meeting the bus and seeing Steve,

143

eight years old and back from a school trip to the seaside, carrying the gnome beneath his arm.

'A present for you and Dad,' he'd said, eyes glowing with happiness.

How she and Frank had laughed that night. Yet behind the laughter, they had both been touched beyond words that, instead of spending his money on sweets or toys, he'd bought them a present.

Today Ruth was struggling to see the gnome through her tears and, when the doorbell rang, she had to rub her face dry. She knew it was stupid and achieved nothing, but she couldn't stop crying today.

News would have flown round the village, and although she'd guessed that people would soon start calling on her, either wanting to help or eager for gossip, she wasn't sure she could face them. On the other hand, she'd never hidden from anyone and it was too late to change the habit of a lifetime.

When she saw Jill Kennedy standing on her doorstep, relief flooded through her. Jill wouldn't be offering platitudes and she wouldn't be hunting out gossip either.

'Hello, love,' she said. 'Come in out of the cold. Frank's taken himself out, the only way he knows how to cope, so I'll be glad of some company. The kettle's on.'

'Excellent. I'd love a cuppa.'

'It's warmer in the kitchen,' she said, ushering Jill inside.

Darkness was already falling and Ruth pulled the curtains closed against the coming night and switched on the light. It made the room seem less depressing.

Jill took off her coat, put it over the back of the chair, and sat at the table. Ruth *was* glad of some company. Time alone, in her experience, meant nothing more than time to brood. No wonder she'd been tearful all day.

'Have you seen Steve?' Ruth asked as she warmed the teapot.

'Yes, I've had a chat with him. He's fine. Really, he is.' Ruth knew he wasn't fine. Still, so long as he was coping, that was something.

'I've called up at the house and had a word with Alison, too,' Jill said. 'I was on my way home from there when I thought I'd pop in and see you.'

'That's good of you, love.'

Ruth had spoken to Alison early that morning, not long after Steve had been taken away by the police. Ruth tried to give her daughter-in-law the benefit of the doubt, but she was still angry that Alison's first thought had been about work.

'I can't go losing my job too,' she'd said irritably. 'It's hard enough living on my wages as it is.'

Ruth could have screamed. As if jobs and wages mattered at a time like this.

'What will happen, Jill?'

'I don't know. I really don't know.'

When the tea was made, Ruth sat down opposite her.

'Is there anything I can do?' It was the sense of helplessness that was the worst. But what could a seventy-six-year-old woman do when her son was being questioned about a murder?

'I don't know that, either.' Jill gave a small smile. 'How has Steve been lately, Ruth? You see quite a lot of him, don't you?'

'Last week, I saw him every night. If Alison's working and staying away overnight, he always comes here for his evening meal. I expect he'd rather be at home eating in front of the TV, but he comes here. He's a great believer in family.'

Jill smiled at that.

'And he hasn't been right all week,' Ruth went on. 'I kept asking him what was bothering him, but he wouldn't tell me. All he said was that it was nothing to worry about.'

'So something *was* bothering him? When was this, Ruth? When did you first notice?'

'On Monday night.'

It was the truth, but it was also the day that poor woman was killed. Ruth could have bitten off her tongue.

'Before that,' Jill asked, 'how had he seemed? Would you have said he was happy?'

Ruth took her time answering that one. Yet what was the point of lying to Jill? The girl wasn't here to trick her. She was here to help.

'I was only thinking the other night,' she said at last, 'that, as a child, he was the one who always made me laugh. He had the sunniest nature you could imagine. He never failed to see the lighter side of things. I was also thinking,' she added quietly, 'that I hadn't seen him happy for years.'

'Oh?'

'Do you think,' she asked Jill, 'that mothers know the state of their children's marriages?'

'Not always. In fact, I think there are only two people who *really* know how good or bad a marriage is.'

'Exactly. And those two are husband and wife.

They can keep a lot from the outside world if they choose.'

Jill sipped at her tea, her hands wrapped around the mug.

'Are you saying that Steve and Alison aren't happy, Ruth?'

'I can't say that because I don't know.' Ruth sometimes wished she did but, more often than not, she knew it was easier to believe that all was rosy.

'Everyone in the village thinks they have the perfect marriage,' Jill pointed out.

'Perhaps they do,' Ruth said.

Jill smiled at that. 'You know your son, Ruth. Better than most people, you would know if he was happy or not.'

'Maybe.'

There was no maybe about it. Steve wasn't happy.

'What about children?' Jill asked. 'Was it a joint decision not to have any?'

The words shocked Ruth but then she realized that Jill was a relative newcomer to the village. She wouldn't know about Maisie.

Even now, Ruth could see Maisie's chubby smiling face. She could almost smell her granddaughter. Could feel those fat fingers clinging to her thumb.

'They had a child,' she said, a lump in her throat.

Jill's head flew up. 'What? I had no idea.'

Steve had been happy then. When Maisie was living and breathing among them, Steve had been the happiest man alive.

Since then...

'They had a daughter,' Ruth explained, trying to blot out the sight of Maisie's little face. 'One night, when Maisie was four months old, Alison was working away overnight. Steve was a smoker then and he ran out of cigarettes. Maisie was fast asleep upstairs so he nipped out to the corner shop to get some cigarettes. He was only gone five minutes.'

She had to stop to take a deep, shuddering breath and she felt Jill's hand give hers a squeeze.

'It was a cot death,' Ruth explained. 'It could have happened at any time. It wouldn't have mattered who was in the house. Steve, Alison or no one. It was just one of those awful tragedies.'

'I'm so sorry, Ruth. I truly had no idea.'

'There's no reason you would.'

'Does Steve blame himself?'

Ruth nodded. 'Alison does too.'

'Oh, I'm sure she doesn't.'

Ruth was equally sure she did.

'You asked when I last saw Steve happy, Jill. Well, that's it. The last time was when Maisie was alive.'

'How long ago did she die, Ruth?'

'Twenty years.'

For twenty long years, Ruth had seen the haunted look in her son's eyes. All that time, she'd known he wasn't happy, known that he longed to turn back the clock.

'With something like that between you,' Ruth said, 'I would imagine it's hard to have a happy marriage.'

'Yes,' Jill agreed slowly. 'Some couples would cling together, others would drift apart. But Steve and Alison haven't drifted apart, have they? Divorce is common enough these days, Ruth. If they really had drifted apart, they would have filed for divorce.'

But they wouldn't.

'Alison's Catholic,' Ruth explained. 'Not only that, her uncle, that's her father's brother, is the priest in Harrington. Divorce goes against all his teachings. They're close, him and Alison. Even if she wanted a divorce, she wouldn't do anything to upset him.'

Ruth didn't believe in divorce either. These days, couples didn't put enough effort into marriage. At the first hurdle, they rushed off to the divorce courts. Good grief, she thought, if she and Frank had been like that, they'd have been lucky to have one child never mind four. Marriage was hard work. It was give and take. Compromise. Forgive and forget.

'What about Lauren Cole?' Jill asked. 'Did he ever mention her to you, Ruth?'

'No, of course he didn't. He didn't know the girl. Why would he?'

Ruth's stomach churned over at mention of the dead girl's name and all her fears rushed at her, sending her dizzy.

'That's what I can't understand, Jill. Why do they think Steve had anything to do with it?'

'Steve sometimes met up with her, that's all.'

That's what Alison had said, but Ruth couldn't believe it. Steve would have told her.

Jill's hand covered hers and gave it another squeeze. 'Try not to worry, Ruth.'

Ruth wished it were that simple.

Chapter Fourteen

The Mill, one of Harrington's most attractive restaurants, was enjoying a brisk pre-Christmas trade. The dining room was decorated with greenery. Candles, surrounded by logs, pine cones and sprigs of holly, burned in the windows. Some diners oohed and aahed at the sight; all Max saw was a fire hazard. But he was in that sort of mood.

He needed to eat, and he needed to see his sons before they forgot who he was so this meal, arranged at the last minute by Jill, was the ideal chance to do that. It was supposed to be a treat for his mother-in-law. Kate was flying out to the States in the morning so it was the only chance they had to wish her bon voyage.

Red candles, sitting in bowls filled with gold baubles, flickered on their table. Everyone had crackers and the chance to wear paper hats. Max wasn't in the mood for any of it. He would far rather be dragging a confession from Steve Carlisle.

'Did I hear you say you were going back to work tonight, Max?' his mother-in-law asked him, disapproval evident.

''Fraid so.' And now he felt guilty. 'Sorry, folks, I know I'm not seeing a lot of you right now, but I need to get this case sorted.'

'Have you found the man who did it?' his

150

youngest son wanted to know.

'I have, Ben. I just need to prove it now.' And that wouldn't be easy.

'Let's not talk work,' his mother-in-law suggested. Max knew Kate liked to keep the less attractive parts of his job from her grandsons. 'Tell us what your new car is like, Jill.'

'It's perfect. Bring on the snow, I say!'

At least the Mill was the closest restaurant to headquarters. Max would eat his turkey, have a quick coffee and then head back to question Carlisle.

'Jill was on the telly the other night,' Harry told his grandmother.

'I know. I saw her and thought she sounded great.'

'Great wasn't how I would have described it,' Jill said with a chuckle. 'I was unbelievably nervous.'

'Is one of your horses paying for this, Jill?' Ben asked, and she grinned at him.

'It is, but I'm not allowed to encourage you to gamble. It's a mug's game and you must never ever go near a betting office. You hear me?'

'I hear you,' the lad agreed. 'But I can bet on there being a white Christmas, can't I? That's not really gambling, is it?'

'Of course it's gambling,' Max said sternly.

'But if Jill puts the bet on for us—'

'It's still gambling,' Max retorted.

Max winced as Jill's heel made contact with his shin. He read the look she gave him easily. It said: 'You're a miserable git, Trentham, and it wouldn't hurt you to be sociable for a change.' At least, that was the polite version. He gave her what he hoped was an apologetic smile, shoved a paper hat on his head and joined in the age-old custom of pulling crackers...

'I'll come back to headquarters with you,' Jill said.

'Oh? Well, yes, why not? It'll be hard work, though. Carlisle's told his story, such as it is, and he's sticking to it.'

'Perhaps it's true.'

'No. He's lied all along.'

'Maybe.'

'You still think he's innocent?' he asked.

'Of murder? Yes.'

They would have to agree to disagree on that. Until they could get a confession from him, at least.

'He is hiding something though,' she added, frowning. 'That's why I thought I'd come back with you, to see if we can find out what it is.'

'Fine. But don't think that, just because he's your neighbour, he can't be a killer. None of us know our neighbours as well as we like to think.'

'True,' she agreed, 'but I know more about him now than I did this time yesterday.'

Max didn't have a clue what she meant by that and he was prevented from asking by the arrival of the waiter. It took too long to choose desserts and then too long for Max and Jill's coffees to arrive.

Finally, however, escape beckoned. First Max had to remind Kate that it was snowing again. She was driving his sons home and for that he was grateful. It was only a couple of miles, but he knew she hated driving in bad weather.

'We'll be fine,' she promised him.

Then it took Jill at least five minutes to say goodbye to Kate.

But then they were walking back to head-quarters. It was a brisk walk, too, with the wind gnawing at their bones. Max lit a cigarette, but it burnt away too quickly to be enjoyed.

They went straight to the interview room where Steve Carlisle still looked to be in a state of shock. He did look pleased, and somewhat relieved, to see Jill though.

'I saw your mum today, Steve,' she began. 'Oh, she's fine,' she added. 'A bit worried about you, but that's understandable.'

The way Jill spoke, they might have been chatting at a village fête.

'Well, when I say a bit worried,' she went on, 'she's *very* worried. It's a shame that, isn't it? I've always liked your mum. I remember my first day in the village. She called on me, brought me some gorgeous flowers from her garden and left me her address and phone number just in case I needed anything. I was really touched by that.'

Carlisle seemed unsure what to make of this.

'She's that sort,' he replied uneasily. 'Always willing to help anyone.'

'She is. It's awful to think of her having to go through this, isn't it? After all, she's no spring chicken, is she? And no doubt the press will soon be camped out on her doorstep. That's always hard to deal with. It'll be very embarrassing for her, too.'

He nodded again, his face filled with all the sorrow imaginable. It wasn't making him con-

153

fess, though, Max thought grimly.

'Tell me about Maisie,' Jill suggested with an encouraging smile.

Max didn't have a clue who the hell Maisie was. Typical of Jill not to discuss anything with him. He did see that mention of her name touched a nerve with Carlisle, though.

'Maisie...' He cleared his throat. A vein was throbbing at his temple. 'Maisie was our daughter. She, um, she died.'

'A cot death, wasn't it?' Jill said.

'Yes.'

'It happened when you were looking after her, didn't it? Wasn't Alison away at the time?'

'That's right.'

Jill leaned back in her chair. 'Tell us about that night, Steve.'

'Oh.' He looked as if he couldn't bear to relive a single second and Max couldn't blame him for that.

'It was this time of year,' Carlisle began reluctantly. 'A bit earlier. The twentieth of November to be precise. As you say, Alison was staying overnight in London. Maisie was four months old.'

His hands shook as he clasped and unclasped them on the desk.

'I used to smoke then and I'd run out of cigarettes. I checked on Maisie and saw that she was fast asleep so I decided to nip out and get a pack from the shop. It was a five-minute walk at the most. When I got back–'

His voice was so low that Max wondered if the recorder was catching it all. He also wondered if this was relevant to the case.

'When I got back to the house, I ran upstairs and she was – gone.'

'That must have been hell,' Jill said softly. 'I suppose you blamed yourself, too.'

He nodded.

'It wasn't your fault though, was it? It was a cot death, one of those inexplicable tragedies that could have occurred on any night at any time.'

He nodded again, but he looked like a man who had been to hell and back many, many times.

'How did Alison react to that?' Jill asked him. 'Was she understanding? Supportive?'

'Yes. Yes, of course she was.'

'Really?' Jill sounded surprised. 'Your mum thought she might blame you.'

He shrugged. 'Perhaps. A little. I was in charge, you see. That night, little Maisie was my responsibility.'

'A terrible thing to happen,' Jill sympathized. 'How old would she have been now, Steve?'

'Twenty.'

The soft, almost inaudible reply shocked Max to the core. Twenty. If she'd lived, Carlisle's daughter would have been the same age as Lauren Cole.

'You must think of her often,' Jill said. 'Especially when you see others of her age. When you used to meet up with Lauren Cole, for example.'

'No!' He knew what Jill was driving at and he was having none of it.

'Oh, come on, Steve, you must have resented her a little. After all, she was alive and your Maisie wasn't. She had her whole life ahead of her and Maisie didn't.'

'No.'

155

'Lauren Cole was wasting her life, too. She'd lost her job, got mixed up with a bad crowd, messed around with drugs. Your Maisie wouldn't have done that, would she? She wouldn't have wasted her life.'

Steve said nothing.

'You must have been very angry,' Jill said in the same matter-of-fact way. 'She was throwing her life down the drain when your poor little Maisie never had the chance to shine.'

Steve thumped the table, then banged his head against it and began to weep.

'Is that why you killed Lauren Cole?' Max demanded. 'Because she had a life and Maisie didn't?'

'No! No, no, no!'

'So why did you kill her?'

'I didn't!'

Apart from Carlisle's sniffles and the whirr of the recording equipment, all was silent.

'I didn't,' he said again, lifting his tear-wet face. 'I swear to God I didn't kill her. I swear on my mother's life even.'

He was damn good. For a moment, he almost had Max convinced of his innocence.

'I did see her, though.' Carlisle's voice was little more than a whisper.

'What do you mean?' Max asked.

'That morning,' he said, 'I saw her. I used to look out for her. She was–' He broke off.

'What?' Max demanded. 'Young? Pretty?'

Carlisle didn't answer.

'You gave her the creeps,' Max said. 'That's how she described you to her friend. As someone who gave her the creeps.'

'Did she?' He looked saddened, but not too surprised. 'Well, why not? I'm old enough – *was* old enough to be her father.'

'Exactly,' Jill said. 'Was that what attracted you to her? The fact that she was Maisie's age?'

'No.' He shook his head. 'She was – young, I suppose. Too young to have been knocked about by life.'

'To get back to that morning,' Max said with all the patience he could muster. 'You claim you saw her?'

'Yes. When you're stuck in a house alone all day, any company is something to be welcomed. Some days, I don't see a living soul. Alison has lots of jobs around the house lined up for me, but, surely, there has to be more to life than that?'

Neither answered his question.

'So yes,' he continued, 'I used to watch out for her. Some days, we'd walk together for a while. Our dogs used to play together. Funny that, because Cally can't usually be bothered but she took to Charlie, the dead woman's dog.'

He cleared his throat.

'She was pretty, yes, but it wouldn't have made any difference to me. She could have been fat and seventy years old and I would still have looked out for her. It was someone to pass the time of day with, that's all. Someone to walk with for a while.'

'So you walked together last Monday?' Max asked.

'Yes.' Carlisle's hands were shaking, and his teeth had started chattering. 'The previous afternoon,

Sunday, I'd seen a branch that had been blown down by the wind so, that morning, the Monday, I took – I took my axe along with me. I'd chopped up the branch and, because it wasn't particularly big, I put it, with the axe, in the sack. I was on my way home when I met up with Lauren, but I decided to walk with her for a while.'

He took a breath.

'After a few minutes, we suddenly realized that, although Cally was trotting beside us, her dog Charlie was nowhere in sight. She loved that dog and she – well, she panicked. I tried to calm her down, told her that he would have been chasing a rabbit or something. I suggested we split up to look for him and then meet back at Clough's Shelter. I left my sack there and we set off.'

He was silent for so long that Max longed to shake the truth from him. He knew, though, that the silence might force Carlisle to talk.

'It was funny,' he continued at last, 'but there was no sign of him. He'd simply vanished. He could be a bit noisy. If he was chasing a rabbit or something, he would have been yapping in that excitable way he has. But I kept shouting to him and, for a few minutes, I heard Lauren calling. Then, I could no longer hear her. I assumed she was out of earshot.'

Max saw the pulse throbbing in Carlisle's neck. The man's heart was racing at one hell of a pace.

'After about fifteen minutes, maybe twenty, I went back to the shelter.' His throat seemed to be giving up on him and he stopped speaking to look straight at Max. 'She was dead.'

'Describe everything,' Jill ordered him. 'Tell us

158

everything you saw, heard and felt when you got back to the shelter.'

He nodded, seeming grateful for Jill's calm tone.

'Cally had trotted on ahead,' he said, giving the impression of concentrating hard, 'and it was the dog who found her lying there. I didn't hear anything. Charlie was there, pawing at her arm.'

As yet there had been no mention of the axe.

'You claim you left your sack – the one with a pile of wood and an axe inside it – at the shelter,' Max reminded him. 'How close to that was Lauren Cole's body?'

Carlisle swallowed as if he had a golf ball stuck in his throat.

'She was lying right by the sack,' he said.

'And your axe?' Max asked.

'It was – someone had...' He balled his hands into fists and rubbed at his eyes. 'Oh, God. Someone had killed her with my axe.'

He began sobbing again.

'Right,' Max said, losing patience, 'let me picture the scene. You've been walking with a friend, acquaintance, call her what you will, and you return to discover that she's been killed with your axe. So you what? I don't suppose you would check for a pulse or call an ambulance? Not much point really because that one single blow would have killed her instantly, wouldn't it? So what would most people do in that situation? They would call the police, wouldn't they? So, Mr Carlisle, tell me exactly what you did when you saw the young woman lying there. Come on, tell me.' He longed to shake him until his teeth rattled. 'What did you do?'

'I panicked.' Still the sobs wracked his body. 'I mean, I knew how it would look. It being my axe and everything. So I took a handkerchief from my pocket and wiped all fingerprints from it. I picked up the sack of wood and I – I ran.'

'But why?' Jill demanded. 'Why run, Steve? Why couldn't you tell the police what you've just told us?'

'Who would have believed me?' he cried.

'I do.'

Carlisle looked at her with the same degree of surprise that Max felt.

Believe him? Max sure as hell didn't!

Chapter Fifteen

'Fancy a pint?' Max asked.

Jill fancied several. It seemed ages since she'd woken to her stalker's phone call that morning. She'd spent time with Steve Carlisle, she'd visited his wife and then his mother...

She'd enjoyed the get-together at the Mill, though. That had been fun.

'Sadly I'm driving and I had champagne earlier,' she reminded him.

'One of the patrol cars can take a drive out to Kelton.'

'Yeah?' It would be silly not to take advantage of that, especially when she fancied a stiff drink. 'Well, you're the boss.'

'Ha!'

They left headquarters and began the short walk to the Green Man. Large fluffy snowflakes had soon covered them. Jill kept her hands deep in her pockets and couldn't believe that Max was willing to risk frostbite by lighting a cigarette.

'Is the pub still open?' she asked. It was gone eleven.

'Open and full of coppers, I expect.'

Just as Max was about to push open the door, a man staggered out. It was Adam Smith, and he was drunk.

'Well, well, well,' he slurred, 'if it's not the fancy detective and his bit of skirt.'

'Good evening, Mr Smith.' Max stood aside to let him pass. 'You're leaving I take it?'

'My girl's out there. At this hour. In this weather.'

Jill could have wept for the poor man. She'd felt bad enough this morning when she'd seen the sheep on the hills with their backs to the blizzard, but it must be unbearable to think of your own child battling with the elements.

'I think you should go home,' Max told him. 'I'll get someone to drive–'

'Go home? How can I go home, you bastard? How can I go home knowing that my Yasmin's out there in this awful bloody weather?'

It was difficult to tell if the raw wind, the alcohol he'd consumed or tears were responsible for his red puffy eyes.

'Mr Smith–' Jill began, but he shoved her back towards the wall.

'You can shut your mouth, an' all.'

'OK,' Max said, 'you can leave quietly or I can

arrest you. Your choice, Mr Smith. A night in your bed or a night in a cell? What's it to be?'

'Bugger off!'

They watched him leave the pub and stand in the car park for a few moments, swaying on the balls of his feet, before heading towards the town centre.

'I shall be eternally grateful when the day's over,' Max muttered as they walked up to the bar.

'You reckon tomorrow will be better?'

'Probably not, but you know me. Ever the optimist.'

He'd been right about the pub's customers being mainly members of the force. There were about twenty people in there and Jill recognized at least half of them. It made her wonder how many coppers were actually working right now.

Max ordered his pint and looked questioningly at her.

'A gin and tonic, please. A double. Not too much tonic.'

They took a table in the corner where no one was likely to bother them and where Max could glance at his watch and glare at members of his team now and again.

'They're not going to dash home to their beds when the boss is out enjoying himself,' she pointed out.

'True, but scowling at them makes me feel better.'

Max drank half of his pint in one slug, and Jill knew how he felt. It was one of those days when a drink definitely helped.

'What do you think about Steve then?' she asked him, already guessing his answer.

'I think he's a lying so-and-so. I also think that, given the time he's had to dream up his story, he could have done one hell of a lot better. Next question.'

She'd known that Max was still convinced of his guilt. She supposed she couldn't blame him. Steve had lied and now it was difficult to believe anything he said.

'He could be telling the truth,' she said.

'So why wasn't anyone else seen in the area?' He picked up a beer mat and tapped it against the table. 'We have three people who saw Lauren Cole that morning. One chap saw her driving up the lane, another saw her parking her car and yet another saw her when she was heading towards the spinney. Added to that, we have two witnesses who can put Carlisle in the area. Five witnesses in total.'

'So? We know that Lauren and Steve were both there.'

'Yes, but given the short time span, one of those five witnesses would have seen someone else. *If* there'd been anyone else to see.'

'Not necessarily.'

Max gave her his 'you're talking crap' look and took another swallow of beer.

'According to your chum Steve,' he said, 'he and Lauren Cole used to meet up and have a pleasant little chat as they walked their dogs. According to Lauren's boyfriend, Ricky Marshall, Carlisle gave her the creeps.'

Jill was aware of that but, without being able to

163

talk to the dead girl, they would never know why. She suspected it was all due to the age difference. Lauren was twenty, little more than a teenager. Steve, on the other hand, was heading towards fifty. To a twenty-year-old, fifty is positively ancient. Added to that, she was an attractive girl and would have been used to members of the opposite sex trying to chat her up. Perhaps she'd thought Steve fell into that category. Come to that, perhaps he had.

'Why,' Max asked, 'would she walk with him if he gave her the creeps?'

'Without being rude, perhaps it was difficult to get away from him.'

'What? She had a masters in being rude.'

'Perhaps with Steve she was different. Look, he's going through a bad patch,' she said. 'He'd worked all his life until a year ago, so he's possibly feeling rejected and worthless. Depressed even. As he said, talking to Lauren brightened his day. Perhaps he was a bit over-friendly. Perhaps he was difficult to get away from.'

Max was right, though; Lauren wouldn't have cared about being rude.

'What about the dog?' she asked. 'Assuming Steve's story is true—'

'Which it isn't.'

'But assuming it is, what happened to the dog? Did someone take the dog to make Steve and Lauren split up?'

'There was no one else there, Jill.'

She refused to believe that. If she did, she would have to accept that Steve Carlisle, a man she liked and respected, or *had* respected, was a killer.

164

'What about the mysterious Josh?' she asked.

'We can't find him. We've spoken to every Josh or Joshua in the area. Nothing. And it's not a particularly common name. I'm beginning to wonder if he ever existed.'

'Maybe he's done a runner to avoid a murder charge.'

'We'd still have records of his existence.'

'Ricky Marshall has no alibi,' she pointed out.

'We don't think he's a killer, but maybe we're wrong. Maybe he was a lot more pissed off about being rejected than he led us to believe.'

'Maybe.' But she could see he was doubtful. She was, too.

'It might be worth having another word with him.'

'It might.' He reached for her empty glass. 'I'll get us another.'

Jill watched him at the bar and was aware of a small inner sigh. There was always something pushing their relationship on to the back burner. Always. Right now the priority was to catch Lauren Cole's killer. Before that, there was the missing Yasmin Smith. And when Lauren's killer had been caught, they would still be hunting Yasmin...

'Why do you believe Carlisle's innocent?' Max put their drinks on the table and sat beside her.

'You know you're always telling me about your gut instincts? Well, this is one of mine.'

Really, she had nothing to back up her claims. If he was found to be guilty though, she would feel let down. Worse, she would feel as if her judgement of character, something she'd always prided herself on, was worth nothing.

'He's a self-contained man,' she tried to explain. 'I don't believe he has illusions about himself. In fact, I think he knows himself well and is happy with himself.'

'How can he be happy with himself when he blames himself for his daughter's death?'

Jill was still surprised she'd lived in the village for five years and yet heard nothing about the Carlisles' child.

'I wonder why they didn't have more children,' she murmured. 'They're practising Catholics, after all.'

'I think a lot of Catholics ignore the views on contraception. If he blames himself, if she blames him...' He shook his head in despair. 'Why the hell do people have to live such complicated lives?'

'It's called marriage,' she said, remembering her own brief marriage and the problems that had brought with it.

'Rubbish!'

'Some people, you and me included, aren't cut out for wedded bliss.'

'Speak for yourself.'

'It's funny, but I always thought Steve and Alison had a good marriage. They always seem easy with each other. Perhaps I've been wrong, though. Who knows what goes on behind closed doors?'

Before Max could comment on that, they were joined by a couple of officers and talk turned to football, a subject that soon had Jill yawning.

She organized a ride home and said goodbye to them all. She needed to get home to her cats who,

166

thanks to her mystery caller, were still locked in.

It was as she walked through her front door that she thought of Adam Smith again. Why had he called her Max's bit of skirt? How could he possibly know they were more than colleagues?

Chapter Sixteen

Ruth Carlisle was pleased to see the first glow of morning light. It had been a long night, one that she'd spent sitting in the kitchen, drinking cups of tea, going back to bed, realizing the futility of that and returning to the kitchen and drinking yet more tea.

On the one occasion she'd managed to drift off to sleep, she'd woken with a start, stiff and aching in the chair in the kitchen, from a dream. Perhaps it hadn't been a dream, maybe her imagination had been playing tricks. Either way, she'd seen Steve being led from a cell with a black hood over his head.

It was stupid. They didn't hang people these days. Evidence had to be gathered, too. Unless they had proper evidence, they couldn't prosecute. Steve would be fine.

What she had to do was keep busy. She'd clean out the kitchen cupboards before Frank came down for his breakfast. Then, when that was out of the way, she would tackle that pile of ironing.

She felt better with her morning planned. By lunchtime, perhaps Steve would be back home

167

where he belonged.

Oh, she hoped so. She couldn't bear to think of him locked up at the police station.

Funny, but whenever she thought about him, it was the child's smiling face she saw, not the adult's world-weary features.

By eleven o'clock, her chores done and her mind refusing to be still, she decided to walk up to the house. If Steve had been released, he would have called her, but if Alison had received news, Ruth would be one of the last to know.

It wasn't snowing, but the ground was frozen hard again, and Ruth chose her steps with care. The last thing she needed was a fall. At her age, that would probably involve hospitalization for a broken hip or some other silly thing.

Years back, she would have crunched her way, slipping and sliding, all the way along the street. It wasn't much fun getting old but, as her dad used to say, the alternative wasn't much better.

When she'd left home, she'd been cold. Then, thanks to the exercise she supposed, she was warm. Now, though, as she walked up the drive-way to Mason's Cottage, she was shivering again. She was well and truly out of sorts today.

Alison opened the door, an earring in one hand and her mobile phone in the other. 'I'll ring you back,' she told her caller, snapping the phone shut. 'Ruth, come in.'

'Thank you.'

Ruth was surprised to see Alison looking so made up. She supposed that, as her daughter-in-law's job was to sell cosmetics, it had become second nature to her. Tall and slim, Alison was always immaculately groomed. In fact, in all the years they'd known each other, Ruth couldn't recall once seeing Alison without carefully applied make-up on her face.

They went into the kitchen and Ruth, still feeling cold and a little shaky, perched on a tall, black and chrome bar stool.

'I don't suppose you've heard anything?' she asked Alison.

'I phoned, of course, but they're keeping him there for the moment and I'm to call again this afternoon. What a mess.' She frowned. 'Are you all right? You look a bit sickly?'

Of course she wasn't all right. Her son was being treated like a criminal. It wasn't that he'd been accused of stealing apples or parking on double yellow lines either. How should she look?

'I'm fine. Just – worried.'

'Would you like a cup of tea?'

Ruth's heart was pounding and she longed to tell Alison what she could do with her tea. She was thirsty though and falling out with her daughter-in-law would achieve nothing. Ruth had managed to be friendly towards Alison for more than twenty years and she wasn't about to stop now. For Steve's sake.

'I would. Thank you.'

Ruth's other children had moved away from the village but, when Ruth saw them and their spouses and their children, she always felt like part of the family. They were still close. Try as she might, she couldn't relax with Alison.

'Has Steve been all right with you lately, Ruth?'

Alison was hunting for tea bags. They always

169

went through this ritual. It was as if Alison needed to point out that she only drank coffee. Steve drank tea, though, so there had to be some in the house.

'He hasn't seemed happy,' Ruth answered. 'But then, he hasn't been happy for years, has he?'

'Thanks!' Alison tried to make light of it. 'Married to the woman of his dreams and you reckon he isn't happy?'

'You know he isn't,' Ruth said, unsmiling.

'It's hardly my fault.'

'I didn't say it was. It's no one's fault. It's just a fact.'

Alison poured boiling water on to a tea bag and went to the fridge for milk.

'You don't take sugar, do you, Ruth?'

For God's sake, how long had they known each other?

'I never have, Alison.'

'Of course not.'

Ruth forced herself to take a deep breath and remember that none of this could be easy for Alison either. Her daughter-in-law might appear cold, unfriendly and uncaring, but there must be more to her than that or Steve wouldn't have married her.

Twenty-two years ago, Ruth had so looked forward to meeting her. Steve had been totally in love with her and Ruth had imagined the two of them growing close, having mother-daughter type days out, laughing together and watching children grow.

But she supposed there were two sides to everything. Just as Steve had been devastated by the

170

loss of lovely little Maisie, so had Alison. Perhaps, if the circumstances had been reversed and it had been Alison looking after the child that night, Steve might have blamed her. Sometimes, it was far easier to apportion blame than it was to accept the cruel facts.

'Last week,' Ruth began, 'you were in Leeds and Steve came to us for his tea, like he always does. I knew then that something was bothering him.'

Alison poured herself a cup of thick black coffee from the machine that was permanently bubbling away in the kitchen. This morning even the smell was making Ruth feel nauseous.

'I knew something was wrong, too,' Alison said at last. 'I phoned him every night from Leeds. I always do if I'm away, you know that. He sounded odd each time. Then, on the Friday night, we went down to the pub for a drink. I was amazed when he lied, and so easily, about not knowing the girl.'

'How do you mean?'

'Exactly that,' Alison retorted, exasperated. 'He'd told me about the woman with the white dog he'd met when he was out walking Cally. Then, because he lied about not knowing the dead woman, I didn't twig it was the same one. He knew her, Ruth. He used to meet up with her. Her dog and Cally used to run around together.'

'But he couldn't have known her.' Ruth was with him when he looked at the newspaper and saw her photo on the front page. If he'd known her, he would have said something. 'No, Alison, you've got it wrong. Someone said they saw him with her, that's all. They must have been mistaken.'

'Of course they weren't,' Alison snapped. 'And

171

do you know how the woman was killed?'

Ruth couldn't say she did. The newspaper and television reports had simply talked of her being 'attacked' and mentioned a 'brutal' killing.

'Not really, no.'

'Well, given that the police were crawling all over this place yesterday, I think it's safe to say she was killed with an axe. They were looking for Steve's axe, Ruth, and it's not here.'

'What?' Ruth felt the room sway and she had to put a hand to her chest to steady her racing heart. 'What do you mean? Why would they think it was Steve's axe?'

Alison walked to the window, peered out across the snow-covered garden and then spun round.

'Hasn't it crossed your mind, Ruth, that there's no smoke without fire? Haven't you thought that maybe, just maybe, the police have some evidence to link Steve to the murder?'

'What exactly are you saying, Alison?'

'I'm asking if you've considered the possibility of your son being a killer!'

Chapter Seventeen

Max turned left at the lights, an action that had Jill looking at him in astonishment.

'This won't take a minute,' he promised. 'I need to call on Vincent Cole. He said he'd try and find Lauren's old diaries for us.'

Having spoken to two shopkeepers who knew

Lauren, but nothing about her, he was driving them back to headquarters. He knew Jill had an appointment, but as he'd told her, it wouldn't take more than a couple of minutes to go via Vincent Cole's house. As well as, hopefully, collecting Lauren's diaries, Max wanted to see how Cole was coping.

'Come in and see what you make of him,' he said, as he stopped the car outside Worcester House.

'I expect I'll see nothing more than a grieving father,' she replied, unfastening her seat belt.

When he opened the door, Vincent Cole looked as if he hadn't washed or shaved since his daughter had been murdered. The shirt and v-necked sweater were those he'd worn when he'd identified Lauren.

Max introduced Jill and, although Cole shook her hand, Max gained the impression he neither knew why she was there nor cared.

'You said you'd try and find Lauren's diaries,' Max reminded him.

'Yes. I did say they were old, though.'

He took them through the hall and into the sitting room where, on a low sideboard, there were half a dozen pocket diaries held together with an elastic band.

'Here they are.' He handed them to Max. 'Every January,' he explained for Jill's benefit, 'Lauren would get a brand new diary and spend hours writing in people's birthdays, and their names and addresses, of course. She'd put in appointments and suchlike, too. By February,' he said with a sad smile, 'her enthusiasm had waned and they'd be thrown in the back of the drawer never to see light of day again.'

While he spoke, Max flicked through them. Cole was right in that they were old, but they were crammed with friends' addresses and phone numbers. Something useful might come to light.

'This is a lovely photo,' Jill said, pointing to a framed print that had pride of place on the mantelpiece.

'Yes.' Cole picked it up and rubbed imaginary dust from the frame. 'Lauren and her mum. It was taken when her mother was well. The last one I had of her, in fact.'

'Were Lauren and her mother close?'

'Oh, yes. Very. Lauren never got over her mum's death. I can't say I ever did, either, but Lauren didn't cope. She just couldn't deal with it.'

'I'm sorry,' Jill said quietly.

The room wasn't quite as neat as it had been, Max noticed. A thin layer of dust covered the surfaces. Three unopened newspapers were lying on the coffee table next to an empty cup. Presumably, Cole had told his cleaner not to bother for a while.

'I need to bury her now,' Cole said, and Max could hear the desperation in his voice. He understood it, too. People hated to think of their loved ones lying in a cold mortuary.

'I'm having her laid to rest next to her mum,' he went on. 'It's all arranged. When can I bury her?'

'Hopefully, it won't be too long,' Max said.

Cole nodded, but he was still agitated.

'I can't rest until then. I want them to be together. Foolish, perhaps, but that's what I want.

I'll feel better then.'

'That's perfectly understandable, Mr Cole,' Jill told him.

Max wished he could promise a swift closure, but he couldn't.

'We'll let you have these back as soon as we can,' he said, nodding at the diaries.

'Thank you. I'd appreciate it.'

They had little else to say to him and were soon back in the car.

'Poor man,' Jill said. 'All those regrets. All that guilt.'

'Guilt?'

'He'll blame himself for not being there for Lauren when her mum died. It's a common problem. Spouses are too wrapped up in their grief to notice how their children are suffering.'

Max knew it worked the other way, too. When his own wife had died, he'd thrown all he had into making sure Harry and Ben were coping. It had stopped him facing up to his own guilt.

Max had a busy morning. Busy, but pointless. In between the briefing, updating his boss, and talking to the press, he'd tried to get something from Carlisle, but the man wasn't changing his story.

It was almost lunchtime when he and Jill sat in the interview room with Ricky Marshall. Max wanted some answers and he wanted them fast, but Marshall was offering nothing other than a smug smile. Given the way he'd learnt how to piss coppers off by parroting 'No comment', he'd been watching too many TV cop shows.

'Let's start again,' Max suggested. 'You were

seen on CCTV in Harrington with Lauren Cole two days before she was killed. Tell me what you were doing with her.'

'No comment.'

'Answer the question or get charged with obstruction. Your choice.'

Marshall looked at Max as if he wanted to kill him. The feeling was mutual.

'I was talking to her, that's all,' he said at last.

'About what?'

Marshall grinned. 'If you must know, I asked her if she'd seen God again.'

'God?' Jill repeated.

'I told you she was bleedin' raving,' Marshall reminded them. 'One night, she got really stoned and reckoned she'd seen her mum. Christ, we had tears, hysterics, the bloody lot. Her mum's been dead for bloody years. Then she reckoned God had come to her in a vision. And get this – according to her, God told her he wanted her to stay off the heroin.' He laughed at the memory. 'Absolutely raving she was.'

'So you asked her if she'd seen God again?' Jill asked.

'Yeah.'

'And had she?'

'How the hell would I know? I asked her, and she just kept saying she'd pray for me. She said she'd been to church to light a candle for her mum.'

'Which church?'

'Dunno.'

'In Harrington presumably?'

'Dunno. So much for seeing God, eh? He must have thought he'd take her up to heaven,' he said

176

with a grin.

'Perhaps he did,' Jill agreed. 'It's a good job that only the good die young, eh, Ricky?'

'Piss off!'

Max nodded at Jill and terminated the interview. They left Marshall to his boredom.

'Get yourself a coffee and I'll make a couple of phone calls,' Max said. 'Lighting candles is a Catholic thing, isn't it? I'd stake my life on Lauren Cole visiting the same church as your good friend Steve Carlisle.'

'If Lauren *did* go to St Mary's,' Jill answered slowly, 'then the priest there is Alison Carlisle's uncle.'

'Exactly!'

Max believed that, finally, they were getting somewhere. He wasn't sure where exactly, but he was convinced they were moving forward.

St Mary's Roman Catholic church, a large red-brick building set back from Princess Street, was more functional than attractive, but today, with its grounds covered in pristine snow that had been falling all day, and a setting sun highlighting the colourful stained-glass windows, it could have featured on the front page of a county magazine.

A board by the gate told everyone that the next service would be at 10.00 a.m. on Sunday morning and would be conducted by the parish priest, Father David Gosling.

Max had phoned the priest and he'd promised to be at the church all afternoon.

The winding path had been cleared of snow, and he and Jill walked along it smartly, eager to

177

find some warmth in the building.

They were out of luck. The temperature plunged as they stepped inside. The lighting was dim, and flames from a few spluttering candles didn't do much to help. Max could see his breath as he walked up the aisle to where a priest was collecting a pile of books.

'Father Gosling?'

'The very same. And you'll be DCI Trentham?'

'That's right.' Max showed his ID. 'And this is Jill Kennedy.'

Father David Gosling was a short man, and looked to be well past retirement age. His face was ruddy and round, his hair thin. Perhaps what struck Max most was the fact that he was all in black, as one might expect, with the exception of brown shoes. The shoes made his feet look enormous.

'Thank you for seeing us, Father.' Max wanted this interview over as quickly as possible. It was far too cold for idle chit-chat. 'We believe you may have known Lauren Cole?'

'Not as well as I wished,' Father Gosling answered. 'I knew her mother very well indeed, God rest her soul.'

'Mrs Cole was a regular at your church?'

'She was. Lauren, too, when she was younger. Mr Cole...' The priest smiled wistfully. 'Alas.'

Somehow, without anyone suggesting it, they all sat on the front pew.

The building had that typical church smell, a mix of dust, damp, musty books and furniture polish.

'And Lauren had stopped coming until

recently?' Jill asked.

'Her mother stopped when she became ill,' Father Gosling explained. 'I visited her at home, of course, and at the hospital. After the Lord took her, I never saw Lauren again. Until recently.'

A police siren was the only sound to penetrate the thick walls of the church.

'How did Lauren seem to you?' Jill asked.

'Sad.' For a moment, Max thought that one word was all they were going to get.

'She was fourteen when her mother died,' the priest went on, 'and it's a difficult age for a child to accept such things. I gather she was losing her way a little.'

'You mean taking drugs, that sort of thing?' Max asked.

'I wouldn't know about that, but I gather her friends left a little to be desired. She seemed confused. Lonely too, I thought.'

'How often did she come to the church?' Jill asked.

'Every Sunday for mass,' he replied. 'But she also called in most days. She would light a candle for her mother and then sit...' He pointed to the far side of the church where there was a carved wooden figure of Christ looking down despairingly on the pews. 'She would sit alone with her thoughts over there.'

'Did you try to speak to her?' Max asked.

'Of course. She didn't want company, though. As I say, she would sit alone.'

'What about confession?' Jill asked and Father Gosling shook his head.

'She never confessed, I'm afraid.'

'Did she ever speak to anyone before or after the service?' Max asked. 'Did she sit with anyone?'

'No. As I said, I think she was lonely. She would slip in a few moments before the service started and sit at the back. As soon as it was over, she was gone. I never saw her speak to anyone.'

'Do you know a man called Steve Carlisle? I believe he and his wife worship here.'

Father Gosling smiled at that.

'I should know them. His wife is my niece, Chief Inspector.'

'Ah, yes,' Jill murmured. 'I heard something of the sort.'

'Her late father, John, was my younger brother. Alison's mother and I were great friends, too, but sadly, Maureen passed away last year.'

'Are you and Alison close?' Jill asked curiously.

'Of course. Alison is all the family I have in the world now.'

'You'll know about Steve then?'

Father Gosling looked at her, a puzzled frown on his old face.

'Know what, my dear?'

'That he's being questioned in connection with the murder of Lauren Cole,' Max enlightened him.

The heavy oak door to the church opened and slammed shut. They all turned to look as a middle-aged woman walked up the aisle carrying an armful of greenery.

'Hello, Elsie,' Father Gosling murmured.

'Father, I won't be in your way,' the woman promised, smiling at Jill and Max. 'I'll take this lot through to the back. I'll come tomorrow to do the flowers.'

'That's fine, Elsie. Thank you.'

Father Gosling turned his attention back to Max.

'When you say he's being questioned, Chief Inspector, what exactly do you mean?'

'He's a suspect in a murder investigation.'

'Steve?'

Father Gosling might be old, even a little frail looking, but Max guessed he had a shrewd brain. It was almost possible to hear it ticking over.

'No, I didn't know that,' he said at last. 'Why Steve?'

Max wasn't going into details.

'Did you ever see him speaking to Lauren Cole?' he asked instead.

'No. Never.'

'You're sure?'

'Quite sure.'

'I'm surprised Alison hasn't told you about it,' Jill said, hands stuffed in the pockets of her coat for warmth. 'As you're so close, I mean.'

'I expect she didn't want to bother me,' he replied. 'I'm sure there's a reasonable explanation for it all. When it's all blown over, then she'll tell me.'

'No doubt,' Jill agreed. 'When was the last time you saw Steve?'

'On Sunday. After the service, the three of us went out to lunch. We often do.'

'How did he seem?' Jill stood up and towered over them. Max guessed she was trying to bring some circulation back to her feet.

181

'Fine.'

'Just fine?'

'Yes. Quite normal. Smiling and talking.'

'Would you say that he and Alison had a good marriage?' she asked him.

'Of course.'

The atmosphere was becoming even chillier, Max noticed. Father Gosling's answers seemed guarded, and he was taking a few moments to think before giving them.

'I only ask,' Jill pushed on, 'because losing a child is so difficult, isn't it? It's hard for couples to cope with such a tragedy. Especially without other children to hold them together.'

'You're talking about Maisie,' he said, and he seemed extremely rattled. 'That was a long time ago, Miss Kennedy. It's over. Forgotten. We can't debate the right and wrongs of God's will, can we?'

'God's will,' she repeated. 'Ah, yes. But even if that were the case, it can't necessarily follow that the parents have come to terms with the loss.'

'Now that's where you're wrong. That's how people *do* come to terms with such things. Christians know and accept that it is God's will.'

'But if one of them didn't accept it–'

'People do, Miss Kennedy.'

'So, having accepted it, one would assume that more children would come along,' Jill said.

'One would,' he agreed, 'but sadly, Alison couldn't have more children.'

'Ah, I didn't know that. So poor Steve–'

'Accepted that,' the priest snapped.

For a Christian, Father Gosling was showing

very little goodwill to all men. Well, Jill at least. His answers were becoming increasingly short and terse.

'Then they're well blessed as a couple,' Jill said, giving him a smile that would chip ice. 'I think many men in Steve's position, men who wanted children, would have difficulty with that. They might grow to resent their wives. They might feel trapped in a sad, poor excuse for a marriage. They might even look elsewhere for–'

'Now look here, I was under the impression that you wanted to talk about Lauren Cole. I can't see that my niece's marriage has anything whatsoever to do with the poor girl. In fact, if there's nothing else, I have things that I need to be doing.'

'You've been most helpful,' Max told him, eager to get outside where it would be warmer. 'Thank you for your time, Father Gosling.'

'A pleasure.'

It had clearly been anything but that.

Outside, darkness had fallen and the wind strength had increased. As soon as they were in the car, Max turned the heater on full.

'I don't think you made a friend back there, kiddo.'

'Miserable git,' she muttered. 'Why is it so wrong for people to have problems with life? And what the hell was it with the brown shoes?'

'God's will?'

'Ha. If I thought God wanted me to look a complete prat, I'd start questioning my faith.' She took off her gloves and rubbed her hands together for warmth. 'It's odd, though, that Alison hasn't spoken to him. Them being so close and all that.

183

And he was rattled when I mentioned their dead daughter, Maisie. I wonder if he's had problems with Alison, or Steve come to that. I wonder how he'd react if they didn't accept that it was God's will quite as easily as he thinks they should.'

'You think they have problems in their marriage, don't you?'

'I think it would be odd if they haven't. The loss of a child, and the inability to have more children, isn't the best foundation for a happy life, is it? And if there *were* problems – no love, no warmth, no fun, no sex – Steve might have found a young pretty girl very appealing.'

Chapter Eighteen

When Jill pushed open the door of her cottage that evening, with Max right behind her carrying their takeaway, the first thing she saw was a brown envelope lying on the mat. There was no other mail and, although she didn't know why, she had an ominous feeling.

She picked it up, let Max inside and shut out the darkness. The envelope was thicker than the average bill and, when she turned it over, she saw that there was no address. It had been delivered by hand.

'Max?'

He'd gone straight to the kitchen and she followed him, holding the envelope in front of her.

'Hand delivered,' she explained, and he took it

from her with the tips of his fingers.

Scowling at it, he took a knife from her cutlery drawer and, very carefully, slit it open. With even more care, still using the knife, he inched out the contents. There were five photographs of Jill. One showed her opening her front door, another getting into her car. In another she was gazing out from her window. In one she was standing at the back door and, in the last, she was bending to fuss a cat.

'Bastard!' she muttered.

'When were they taken?'

Jill looked more closely and tried to remember what she'd been wearing yesterday.

'At a guess, I'd say those three were taken yesterday. These were taken this morning.'

'Sure?'

'Yes.' Today was the first time she'd worn her long grey coat.

She'd known he'd been close, of course. Close enough to kill a cat. To know he was hanging around long enough to use a camera was unsettling, though.

At least her cats were safe. They were sulking because they couldn't come and go as they chose, but they were pleased to see her and would be even happier to see the tin opener.

'Let's eat,' she suggested, 'before it gets cold.'

She didn't want to think about cranks phoning her in the small hours or taking photos as she went about her day.

Max went outside to his car and returned with an evidence bag. The envelope and photos were put inside and Jill hoped they could forget it for a while.

She was trying to enjoy her spicy chicken wings, without the appetite she'd had before arriving home, when Max brought up the subject again.

'At least we know Steve Carlisle isn't stringing up cats,' he said.

'Well done, Max, you've managed to narrow it down to sixty million suspects minus one. No wonder you're a detective.'

He ignored her sarcasm, and she supposed she couldn't blame him.

'We need to get you away from here,' he said instead.

'No way. I'm not being frightened out of my own home. Besides, I can take care of myself.'

He rolled his eyes at that.

'For all we know, Lauren Cole had a few Thai boxing lessons, too.'

'I can take care of myself, Max.'

She could tell he wasn't convinced.

In truth, she was beginning to feel a little anxious herself. Looking on the bright side, though, she knew that this particular nutter was merely trying to frighten her. Phone calls were the act of a coward. As was hanging an old frail cat. He'd been near enough to take photos, so near enough to put an axe through her head.

'We'll get a couple of cameras rigged up,' Max said and she nodded.

She watched him start his second glass of wine. She wasn't going to suggest he stayed the night but she had to admit that she'd feel a whole lot easier if he did.

'Why was that priest so antagonistic this afternoon?' she asked, changing the subject.

'I don't know. Perhaps he didn't like us prying into the lives of his family members.'

'Maybe.'

But Jill wasn't convinced. She thought it went deeper than that. Then again, hearing that a family member was being questioned in connection with a murder would be a shock for anyone.

When their food was eaten, she put plates and cutlery in the dishwasher, and then they carried their wine through to the sitting room.

The room was warm, but Jill lit the stove. She liked to see the flames and hear the logs crackling. It was cosy, a place to relax, yet Jill was struggling to do that. She kept wondering if someone was outside.

So when her doorbell rang, a quick short ring, it frightened her half to death. Yet again, she had to remind herself that maniacs rarely announced their presence.

'I'll get it.' Max was at the door before she could argue, but she followed, curious as to who might be calling so late.

She was surprised to see Ruth Carlisle standing there.

'What are you doing out on a night like this, Ruth? Come in, quick.'

'I'm sorry to bother you, Jill.'

'It's no bother at all. We were doing nothing, just sitting by the fire. You've met Max, haven't you?'

She realized that although Ruth most likely knew Max, he couldn't be expected to know her.

'This is Ruth Carlisle, Max. Steve's mother.'

187

They went through the social niceties as Jill ushered Ruth into the sitting room.

'A glass of wine, Ruth?'

'Oh, no, love. Really, I'm not stopping. I wouldn't have bothered you at all, but–'

'You're not bothering us,' Jill assured her again. 'Let me take your coat. Come and sit by the fire and get warm.'

Jill wasn't normally so pushy with her visitors, but Ruth looked a breath away from collapsing. Her face wasn't so much white as a pale grey, and it was dominated by red-rimmed eyes.

Ruth sat down and Rabble, the cat who was usually wary of strangers, jumped straight on to her lap. Instinctively, Ruth began to stroke her.

'I only came – well, I wondered what was going to happen to Steve,' Ruth said. 'I don't suppose you can tell me anything but–' Her voice cracked. 'Oh, Jill, you can't imagine what a worry it is.'

'I can.' Jill sat beside her and patted her hand. 'At the moment, Steve's trying to tell us everything he can about the morning Lauren Cole was murdered. That's all.'

It wasn't quite 'all', but Jill didn't want to add to Ruth's panic.

'But why? I mean, what would make you think' – she looked at Max as she spoke – 'that Steve had anything to do with it?'

While Max prepared his answer, she rushed on, 'And Alison said something about the poor girl being killed with Steve's axe. Surely, that can't be true.'

'I'm afraid it is,' Max said.

'Oh!' Ruth seemed incapable of anything more

than that one anguished word.

'Have a glass of wine,' Jill urged her.

'Perhaps I will. If you don't mind, Jill. I won't stay long. I know you'll not want me—'

'Don't be silly,' Jill insisted. 'It's good to see you. I just wish the circumstances were different.'

Jill went to the kitchen for another glass. The photos, safely packed away in the evidence bag, were still on the table and, once again, she wondered if the photographer was outside. Perhaps he was watching them. Perhaps he'd seen Ruth arrive. And perhaps he would see Max leave...

'Here you go, Ruth.'

With a glass in her hand, Ruth seemed to calm herself slightly.

'Tell me,' Jill began, 'how do you get along with Alison?'

She could see that her question had taken Ruth completely by surprise.

'Alison?'

'Yes. I know that, on the surface, everything is fine, but—'

'I know what you mean,' Ruth said. 'Yes, if we're out in public, we smile and give the impression that we're the best of friends. The truth? We've never really taken to each other.'

'Oh?' And that took Jill by surprise. Ruth was the typical mother hen, the sort who would welcome anyone into her family. 'Why's that?'

Ruth managed a weak smile.

'We're chalk and cheese. Alison is always dressed up to the nines. Her house is the same, one of those where you have to ring for an appointment to visit.'

She took a small sip of wine and Jill could see her considering the question more seriously.

Max, Jill was pleased to see, was looking fairly relaxed. He was paying attention to every word, but at least he wasn't firing questions at Steve's mother.

'When Steve first met Alison,' Ruth explained, 'I thought she was the best thing that had ever happened to him. He wore a smile as big as Lancashire. He was so deeply in love that it touched my heart. I couldn't wait to meet the girl responsible.'

'And?' Jill prompted.

'She only came from Harrington, but it might as well have been a thousand miles away. She simply didn't have time to meet Frank and me.'

'Really?'

'We saw her twice before the wedding, and then only briefly. She called at our house both times to tell us of the wedding plans. Of course, as I wanted to welcome her, I'd prepared a big spread. I know she likes to watch her weight, but she wouldn't have so much as a cup of tea. I felt, well, we both felt a bit uneasy with her. It was as if we weren't good enough for her. We felt – on edge.'

On edge and deeply hurt, Jill guessed. She could imagine Ruth fussing for days over Alison's impending visits. Everything would have been done to ensure Alison had the warmest of welcomes to the family.

'A year later,' Ruth went on, 'little Maisie was born.' She smiled at the memory. 'I don't think I've seen a prettier baby. She was just beautiful.'

'Alison and Steve were happy, yes?'

'Oh yes.'

'And you were chief babysitter?' Jill guessed with a smile.

'No.' Ruth stared into the depths of her glass. 'No, Alison preferred to leave her with a young woman called Valerie Easton. She's left the village now. Left Kelton about ten years ago. She was a qualified child minder, you see. It didn't matter that I'd managed to raise four children. Alison insisted that an expert looked after Maisie.'

It was no wonder Alison and Ruth didn't get along too well. Jill could imagine her own mother's reaction if Prue left her kids with anyone but their grandmother.

'I had such hopes,' Ruth said, her expression wistful. 'I thought it would be wonderful to have Steve and his wife living in the village. I thought we'd be close, you see. I imagined me and Alison going round the shops together, planning Maisie's birthday parties together – you know the sort of thing?'

'Yes.'

'The reality is that I rarely visit the house without phoning to see if it's convenient. That's the way Alison likes it. She's polite enough, of course, and she always buys me something nice for Christmas and on my birthday.'

Something 'nice'. That one word summed up the relationship perfectly. Ruth wouldn't want a silk scarf or the latest fragrance. She would prefer something that a little thought had gone into. Homemade biscuits would have given her more pleasure.

'What about Alison's uncle, Father Gosling?'

Max asked. 'How do you get along with him?'

'I don't,' she answered simply. 'I've only met him twice. Once at the wedding, and once when he visited Steve and Alison.'

'Alison is close to him,' Max pointed out.

'She would be, wouldn't she?'

Jill was alerted by something in Ruth's tone.

'What do you mean by that, Ruth?' she asked.

'Nothing,' she answered quickly. 'It's nothing. Just something that me and Frank say.' She sighed. 'Her uncle, the vicar, priest, whatever you call him, is very well off,' she explained. 'He's had people leave him a lot of money in their wills. Perhaps we're being unkind, but me and Frank both reckon that's why she keeps so friendly with him.'

She emptied her glass.

'I shouldn't say such unkind things, true or not,' she said as she stood up. 'Put it down to worry about Steve. And now it's time I left you two young people alone.'

'I'll drive you home,' Max said, already on his feet as Jill went to fetch Ruth's coat.

'Thank you, but there's no need. Really.'

'It's no trouble.' Max had his car keys in his hand to allow no argument.

Ruth smiled at Jill. 'You've got a real gentleman here, love.'

'Don't you believe it!'

Jill gave her a quick hug, watched her being helped into Max's car and then closed the door on the night to think over what Ruth had told them about Steve and Alison's marriage. It was preferable to thinking that someone might be lurking outside her cottage, someone who had

192

seen Max leave and knew she was alone.

Five minutes later, Max was back and Jill was glad of that.

'Ruth OK?' she asked him.

'Probably.'

He looked at the empty wine bottle, picked it up and went to the kitchen for a full one.

When their glasses had been filled and they were, once more, enjoying the warmth from Jill's stove, she thought how civilized this was. She still didn't know if Max planned to stay the night, but the later it became, the more optimistic she grew.

'She seems nice enough,' he said.

'Ruth? She's a lovely woman. Completely genuine. What you see is what you get. She has a nice family, too. Steve, believe it or not, is just the same.'

'When he's not lying through his back teeth,' Max pointed out and Jill knew he had a point.

'I expect a lot of it is due to low self-esteem,' she excused Steve. 'He's probably spent twenty years blaming himself and being blamed for the death of his daughter. Add to that the fact that he's lost his job. He'll be feeling totally useless and inadequate, far too worthless to imagine that anyone will believe his story about finding Lauren Cole like that.'

Max could think what he liked, but Jill was convinced of Steve's innocence. What's more, she was determined to prove it. With or without Max's help.

'Ruth's views on Father Gosling were interesting,' Max murmured. 'Well, her views on Alison Carlisle keeping well in with the bloke.'

'Yes, I thought that. It makes sense, too. Alison isn't the type to trot off to church every Sunday.'

'We'll have to delve into his finances.'

Jill leaned back on the sofa and lifted her feet to rest on the footstool. 'Give me an alternative, detective,' she said.

'For what?'

'In very different ways, using different methods, we both believe we can get inside a killer's mind. So give me an alternative. Tell me how someone could murder Lauren Cole and pin the blame on Steve.'

He smiled at that. 'You think Steve's been set up?'

'Stranger things have happened.'

'True, but not much.' He kicked off his shoes and rested his feet beside Jill's. 'OK. Someone somehow manages, and God knows how, to get to the shelter without half of Kelton Bridge seeing him. He knows Steve walks that way each morning, and he knows that Lauren sometimes does, so he lies in wait with a lamb chop in his pocket.'

'What?' She spluttered with laughter.

'He'll have known that he can't call Lauren's dog,' Max explained, 'so he'll try and entice the dog without being heard.'

'Hey, that makes sense.'

'Hm. So he produces his lamb chop and, according to plan, Lauren's dog goes to investigate. He grabs the dog and ties it up. Oh, he gags it, too, so it can't bark.'

Jill knew he wasn't taking this very seriously, but she was determined to find something, somewhere, that was feasible.

'So he lies in wait,' Max continued, 'with the dog bound and gagged until Lauren returns to the spot where she's agreed to meet Carlisle. He then takes the axe from Steve's sack. Did I mention he has X-ray vision? That's how he knows the axe is there. He kills Lauren with one swift blow. He then unties the dog and scarpers without a single soul in Kelton Bridge seeing him.'

Put like that, it sounded absurd. Impossible.

'There has to be an explanation,' Jill insisted.

'No one else was seen in the area,' he reminded her.

'But they wouldn't be, would they? Everyone saw Lauren and Steve because they were walking their dogs as they often did. They had no reason to hide. The killer, on the other hand, would have made sure he wasn't seen.'

'How?'

'There are plenty of stone walls to hide behind. And trees.'

All the same, it didn't make any sense and she was too tired to think. Either that or the wine had turned her brain to mush. She closed her eyes and listened to the crackling of the logs.

Chapter Nineteen

Frank Carlisle lay in the bed he'd shared with his wife for more years than he cared to remember and longed for the first hint of daylight. At this time of year, it was slow to come.

For once, Ruth was sleeping soundly. Perhaps the glass of wine she'd had at Jill Kennedy's had helped.

She needed sleep. They both did, but Frank's mind refused to switch off. The last thing he wanted was to wake Ruth, but his body ached from holding it so still.

Not, he decided, that an aching body was anything new. At seventy-eight years of age, he was used to that. The slightest movement out of the ordinary always brought with it a painful reminder of his age.

It seemed no time at all since he'd been able to run up these hills and think nothing of it, or race the length and breadth of the football pitch for an hour and a half and barely be out of breath.

All that was a long time ago. Now, he often wondered how long it would be before even climbing the stairs was too much for his old body.

To hell with it. Coaxing his stiff limbs into an upright position, he sat on the side of the bed for a moment, waiting to see if the movement had woken Ruth. Pleased that it hadn't, he stood up and padded barefoot to the door where his dressing gown hung from the hook.

He shrugged that on and tiptoed down the stairs and into the kitchen. Perhaps a hot mug of tea would settle him. At least it would give him something to do until the light finally ushered in another day.

With his tea made, he carried it into the sitting room and sat by the window in the upright wooden chair. The chair had belonged to his father and his grandfather and, what it lacked in looks, it made up for by easing his aching back.

On the sideboard, on the opposite side of the room, were several photographs, all showing members of the family on important days. There were birthdays and graduations. The one that held Frank's gaze showed Steve and Alison smiling for the camera on their wedding day. He felt like flinging it across the room. What hurt most was the broad smile on Steve's trusting face as he stood next to his young beautiful bride. Sometimes beauty was only skin deep, Frank thought as he tore his gaze away.

For years, ever since young Maisie had been snatched from them, Ruth had been worrying about the state of Steve and Alison's marriage.

'Don't be daft, woman,' Frank had scolded at first. 'They've lost a baby so of course they're unhappy. But they'll have more. It'll all come right in the end, you'll see.'

No other children had come along though, and Frank had begun to wonder if perhaps Ruth was right. But Steve had seemed happy enough with his lot.

Frank had chosen to believe that all was well in his son's marriage until, six weeks ago, he'd seen that it wasn't. Although he could remember things that had happened sixty years ago, he often struggled to remember what he'd done yesterday, but he could remember everything about that day with a perfect clarity.

His friend, Bill, had been going into Burnley to get his car serviced and Frank had said he'd go along to keep Bill company while he waited. They planned to walk into town and have a look round.

As Bill drove them over Deerplay Moor, they spoke about Burnley's football team and how their recent success had given the town a much needed boost.

It had been drizzling, and the windscreen wipers had screeched their way back and forth. While Bill was complaining about that, Frank spotted a car like Alison's in front of them. He paid it no real attention. He was too busy talking.

It was when they were a couple of miles further on, where roadworks had narrowed the road near the lay-by, that he realized it *was* Alison's car.

As Bill's car was stationary at the temporary traffic lights, Frank watched, a sick feeling thudding in his stomach, as Alison parked her car, jumped out, and ran a couple of yards to another car. The owner of that car got out to meet her.

Bill was easing the car forward when Frank saw his daughter-in-law kiss the driver of that other car. It was a long kiss. The man had been sliding his hands over Alison's buttocks...

Frank hadn't said a word to Ruth about it. Nor Steve, nor Alison. He hadn't mentioned it to a soul, but he couldn't get it out of his head.

That Alison could cheat on Steve – and what other explanation could there be? – sickened him to the pit of his stomach.

More than anything, Frank hated liars and cheats, hated people running around behind their partners' backs.

And now, Steve was alone. He was being held in a cell while the police quizzed him about the murder of a young girl. And it was tearing his mother apart.

It would be sorted out, Frank had no doubt about that, but what did Steve have to come home to? A cheat and a liar, that's what.

For two pins, he'd go to their house and tell Alison exactly what he thought of her. He wished to God Steve had never set eyes on the blasted woman.

Chapter Twenty

Jill opened her eyes, sat up with a jolt and felt a stab of pain in her neck. She'd fallen asleep on the sofa. Max had too but, as she moved, he woke up.

'What time is it?' he mumbled.

'Early enough to go to bed, I hope.'

Max rubbed his eyes then checked his watch. 'Hell's teeth. It's almost eight. Time for a quick shower and then I need to go.'

Jill liked to wake up slowly, preferably with coffee in bed. That was out of the question, but she had no intention of doing a single thing before she'd had a caffeine hit.

'You have a shower,' she said, 'and I'll sort the coffee.'

While it was brewing, she let the cats out, peering into the garden as she did so just in case any lunatics were out there. It was deserted, of course. All the same, she wouldn't rest easy until the cats were on the right side of a locked cat-flap again.

She was sitting at the table, a large mug of coffee in front of her when Max came downstairs. Not only had he showered, he'd managed to find a clean shirt. He looked wide awake and smart; she looked as if she'd spent an uncomfortable night on a sofa.

She poured him a coffee and glanced out of the window again to see what her cats were up to. Sam was sitting on the shed's roof surveying his world. Rabble and Tojo were having their usual morning fight.

Max's phone rang and Jill wondered why they couldn't even manage a coffee without interruption.

'Oh, no,' she heard Max say. 'How?... Do we know when?... Yeah, OK.'

He ended the call and shook his head in despair.

'What's happened?' She hardly dare ask.

'Vincent Cole is dead. He killed himself.'

It took a moment for his words to sink in.

'No,' she said with absolute certainty. 'I don't know what happened, but no way did he kill himself.'

'Believe me, he did. He's hanging from the beam in his sitting room.'

'No, Max. He didn't.'

'Jill,' he said patiently, 'the bloke never got over losing his wife. Now his daughter is dead. In his shoes, I'd probably top myself, too.'

'Trust me, Max, this isn't suicide. Yes, he might have been having thoughts about ending it all but there is no way he would do that before he'd buried Lauren.'

He was perfectly still, considering that.

'We do all we can for our loved ones,' she reminded him, 'and the last thing we can do is lay them to rest with the dignity they deserve. Believe me, Vincent Cole wouldn't have killed himself before Lauren was at rest beside her mother. When we visited, that's all he cared about.'

'Shit!'

Max was on the phone again.

'Vincent Cole,' he told the person at the other end. 'I want everyone available out there. And nothing is to be touched. Nothing at all. I'm on my way. I'll be there' – he glanced at his watch – 'half an hour at most.'

He ended the call and gave Jill a quick kiss. 'I'll have to dash. Catch you later.'

Jill stood at the door to watch him jump in his car, fire the engine and take off down the lane at a speed that was far from sensible given the icy state of the road. Then she went to see if she, too, could shower and find clothes smart enough for the interview she was doing later.

It was mayhem when Max arrived at Worcester House. Tape sealed off the property. A crowd of neighbours stood in the cold air to see what was going on.

Max changed into his protective suit in the hallway and then walked into the sitting room where SOCOs in similar suits were gathering evidence. The photographer was busy, bursts of flash lighting the room – and the body – every few seconds.

Hanging from the centre beam in the room,

wearing blue striped pyjamas, was Vincent Cole.

Beneath Cole was a kitchen chair that had, possibly, been kicked away.

'Who found him?' Max asked.

'A neighbour. She's in the kitchen.'

Max went to the kitchen where an elderly woman was sitting at the table, an untouched cup of tea in front of her and a young WPC opposite her.

'This is Mrs Hollingsworth,' the WPC told Max. 'She cleans for Mr Cole and has a key.'

Max sat opposite her and gave her an encouraging smile.

'You've had a terrible shock,' he said, and she nodded at the understatement.

'What made you come here at this time?' he asked. 'It's a bit early to start cleaning, isn't it?'

'The wheelie bin,' she replied, her voice trembling. 'Oh, I live in the bungalow across the road,' she explained, 'and I've been coming in to clean for Vince since – since his wife died. Not yesterday. I don't do Tuesdays. Yesterday, I went into Manchester and didn't get back till six.'

'You said something about the wheelie bin?'

'Yes. Knowing it would be dark when I got home, I put my bin out before I left. I always put mine out the night – or day – before because they come early to empty it. This morning, I was up early. Couldn't sleep for some reason. Anyway, I saw that Vince hadn't put his bin out. You can see it now. It's still round the corner of the house.'

'And that's unusual?' Max asked.

'Oh, yes. He's a stickler about it. He likes to get up very early and normally he'll put it out about six o'clock. The bin men are always here by seven in the morning. Always.'

She looked at the tea in front of her and took a hesitant sip.

'I spoke to him when I put mine out,' she said. 'He was getting his car out of the garage. He told me he'd probably put his out later because it's so dark in the mornings.'

'And that's all he said.'

'More or less, yes. I told him, yet again, that if there was anything I could do, he just had to say the word. I don't suppose there is – *was* – but I did feel for him. That girl meant the world to him, poor man.'

Max nodded at that.

'How did he seem?' he asked her.

'The same as usual,' she replied. 'He thanked me, said he was doing all right. Mind,' she added, 'he used to be in the army so I suppose he thinks it's weak to show his feelings.'

'Did he say anything else?'

'No. But it was cold and we were both keen to get back inside.'

That was understandable.

'I wouldn't normally dream of going in the house,' she went on, 'using my key, I mean, unless it's my day to clean. But, like I said, it felt wrong. In fact, it felt so wrong that I nipped over here and rang the bell a couple of times. There was no answer. I even shouted through the letter-box a couple of times. Nothing.'

'So you came inside?' Max asked.

'Not then, no. I thought he must still be in bed or – to be honest, I didn't know what to think.'

She took a long, shaky breath. 'Then I thought he might have taken a fall, or had a heart attack. I just didn't know. So I took his keys from the hook and came across here again. I rang the doorbell a couple of times, shouted through the letterbox, and then – and then I let myself in. I shouted up the stairs, but it felt horrible. So quiet. I pushed open the sitting room door, switched on the light, and that's when I saw him.'

Tears welled in her eyes and she took a white lace handkerchief from the pocket of her coat.

'I can't believe he'd do such a thing,' she said on a sob, mopping at her eyes. 'I mean, I know losing his wife hit him hard. And now this. This is just the worst thing that can happen to anyone. Losing a child, it's the worst thing imaginable. But even so...'

Max nodded his understanding.

'Did you touch anything when you came in?' he asked and she looked surprised by the question.

'No. Why?' Before Max could answer, she said, 'Well, I used the phone to dial 999. But no, nothing else. The woman who answered the phone asked me to stay here. I sat on the stairs.' She pointed in the direction of the staircase. 'I couldn't bear to see him like that so I sat on the stairs. It wasn't many minutes before two policemen arrived.'

'OK. Thank you.'

Max left her with the WPC and took a look around the rest of the house.

There was nothing at all to suggest that this was anything other than a suicide.

He stood in what had to be Cole's bedroom and

gazed around him. It was a large room, the ceiling lower than those downstairs, and was dominated by a double bed with a mahogany headboard. The bed was unmade, the pillows crumpled.

He pulled open the wardrobe doors. Trousers, shirts and jackets were hanging from the rail, some beneath dust covers. A poppy was pinned to a blue blazer, a reminder of Remembrance Day. Highly polished shoes were lined up neatly on a low shelf.

A comb sat on the mirrored dressing table, alongside a small trophy engraved with Harrington Amateur Dramatic Society, but, other than that, it was bare. Max pulled open drawers and frowned at what he saw. Here, unlike in the rest of the house, was the sort of mess that would have driven a man like Cole crazy. Underwear had been thrown in untidily. A couple of T-shirts would need ironing again before they could be worn. A belt, pushed in haphazardly, stopped the drawer opening smoothly.

Odd.

He walked down the stairs and into the sitting room where Cole's body was finally being released.

Max walked over to the sideboard and opened the drawers. Here, the same mess existed. Perhaps Cole was only tidy where things were visible.

No, that didn't make any sense. The man had been tidy to the point of obsession.

It seemed to Max that someone had rummaged through drawers looking for something. But what? An officer was examining the vacuum cleaner. 'Looks like he used the cable from this, Max.'

So Cole had donned his pyjamas, gone to bed, decided to end it all, come downstairs, cut a length of cable and hanged himself? No way.

This wasn't suicide. Vincent Cole had been murdered, Max was sure of it.

Max spent much of that day pacing his office, reading through paperwork and waiting for reports that didn't come.

You could gather all the evidence in the world, he thought irritably, but until it had been analysed, it was worse than useless. And the waiting was driving him crazy.

Jill was doing a TV interview today so he couldn't even moan to her.

Phil Meredith thought Max was going mad. As far as Max's boss was concerned, the fact that Cole had decided to end it all should be obvious to anyone.

'Even you, Max! Christ, there's no need to go looking for trouble...'

Max stepped into the bustling incident room. He stared at a wall of photos and annoyed everyone who didn't have a phone glued to their ear by demanding answers they couldn't give him. The collective sigh of relief as he left the room was audible.

In Cole's situation Max knew that he too would want to see his daughter buried. He wasn't religious, he had no belief in any afterlife, but it was something you did. You did your best for your loved ones whether they were alive or dead. The only thing Cole could do for Lauren now was see her buried next to her mother. No way would he have killed himself before he'd performed that one last act for his daughter.

As he walked along the corridor, he peered through a glass door and saw Doug leaning back in a chair staring at CCTV footage. While doing that, he was chatting to Clive White.

Max pushed open the door.

'Hello, Clive. You're spending more time in the building since you've been suspended than you did when you were working.'

'I'm still trying to get sponsorship, guv. Coppers are the most tight-fisted bastards imaginable.'

'We're all overworked and underpaid.'

'True.'

'So how's it going?'

'I'm bored rigid,' Clive admitted.

Max could understand that. God alone knew what he'd do with his time if he ever found himself in the same situation.

'I've had a clear out in the house,' Clive went on, 'and taken a load of junk to the tip. I thought I'd call in here on the way back and see if I could get more money out of anyone.'

'I've had to cough up,' Doug said, his eyes not leaving the screen.

'What's that?' Max asked, nodding at the fuzzy town centre pictures. 'And where is it?' It wasn't Harrington.

'Blackpool,' Doug said with little enthusiasm. 'There was a robbery last night and guess who gets lumbered with this job.'

Max had heard about the robbery, but it didn't interest him.

'Hey, go back a bit,' Clive said suddenly. 'Back

to where that white car was.'

'If you see a couple of blokes wearing bala-clavas, I'll double my sponsorship,' Doug pro-mised as he rewound the tape. 'I hate this job.'

'There!' Clive said.

Something in his voice had Max peering closely at the image.

'What?' Doug, like Max, was none the wiser.

'That girl,' Clive said, tapping a finger against the screen.

'Good God!' Now, Max knew exactly what Clive was thinking. 'Go back a few seconds, Doug.'

The three of them watched as a young girl, her arm gripped by a tall man, was helped into a white car. The man was wearing what looked to be a leather coat with the collar hiding most of his face.

'See what you can do with it, Doug, and let me know when you've got something clear. If you can't get the car's registration, see what else there is – scratches, dents, furry dice in the windscreen – anything.' Realizing that Doug knew exactly what was needed, he nodded at Clive. 'Good work.'

'Thanks, guv.'

As far as Max could remember, none of the possible sightings of Yasmin Smith had been in Blackpool. But that meant nothing. She might, just might, be the girl on the screen.

He refused to get too hopeful. And he wasn't letting Adam Smith know about this yet.

Instead, he rang Jackie Ingram to see when her postmortem report on Vincent Cole would be available. Needless to say, her greeting was less

208

than warm.

'I've told you, Max, you'll have my report later today. Believe it or not, I have other things to do.'

'I know, I know.' He put on his grovelling voice. 'Is there nothing you can tell me? Nothing at all?'

There was a long pause, followed by a sigh. 'I can tell you that he was already dead before that cable went round his neck. Something heavy to the back to the head.'

Bingo!

'If a victim falls several feet, the noose will fracture his neck, bringing a fairly quick death,' she said. 'If the fall is short, as in this case, death is through strangulation, which is slow and painful. The victim's eyes would protrude and his face would be engorged with blood. This definitely wasn't suicide, Max.'

'Thanks, Jackie. I appreciate it.'

'You owe me,' she said, and cut the connection.

It wasn't until their food was brought to their table that evening that Max realized he hadn't eaten all day. He'd had enough coffee to keep him awake for a week, but he was ravenous. Jill, sitting opposite him and looking unusually smart having come straight from the television studios, was always hungry.

They were in the Black Bull, a large pub on the outskirts of Harrington that was winning acclaim for its simple home-cooked fare.

'Anything new?' Jill asked him.

'Let me see.' As it turned out, he'd had a busy day, one of those where surprise had followed surprise. 'Firstly, your friend Steve Carlisle has been released.'

'You're kidding me. I bet that wasn't your decision.'

'It wasn't.'

Max's boss had gone from being convinced that Cole had committed suicide to being equally convinced that the same person had killed both Lauren and Vincent.

'Which means Steve Carlisle is innocent,' Phil Meredith had said.

'It means no such thing,' Max had argued.

'You haven't got anything that will secure a conviction, Max. You'll have to let him go.'

Max wasn't happy about it, but Meredith was right. They didn't have anything that would qualify as hard evidence so Steve Carlisle was a free man again. For now.

'As you thought,' he told Jill, 'Cole didn't hang himself. He suffered a fatal blow to the back of the head before he was strung up in his sitting room.'

Jill shuddered, but he knew it wouldn't put her off her food.

'Why?' she asked, and Max had no explanation.

'That remains a mystery.'

'But why the delay? Why kill Lauren and then wait over a week before killing her father?'

'You're assuming we're looking for one killer,' he pointed out. 'Just as Phil Meredith is.'

'Aren't you?'

'I'm assuming nothing.'

He was completely in the dark. If they were looking for the same man, he could only imagine that both Lauren and her father knew something they shouldn't. At least, the killer thought they

210

did. But if that was the case, why wait a week?

As he enjoyed his food, officers were out there knocking on doors and begging for information. Max only hoped they were successful.

'On top of that lot,' he went on, 'we may, and I stress the may, have captured Yasmin Smith on CCTV in Blackpool.'

'Really? God, no wonder you're looking pleased with yourself.'

But he wasn't. He was no closer to finding Yasmin than he had been four months ago. He was no closer to catching Lauren Cole's killer, either. Or her father's.

'Your friend and mine, Clive White, was the one to spot Yasmin,' he added. 'If indeed it was Yasmin.'

'Clive?' He saw the way her lips tightened. 'What the hell was he doing looking at CCTV?'

'He called in–'

'Why?' she demanded. 'What's the point of him being suspended from duty when he's spending more time at the blasted nick than away from it?'

'He called in to try and get some more sponsorship,' Max explained patiently. 'He wasn't there above five minutes.' He had no idea how long Clive was actually in the building, but he couldn't see that it mattered. 'While he was chatting to Doug, he spotted a girl who looked a lot like Yasmin.'

'He's suspended from duty, Max. He shouldn't be there.'

'If he hadn't been, we wouldn't have spotted Yasmin.' Seeing that she was about to argue, he quickly changed the subject. 'How's your food?'

'Very nice,' she said, refusing to be diverted that easily, 'but Clive White is supposed to be at home. I'll have to speak to him. Or to Phil Meredith. It's ridiculous.'

'I'll speak to Clive,' he promised.

He would, too. He'd warn him to keep out of Jill's sight.

'So how was your day?' he asked her.

'It was good. Nerve-wracking, but good. It's difficult to convince people you know what you're talking about when you're conscious of God knows how many viewers tuning in. Not that many people watch a programme like that during the day, I suppose. But all I could think was that my mum might be watching.' She grinned at that. 'Why that mattered, I don't know.'

'Aw, the shame of seeing her daughter on TV with no wedding ring to her name.'

Jill laughed at that. 'Don't!'

The pub was busy and most of the tables in the dining area were occupied. Max wasn't surprised. He'd just eaten the best steak of his life.

Jill, who'd eaten chicken with an avalanche of roast potatoes and vegetables, still had room for dessert.

'Death by Chocolate, please,' she told the young waitress.

'Oink.'

'I don't care. I was too nervous for lunch and it's ages since breakfast. Besides, who can resist Death by Chocolate?'

She was soon demolishing the sickly pudding.

'So who could have killed Lauren and her father?' she mused, fork poised in the air between mouthfuls. 'And what does any of it have to do with Steve? It seemed to me that someone was out to lay the blame for Lauren's death on him. Perhaps he had nothing to do with it at all. Maybe he was simply in the wrong place at the wrong time.'

'There's something we're missing.'

'Ten out of ten, detective.'

'But what?'

Jill was busy scraping her plate clean. 'I don't know.'

Max didn't either. They'd thought Lauren's murder had been committed on the spur of the moment. Now, with Vincent Cole dead, that didn't ring true. Unless, of course, Cole had learned something about his daughter's killer.

If Steve Carlisle was innocent, and Max was far from certain about that, their killer had to be someone who knew his movements, someone who knew that, unlike every other dog walker in the area, he carried an axe with him.

And what about the dog? Had Charlie wandered off or had he been enticed away? The dog was still at the boarding kennels waiting to be re-homed and Max had paid a visit. Charlie was wary of strangers. It was unlikely he would have gone off with someone he didn't know.

'Perhaps Vincent Cole's killer will prove less elusive,' he said, looking on the bright side. 'We may have a shoe print. There was a size-eight print in the back garden and it's not Cole's.'

'That's something then.'

'Yeah. And maybe someone in the neighbourhood saw something.' And maybe they didn't. 'Mrs Hollingsworth, his cleaner, is going to have a good look tomorrow and see if anything has been stolen. She tried today, but got too upset by it all. Hopefully, she'll be calmer tomorrow.'

'Maybe that's it,' she said. 'Maybe Vincent Cole disturbed a burglar.'

'But only someone who knew Cole and knew of his daughter's death would think of conjuring up a suicide story.'

There were a lot of theories, but precious little else.

'Let's forget it for a while,' he suggested.

It was impossible to forget, even for a minute, but he knew he had to try. When he pushed problems to the back of his mind, his sub-conscious often worked away on the puzzle and came up with a solution.

'Good idea.' She caught the attention of the young girl who'd brought her Death by Choco-late. For a moment, Max thought she was going to order another. But no. 'Could we have more coffee, please?'

Max had banished Lauren and Vincent Cole from his mind only to come up with another puzzle. Like who the hell was phoning Jill in the middle of the night and delivering photographs to make sure she knew she was being watched.

Max had checked the camera they'd had installed at her cottage, but it had captured noth-ing, or no one, out of the ordinary.

She was right about one thing, he supposed. The person stalking her was a coward. Phone calls were the act of a coward. Photographs, too. Someone was trying to frighten her.

'You're frowning,' she said.

214

'Sorry. I was thinking about Christmas,' he lied.

'Ah.' She smiled at that. 'You'll have a great time and your dad will be fine.' Another thought struck her. 'Who'll be cooking lunch? I know Kate will leave the freezer and cupboards stocked up when she's goes to America, but she can't leave a Christmas dinner to be warmed up, can she?'

'Trust you to think of food. Actually, I'll be cooking it.'

She stared back at him as if he'd said he'd be performing brain surgery with a butter knife.

'Come on, Jill, it's hardly rocket science, is it? A turkey gets banged in the oven for however long and that's that. Vegetables are peeled and thrown in a saucepan.'

'*You* are going to cook Christmas dinner?'

'Why not? How difficult can it be?'

'Good grief. You can't cook it on the barbecue, you know. At least, I don't think you can.' She grinned at him. 'Am I getting an invite? I wouldn't miss this for the world.'

'Of course. You have an open invitation, you know that. Besides, I can't cope with Dad on my own.'

'He'll be fine. Tell you what, I'll bring the mince pies. Hey, don't look like that, I wasn't offering to make them. They'll come straight from Tesco...'

It was easy to laugh and joke; impossible to know who had wanted Lauren and Vincent Cole dead or who was hell bent on frightening Jill.

Chapter Twenty-One

When Jill drove up to her cottage that night, she knew the rich dessert had been a mistake. She had a habit of not eating all day and then over-doing it at night. Instead of eating out with Max again, she should have been at her Thai boxing class. Too late to worry about that now though.

She killed the engine, thought about putting the car in the garage for the night, and decided she couldn't be bothered. It meant struggling with the lock to open the garage door, going back to her car and driving it in carefully so as to avoid the pile of junk that was accumulating, inching her way out of the car without scraping the door, and then battling with the lock again. Life was too short.

She grabbed her bag, got out of the car and locked it.

A straggly clematis that would provide a splash of colour in the summer months clung to trellis by her front door and, hidden among the spindly twigs was a small camera. She was smiling as she waved at it. Given that the security light had bathed her in white light, she must look ridiculous.

Her breath caught as she heard a noise. She spun round.

Someone was out there. Someone had stepped on a twig.

She stood still to listen, but all she could hear

was the drumming of her own heartbeat. Perhaps a fox or a cat was moving through her garden, hunting for food.

She had her back to the dark garden as she put the key in the lock and turned it, but she was ready for anything. At least, she hoped she was.

She closed the door behind her and made sure the locks were secure.

Perhaps her imagination had been playing tricks on her. That's what happened when young women were murdered less than half a mile from your front door. Not that her imagination was responsible for crank phone calls or the photos that had been pushed through her letterbox.

Her three cats strolled up to meet her. She knew they'd missed the can opener more than her, but it was good to see them and hear their purrs at the thought of food. She went to the cat-flap, ready to unlock it, but changed her mind. Until she was sure there was no one outside, and that wouldn't be until morning, it would remain closed.

She checked that all windows were locked before drawing curtains as a defence against the blackness outside.

She wasn't frightened exactly, but she wished Max was there. Or she wished she'd taken him up on his offer and gone to his place with him. Instead of wondering if some axe-wielding maniac was outside her house, she'd be enjoying the company of Max, Harry and Ben.

She thought of having a bath, but dismissed that idea. If there was anyone creeping around and she had to put her boxing lessons into prac-tice, she would rather do it fully clothed.

The idea of a quick shower was also dismissed as the famous scene from *Psycho* leapt into her mind. She had a glass door rather than a shower curtain, but even so...

She poured herself a generous gin and tonic and went into the sitting room with her copy of the *Racing Post*. Studying the runners and riders for tomorrow's race card would calm her down.

All she could hear was the gentle rumble of the central heating boiler, and Tojo hitting the cat-flap with her paw.

In a way, it would be a good thing if someone *was* outside. Better still if they held a steady head and shoulders pose in front of the camera. At least that way she would know what she was dealing with.

With her horses chosen and bets ready to be placed in the morning, she took herself off to bed.

She was still awake at 1.34 a.m., possibly because she was sharing her bed with three cats, and when her phone rang she snatched it from its cradle.

'Right, you sick pervo–'

There was a laugh before the line went dead.

'Shit!'

She was a psychologist, for God's sake, a highly respected one at that. What she had planned, and what she would do in future, was try to engage him in conversation. If she didn't know how to get him to talk, she might as well get a job as a window cleaner.

She dialled 1471, just in case he'd forgotten to withhold his number. Of course, he hadn't. He wasn't that stupid.

She was mentally holding a conversation with him as she drifted off to sleep...

When she awoke, just after six, it was to yet another hard frost. Snow still lay thick in parts of her garden where yesterday's sun hadn't reached.

It wasn't light yet, though, so her cats would have to wait a while for their highly anticipated adventure in the garden.

She showered, dressed, then made herself a good strong cup of coffee.

When she opened the front door, her cats sped past her, tails high, noses in the air scenting for mice. Sam leapt straight on to the roof of the shed to view the land from a superior position.

Jill pulled on walking boots and followed them. Funny how nothing was quite so worrying in daylight. She walked all round her cottage, looking for pawprints. Or footprints.

There was nothing.

At eleven o'clock that morning, Max was perched on a stool in the kitchen of Hill View, Longman Drive, four properties away from Vincent Cole's home. He was with Tony Swift, an energetic-looking man in his forties. Keeping a close eye on Max was a lively German Shepherd.

'Don't worry about the dog,' Swift said. 'She's fine with people.'

Max would have to take his word for that and try to ignore the way the dog's enormous yellow teeth glistened from behind a lip that was permanently curled back.

'Mr Swift, I believe you saw someone running

along Longman Drive on Monday night? What can you tell me about that?'

Max had decided to visit Longman Drive because he wanted to make sure Vincent Cole's cleaner, Mrs Hollingsworth, checked every item in her late employer's home. As Swift had told one of the house-to-house officers that he'd seen someone looking suspicious, Max thought that, as he was passing the door, he'd have a chat with him, too.

'I can't tell you anything else,' Swift said. 'As I told the chap last night, I was late getting back from work—'

'You're in the fire service, yes?'

'That's right. It was almost eleven o'clock when I got off shift,' he explained, 'and probably closer to midnight when I took Tess' – he nodded at the slavering dog – 'for a walk round the block.'

'Where did you go?'

'Up to the top of the road and then I turned into Kingfisher Drive. I always take the same route, every night. From Kingfisher Drive, I go into Cuthbert Street and then back into the bottom of Longman Drive.'

Max pictured the route in his head. It was a perfect square, and the ideal late-night walk.

'It was as I got on to Longman Drive,' Swift went on, 'that I saw a lad running towards me.'

'Can you describe him?' Max asked, hoping the man had remembered more than he'd been able to tell his officers.

'Not really,' he admitted. 'He was wearing one of those hooded sweatshirt things. Grey, at a guess, but the streetlights aren't very good along here. Quite a light colour at any rate.'

'He didn't say anything?'

'Not a word. He was too busy running. But, like I said, he had a holdall hoisted on his shoulder. Had I seen him during the day, I would have assumed he'd been to football training or something like that. Seeing him around midnight, I thought it was a bit late to be coming back from a gym. I guessed he'd been up to no good. Cars get pinched, taken for joy rides – I thought something like that. Or maybe, given the holdall, I wondered if he'd been breaking in somewhere. Six months ago, several people had their garages broken into.'

'I see. And there's nothing else you can remember? Footwear? Height? Skin colour?'

Swift shook his head.

'It was too dark to see much. I'd say he was around the five feet nine or ten mark. I think he was young, too.'

'What makes you say that?'

'The way he ran. Sort of leggy.' He gave Max a knowing look. 'Because I thought he was up to no good, I did think of setting Tess on to him.' He patted the dog's head. 'A word from me and she would have pinned him down. But you can't go around doing things like that, can you?'

'No, Mr Swift.'

Max wished Swift *had* taken the law into his own hands. He'd give a lot to know what had been in that holdall. He gave Swift his card.

'If you think of anything else, anything at all, no matter how insignificant it seems, will you call me?'

Swift examined the card. 'Of course. This is to

do with that bloke Cole, I assume? Some said he committed suicide but, as I told folk, you lot wouldn't seal off the whole place if he'd topped himself.'

'We're asking questions in connection with Mr Cole's death, yes. Did you know him well?'

'Not really. He kept himself to himself. Out at work all day. At home most nights if he wasn't at his amateur dramatics thing. That's not my scene. We were on nodding terms, but that was all.'

'OK, Mr Swift, thanks very much for your time. I appreciate it. And if you remember anything else–'

'I'll be sure to let you know,' Swift said, waving Max's card in his hand.

'Thanks.'

Glad to be away from the dog, Max left Swift's house and strode down the bank towards Mrs Hollingsworth's bungalow. He hoped she was calmer today because he needed her to check Cole's house thoroughly.

He walked up the short drive and rang the bell.

She looked dismayed to see him on her doorstep, as if she realized the time of execution was upon her.

'But I've just made myself a cup of tea,' she said uncertainly.

'That's fine,' Max said. 'You can drink it before we go and look at Mr Cole's house.'

'Thank you.' She brightened immediately. 'I'll make you one too, Chief Inspector.'

She led him into the sitting room where a decorated tree dominated. Christmas cards were strung across the walls and china dogs and horses competed for space on the surfaces.

'Now then, you sit yourself down and I'll make you that cuppa.'

Max gazed at the house directly opposite. Vincent Cole's. Everything about the exterior was neat, from hedges that looked as if they had been hand-trimmed with scissors to the perfectly shaped dwarf conifers that sat either side of the driveway.

Mrs Hollingsworth carried in a tray, put it on the sofa, cleared some space on a long, low table and then set it down on that.

'Milk and sugar?' she asked, pouring tea into cups. Presumably, she'd decided to make herself a fresh cup. Either that, or the excuse of having made herself tea had been just that, an excuse.

'Milk, no sugar, thanks.'

Max would bet she knew the history of every single china cat, dog and horse she shared her home with. She would know how long she'd had them, whether she'd bought them herself or if they'd been gifts. He hoped she was as observant with other people's belongings.

'I realize you want me to look at his things,' she said, nodding in the direction of Vincent Cole's house, 'but, for the life of me, I can't understand why.'

She believed her neighbour had taken his own life so she would think it beyond strange that they were wanting her to check the contents of his house. On the other hand, if Max told her that someone had killed him and then strung him up from his own beams, she would probably go into a faint.

'It's routine procedure,' Max said, opting for the well-worn phrase. 'We always have to check everything in the case of a suicide. We have to make sure that it really was suicide.'

'Oh, I see. Well, that's a waste of time, isn't it? No one can have any doubt about that.'

Max simply shrugged in answer.

'How long had you known him?' he asked in a swift change of subject.

'Ever since he and his wife first moved to the street,' she replied. 'That would have been...' She searched her memory. 'Young Lauren was about to start school so it would have been about fifteen years ago.'

'A long time,' he said.

'I knew his wife better back then. She invited me in for a cup of tea a few times and she came round here maybe half a dozen times. It was six years ago, when she died, that I really got to know him and young Lauren. The pair of them were lost without her and I used to pop round and see if there was anything I could do. When I mentioned I did a bit of cleaning for folk, he asked if I'd clean over there a couple of mornings a week.'

'You knew Lauren well?'

'At one time I thought I did.' She sighed. 'But children grow up, don't they? Seeing her shouting at her dad, swearing at him even – it was like seeing a stranger in the house.'

'Did they argue a lot?'

'*He* didn't. Lauren was always short of money and she kept trying to persuade her dad to lend her some. Or give her some. Usually, he handed it over. A bit of a foolish thing to do I thought but who am I to say? He'd always try and talk some sense into her though and that's when the young madam would fly off the handle at him. The language she used made me blush, I can tell you.'

Max sipped at his tea, more than willing to let her talk.

'I'll tell you something else,' she said in a confidential tone. 'A couple of times, I saw her and a young man visit the house. They hadn't called to see Vince because it was in the middle of the day when they'd have known he was at work. Both times, they were only in the house a couple of minutes. Now, the day after I saw them the last time, I happened to notice that a pair of silver candlesticks weren't where they should have been. He had a bit of silver did Vince. He attended classes and made stuff himself. Anyway, I used to clean it. He was quite fussy about that. So, like I said, I noticed those candlesticks had gone and mentioned it to him.'

'And was he able to tell you where they were?'

'Well, it was funny that. He looked at the table where they should have been, and seemed quite surprised. Then he said he remembered. He'd taken them to have them valued.'

Max wondered why none of this had come out before. Sometimes the only thing you could do to drag information from people was sit and drink tea with them and let them talk.

'Did he get them valued?' Max asked, guessing the answer. 'Did you see them again?'

'Never. I couldn't swear to it, of course, but I always thought that little madam had pinched them.'

225

'The young man you saw with Lauren on those occasions, what was he like?'

'I never saw his face. He had one of those hood things on. You know the sort I mean, like a jumper but with a hood?'

'I know the sort you mean.' The same as worn by the man Tony Swift had seen running down the road.

'Although,' she said, 'I did see Lauren in town with him once. At least, I'm fairly certain it was the same one. It was back in the summer. He had a shaved head. You know how they have it these days? They used to call them skinheads years back.'

A shaved head. They weren't talking about Ricky Marshall then.

'Would you recognize him if you saw him again?' he asked.

'The one in town? Possibly. I don't know really. And as I said, I'm not even sure it was the one who came to the house with her. I think it was, but it's hard to tell.'

Their tea was drunk and Max decided to get her across the road while she was in a calmer state of mind.

'Shall we go and see what's what over the road then, Mrs Hollingsworth?'

She gave Vincent Cole's house a swift look as if she expected all sorts of demons to be lurking behind its walls.

'If we must,' she replied, resigned.

They left her bungalow and walked slowly across the road to Vincent Cole's house.

Max went straight to the sitting room. She

followed, and her gaze, as Max had guessed it would, went straight to the old ceiling beams.

'Right,' she said, shaking herself. 'Let's see.'

She walked to the large mahogany sideboard, pulled open the doors and looked inside. Then she spun round to face him. 'Have you lot moved stuff?'

'No. Why? Is something missing?'

'A large silver rose bowl. And a chess set. I can't think what it was made from, but it was a gift from a friend of his in South America and I think it was valuable. They should be here. Of course, Vince could have put them somewhere else, I suppose.' She looked up at him. 'I can't imagine why he'd do that though, can you? It would make no sense at all.'

Max wished he could remember the last time anything had made sense.

Chapter Twenty-Two

Frank Carlisle walked round the corner into the driveway of Mason's Cottage, and was relieved to see that there was no sign of his daughter-in-law's car. With luck, she'd be working. He guessed it would take more than her husband's release from a police cell to stop Alison earning commission.

As he knocked on the door, he wondered if every father did that. Frank had three other children and, when visiting their homes, he simply walked round to the back door, pushed it open and shouted out to announce his arrival. They didn't mind. If they'd considered it an invasion of their privacy, they would have said so.

There was no response so he knocked again. He was about to turn round and go home when his son's dog ambled into view.

'Hello, Cally. Is he round the back?'

Frank walked up the path between house and garage, and saw Steve shovelling snow from the patio.

When his son straightened, Frank realized that Ruth hadn't been exaggerating. She'd called in yesterday afternoon and said he'd looked worse than she'd ever seen him. Frank had dismissed her concerns. After all, he'd only been released a few hours.

'Give him a good night's sleep in his own bed,' Frank had told her, 'and he'll be as right as rain.'

A night's sleep had done nothing to help, it seemed.

'This is a surprise, Dad. Is everything all right?'

'Yes. Just thought I'd call and see how you are. Is Alison working?'

'She is, yes.'

As they spoke, Cally nuzzled Frank's hand. Even the dog seemed sad.

'I'll get myself a spade,' Frank said. 'We'll soon have this cleared.'

'Don't be daft. It can wait.'

'Never put off till tomorrow what you can do today,' Frank said, heading down the garden to the shed. 'I'm not totally buggered yet, you know,' he called over his shoulder.

He found a spade and was soon working alongside Steve.

'It's a cheap way of keeping warm,' he said, enjoying the exercise.

'It is, but don't do your back in, Dad.'

'I'm used to digging on the allotment,' Frank reminded him, 'and this is nothing. I remember when the snow was up to the – what?' he asked, spotting Steve's smile. 'Ah, you've heard that before, haven't you?'

'A few times, Dad.'

It was good to see Steve smile, but it didn't take the dark shadows from his eyes. The lad must have been to hell and back.

Frank felt guilty as they quietly cleared the snow. He should be supporting Steve, not bringing him bad news. But he'd come here determined to have some straight talking. If they were closer as a family, if they said what was on their mind, maybe Steve would never have been in this mess.

'It's not often we see you here,' Steve remarked after a while.

'It's not. To be honest, I can't say as I've ever felt particularly welcome.'

'I know, Dad, and I'm really sorry about that.'

The apology hurt, and Frank wished he'd kept quiet. But what was the point? Families *didn't* keep quiet. They didn't keep feelings to themselves for fear of hurting one another.

'So where's Alison today?' Frank wasn't interested but he felt the need to make conversation.

'The company's holding an exhibition in Liverpool. Today and tomorrow. She'll be back on Saturday morning.'

'Liverpool?' Frank scoffed. 'Can't she drive home from there?'

'She has customers to entertain in the evening, Dad. You know how it is.'

Frank knew exactly how it was and he very much doubted if customers would be entertained.

Cally, not a fan of the outdoor life, took herself off to the shed. She'd find a warm spot and settle down to sleep.

'I bet you're glad to be home?' Frank said quietly, and Steve nodded.

'More than you'll know. It was a bit – worrying.'

'I daresay it was.'

'In future I'll only buy logs by the load and, instead of walking Cally over the hills, I'll walk her through the village.'

'Don't be daft. You can't let something like this change you.'

'But it does.' He gave Frank a weak smile. 'So what have you *really* called in for?'

Such directness took Frank by surprise. It shouldn't have. When you didn't feel welcome, you didn't visit unless you had to.

'How are you and Alison getting on?' he asked, hedging around the subject.

'The same as ever.' Which didn't answer the question. 'Why do you ask?'

Damn it, Frank had come with the intention of telling his son the truth and he was determined not to leave until he'd done just that. Maybe it wasn't his place to say anything.

God knows, he'd never interfered in his children's lives before. But Alison had no right to cheat or lie.

'I saw her,' he confided, wishing his voice was a little stronger. 'About six weeks back. I was in the car with Bill going to Burnley. Alison was in the car in front of us. She stopped at the lay-by, left her car and went to someone else's, someone who was waiting for her. She kissed him.' He realized he'd been holding his breath and he exhaled. 'It wasn't the sort of kiss she'd give a friend either.'

There, it was said.

He waited for some reaction from Steve, but there was nothing. The haunted look in his eyes didn't change. The shoulders didn't droop any lower.

'I see,' was all he said.

'You knew?' Frank asked.

'No. But I'm not surprised.'

A blackbird landed on the snow-covered wooden bench about a yard from them. Perhaps it thought they were digging for worms. The ground was frozen too hard for beaks to drag out food, but there was plenty in the garden. Seeds, nuts and fat balls hung from the trees.

'Does Mum know?' Steve asked.

'I haven't told her, no.'

'Probably best not to,' Steve said. 'You know how she worries.'

'Tell me about it.'

They smiled at that, and carried on clearing snow in a silence that, surprisingly, wasn't uncomfortable.

'Don't worry about things,' Steve said after a

231

while. 'I've done a lot of thinking. I've realized what's important and I'm going to sort things out. Everything will be fine, you'll see.'

'I'm glad. And I'm sorry if I was wrong to tell you about Alison. I just had to and that's all there is to it. It was on my mind. I don't like cheats.'

'Who does?'

'And at a time like this—'

'It's all right, Dad. Don't worry about it.'

Their spades clanged against the paving slabs as they worked, and the patio was soon clear.

'Time to put the kettle on,' Steve said, and Frank nodded.

It was a long time since he'd felt so close to his son.

Chapter Twenty-Three

That evening Jill sat in on the briefing. Given the mood Max was in, she soon wished she hadn't. He was snapping at everyone. He wasn't getting answers and patience had never been one of his virtues. He looked stressed, too. His shirt sleeves were rolled up and his tie had been loosened.

'OK,' he said. 'The guy wearing the hoody who was seen running down Longman Drive on Monday night is our number one priority. If he's the same person Mrs Hollingsworth saw, he's visited the house with Lauren and knows his way around.'

'We're getting CCTV checked in the area,' someone said.

'Good. And we need to speak to everyone who might have known Lauren. Her diaries haven't given us anything yet. Make sure every number is checked and double checked.'

Jill knew they'd checked those numbers. Most entries consisted of an initial, maybe two, and a mobile number. The mobiles had long gone and it was proving almost impossible to get details of past owners.

'Ask her flatmate again,' Max said. 'She might know of someone fitting an admittedly vague description. Speak to Ricky Marshall again. It might be worth talking to Father Gosling again, too. Perhaps he saw Lauren with someone wearing a hoody.'

'What about the mysterious Josh?' Jill asked. Have you found him yet?'

'No.'

'You need to,' Jill said with certainty. 'If he was constantly on the phone to her, she knew him well. She would only take someone she trusted to her dad's home.'

'We've only her flatmate's word that the bloke even existed,' Max pointed out.

'But surely you've checked Lauren's phone?'

'She changed her sim card,' Max reminded her impatiently. 'Now then–' Dismissing Jill, he held up a sheet of paper.

'This is the list of items missing from Vincent Cole's home. It adds up to a fair sum. We need to ask around and see if someone's tried to sell any of it.'

Jill's mind began to wander. If this hoody-wearing young man had killed Vincent Cole, it must stand to reason that he'd also murdered Lauren.

He must have known of Lauren's movements on the day in question. Had he also known Steve Carlisle's? Had Lauren mentioned Steve to this person? Why? And in what context?

'Given Lauren's lifestyle,' Max was saying, 'it's a fair bet that whoever stole these items is feeding a drug habit.'

'What about the keys found on Lauren when she was murdered?' Jill piped up.

'One for her car and one for her flat,' Max said, frowning to indicate she'd interrupted his train of thought.

'But what about the key to her dad's house? She'd called at her dad's that morning expecting him to be out, right? So she must have had a key on her.'

'We haven't found it,' Max said.

'So it stands to reason the killer took it?' Jill asked.

'Nothing stands to reason,' Max muttered. 'All I can say is that we're still looking for it.'

'OK,' she said. 'So, if we assume–' She saw the look on Max's face. 'I know, I know. Assume nothing. But my guess is that Lauren and this unknown wearer of the hoody were stealing stuff from her dad's place together. That means she knew him well and trusted him. Deep down, she was a good girl and she loved her dad so–'

'How do you figure that one?' DS Fletcher called out in amazement. 'She was stealing from him. She had a row with him and stormed out on the morning she was killed. Not the sort of love

I'd want.'

'She was a bright, happy girl who was doing very well at school until her mother died,' Jill reminded the room in general. 'They were a close family and Mrs Cole's death was devastating for both Vincent and Lauren. Lauren turned away from the church *and* her father. She began playing truant and left school instead of going to uni as her dad had expected and hoped. She got herself a job, but couldn't stick at that. She mixed with people who were afraid of nothing, who were experimenting with drugs. She tried anything that might ease the pain. She would have craved love from her dad, but he was lonely, and too wrapped up in his own pain to give it. She tried to get money from him, another attempt to get some attention. She boasted to her flatmate that her dad would give her anything. She wanted to be loved, told people that she was loved. In truth, she was lonely. Her dog was well cared for because he was all she had. Recently, she'd returned to the church and she would have returned to her father, too. Given time to heal, she would have been a bright happy woman again.'

She saw the smirks on their faces and heard a couple of whispered quips.

'Sorry,' she said, 'was I stepping into the realms of psychology bollocks then? All I'm saying is that Lauren Cole loved her father. If she was allowing someone to steal from him, she would have known and trusted that person for a long time. It may be that she went to school with him even.'

Max must have decided to humour her.

'There might be something in that,' he said, but

235

he sounded doubtful. 'Talk to everyone who knew her – those who've known her for years as well as more recent acquaintances.'

'And I bet his name is Josh,' she couldn't resist adding. When the briefing was over, Jill was about to head to her office for her coat and then go home.

'Jill, can I have word?' Max called to her.

'Yup.' She walked over to him.

'My office,' he said, taking her by surprise.

They walked along the corridor to his office.

'Well?' She was curious now.

'You're staying at my place tonight.'

He perched on the edge of his desk and she could see he was waiting for an argument. Jill was too taken aback to give him one.

'You what?' she said.

'You're staying at my place.'

'Blimey, quite the caveman, aren't you? Why might I want to do that?'

For answer, he moved a couple of files on his desk and produced a large black and white photograph.

'What's this?' she asked.

But she guessed that the hooded person in the photo might be fond of making late-night phone calls.

'This person was outside your cottage. Now, I don't suppose you get too many visitors wearing balaclavas, do you?'

'Can't say I do, Max.'

She was trying to make light of it to cover her shock.

'Was this taken by the camera near my front

door?' she asked.

'Yes, about five minutes before you got home last night.'

So it hadn't been a fox after all.

'Right,' she said, unable to think of anything more appropriate.

'So,' he said briskly, 'we'll call at your place so that you can pack a few things and collect the cats. We'll leave your car there. That way, he might think you're inside. We'll get all the lights put on timers. Also, we're going to set up a caravan in Mrs Johnson's drive. From there, we should be able to see anyone trespassing.'

Jill knew her neighbour would love that. She already saw herself as Miss Marple.

'Right,' she said again. 'But I bet I could still–'

'Flatten him? Maybe. Maybe not. I'd rather not take any chances just in case he's an expert in Thai boxing, too. OK?'

She nodded. It was one thing being brave in Max's office, but she knew from experience that it was a completely different matter when you wanted a shower and couldn't banish that confounded scene from *Psycho* from your head.

'He must phone first,' she mused, 'to see if I'm there.'

'Maybe. He certainly doesn't hang around on the phone for more than a second or two. Anyway, don't worry, we'll soon have him. Tell you what,' he went on, 'I need to call on Adam and Vivienne Smith but, when I'm done there, we'll all go out for a meal. Me, you and the boys. I'll even pay.'

'Sounds good to me.'

'Oh, and one other thing,' Max added. 'You

don't tell a living, breathing soul, right?'

'Right.'

'I mean it, Jill. We're dealing with someone who knows you. Someone who knows we're a couple.'

She was fully aware of that, and it wasn't a comforting feeling.

Max had hoped that, as was usually the case, Adam Smith would be pounding the streets looking for his daughter. His wife, Vivienne, was far easier to deal with.

His luck was out, however. Adam Smith opened the door to him.

Max watched as Smith swayed in front of him. Not alcohol this time, Max suspected, but nerves. Smith might try to convince himself, as well as everyone else, that his daughter was lost on the streets, but even he must realize that, after so long, there was a very strong possibility that she was dead.

'Nothing's happened,' Max assured him, 'but I'd like a word if that's all right. May I come in?'

Smith pulled the door open fully to allow him access. 'What do you mean, nothing's happened?' he demanded.

'I mean I don't have anything to tell you other than that we may, and I stress the may, have had a positive sighting of your daughter in Blackpool.'

'Blackpool?'

That threw him. It made a mockery of the hours he'd spent walking the streets of Harrington.

Vivienne Smith had been sitting in the lounge, but she rose to her feet, panic etched in every facial muscle.

No TV or radio had been on and Max guessed they had either been talking about their daughter or, more likely, simply staring into space, too terrified to voice their personal nightmares.

'Hello, Mrs Smith,' Max said, giving her what he hoped was a positive, upbeat sort of smile.

'Did you say Blackpool?' she asked, and Max nodded.

This room was like any other in the row of semi-detached houses on West Street, but it had a sadness to it that seeped into your bones. He wondered what it had been like when Yasmin was living there. Filled with noise? Echoing with laughter? It was difficult to imagine.

The plasma TV screen was huge and to the side of that was an impressive audio system. There was a pebble-effect gas fire, a tan-coloured leather suite and cream carpets.

Max handed Adam Smith the photograph they'd pulled from the CCTV footage.

'It's the best we can do, I'm afraid,' Max told them. 'Would you say this is Yasmin?'

Max saw the way Smith's chin quivered, and the way his jaw tightened as he strove for a tight grip on his emotions. At first, Max thought the pain was from seeing his little girl in the photo. Then he realized it was because Smith couldn't say for sure if it was Yasmin or not.

Wordlessly, he handed it to his wife.

'That's Yasmin,' she said. 'That's our daughter, Chief Inspector.

'You're sure?'

'Positive.'

'When was this taken?' Smith asked.

'Two nights ago.' Max knew the couple expected him to go to Blackpool, collect Yasmin and bring her home. He only wished it was that simple. 'The car she's getting into is a white Mercedes,' he went on, 'but we can't see anything to give us a clue as to its owner. No registration, no identifying marks, nothing. We're scanning all other CCTV in Blackpool to see if we can get another sighting of either Yasmin or the car.'

Smith took the photo and stared at it for a few moments. Once again, emotion threatened to take over. Max was wrong; the emotion wasn't due to not being able to recognize his own daughter, it was due to not daring to believe it could be her.

'I wondered if you have more photos of Yasmin,' Max said. 'Or, even better, videos of her. We'd like to see the way she moves and talks, any gestures unique to her—'

'We've given you photos,' Smith muttered.

They'd given them two photos. In both, Yasmin had been smiling for the camera. The stance was too posed.

'I know, and I'm asking for more. We have a lot of highly trained officers working on this, and it will be a great help if they can study Yasmin in more detail. If you have pictures where she's been caught unawares, where she's doing something other than looking at a camera, we'd be grateful.'

'I'll get them,' Vivienne said.

She left the room briefly and returned clutching a large cake tin to her chest.

'We'll return them to you as soon as possible,' Max promised.

When she lifted the lid, Max saw hundreds of photographs. They must have sorted them out over the last few months.

'There are lots taken when she was a baby or a toddler,' Vivienne warned.

'They won't be any use, will they?' Smith snapped at his wife.

'Let's have a look, shall we?' Preparing himself for the long haul, Max sat beside Mrs Smith and looked through them with her. Picture after picture.

One in particular caught his eye. It would have caught anyone's eye. Fairly recent, it showed Yasmin dressed as Madonna. Instead of an innocent fifteen-year-old schoolgirl, she looked seductive and experienced. In short, she looked like every red-blooded man's fantasy.

'This one...' Vivienne shot her husband an anxious look and spoke softly. 'It was for a party at her friend's house. They all dressed up like this. Yasmin thought it was a bit of fun, but then Beth, her friend, put pictures of everyone on the internet. Yasmin didn't like that. She's quite shy, you see, and she hates other people seeing her photo.'

Max longed to grab them both by their throats and shake them. Did they seriously imagine that finding a lost teenager was simply a case of having a couple of patrol cars on the streets ready to bring her home? Why in hell's name hadn't they mentioned this before?

'Which internet site was it?' Max asked, and Vivienne shook her head.

'I don't know about the internet,' she apologized.

'I need Beth's address.'

'Beth?' Smith snapped. 'You've got Beth's address. You were given all her friends' names and addresses.'

Yes, and they'd spoken to every last one of those friends. But while they'd checked everything on Yasmin's computer, they hadn't checked Beth's.

Vivienne didn't argue. She simply went to the address book by the phone, tore a page from the back, and carefully, stopping to double check, wrote down Beth's address and phone number.

'Thank you,' Max said. 'I need to take this photo, but I will let you have it back.'

They looked at every photo in that tin and, while there were several pictures of Yasmin that interested him, the Madonna lookalike was at the top of his list.

All the time, Adam Smith paced the room. Max guessed he was mentally packing a bag. Without doubt, he would be on his way to Blackpool first thing in the morning.

Max knew better than to argue with him.

Chapter Twenty-Four

Jill was striving for normality but having breakfast with Max and his sons was a disturbing experience. It was a painful reminder of how good *and* how bad things had once been between them. She was trying hard not to remember any of it.

She had a slice of toast, something she never bothered with at home. Usually coffee was her first meal of the day. Perhaps she was trying to set an example to Harry and Ben by showing them she knew all about the most important meal of the day. Or, more likely, she was too greedy to refuse.

'Bus,' Max mumbled through a mouthful of food, nodding up at the clock.

'It's always late,' Harry said, but he picked up his schoolbag.

'Yay! Last day of school,' Ben said happily.

'Trousers, Ben,' Max pointed out.

Ben looked down at his legs and seemed surprised to see the old jeans he'd worn in the garden while playing with the dogs.

'Oh, yeah,' he said, and he ran upstairs to change, leaving Max to roll his eyes in despair.

Five minutes later, in full school uniform and with bags slung over their shoulders, the boys headed off for the school bus.

'It's lucky Ben doesn't want to be a rocket scientist,' Max said, shaking his head. 'Do you want another coffee?'

'Please.'

The caffeine would help to keep her awake. She'd been too conscious of Max in the adjoining room to sleep well. The offer had been there, so she could have shared his bed. They'd had some wonderful times when they'd lived here together, but it had ended in disaster, and she didn't want his sons thinking she was a permanent feature.

'I'm a bit stuck without a car,' she said, pushing the memories aside. 'I wanted to go over to Kelton this morning and have a chat with Steve.'

'About what?'

'I won't know until I get there.'

'You can come in with me and then take a pool car.'

He was ready to leave but first Jill needed to sort out her cats. Apart from Fly, who always looked as if he was contemplating a tasty snack of cat, Max's dogs were polite around the felines. There was a reasonable harmony between them all, and Jill marvelled that animals, unlike humans, could exist fairly happily side by side. All the same, she locked her cats in the conservatory, well away from the dogs.

'Are you ready to go?' Max asked.

'Yes, and thanks for letting me stay last night. I'm sure I was perfectly safe back at my cottage, but, well, until we have some idea who's out there–'

'Quite. Good to see you showing a bit of sense for a change.'

'Although, my stalker isn't planning to harm me,' she added confidently. 'He's a complete coward.'

'We're safer not testing that theory.'

Most of the snow had thawed, but Max had the radio tuned to the local station as he drove and more heavy falls for the north-west were expected overnight.

Once they reached headquarters, Jill went to her office to check emails. Finding nothing urgent, she dashed off a couple of replies and then went to sort out a car. It wasn't quite as simple as Max had suggested but half an hour later she was driving an ancient Vauxhall Astra in the direction of Kelton Bridge.

She wasn't surprised the car had been available and was merely glad she wasn't in a hurry. The interior smelt of stale fish and chips and something that she couldn't identify. She didn't try too hard.

When she reached the village, she drove straight to Steve Carlisle's house.

She wasn't sure what she wanted to talk to him about. She believed though that, whether he knew it or not, he held some of the answers to this.

She knocked on his door, but no one answered. It was after nine o'clock, so he would have listened to the news headlines and taken Cally for her morning walk. Jill decided to wait. Her copy of the *Racing Post* was in her bag, so she passed the time by looking at the runners and riders.

She couldn't concentrate, though. Her mind went round in circles as she thought of Lauren Cole and her father. Father and daughter murdered. Why?

She was trying to mentally gather all she knew about Lauren and Vincent Cole when Steve walked up his drive, the dog ambling by his side.

She jumped out of her car.

'Morning, Steve. I was passing so I thought I'd call in and see how you are.'

'Hello, Jill. Come on in. You haven't been waiting, have you?'

'No, I've only just pulled up.' She'd been sitting there for half an hour.

Steve shrugged off his coat, scarf and hat, and kicked off his walking boots, then they went into the sitting room where Cally immediately jumped on to her chair and settled down to sleep.

The stove hadn't been lit, but the room was a lot warmer than the pool car had been.

'So how are you doing, Steve?'

'Fine, thanks,' he replied. 'The reporters seem to have given up on me for the time being. Fingers crossed they stay away.'

Jill knew what he meant. Journalists would try any ploy to get a story and having them camped out on your doorstep was a daunting experience.

'How's Alison?' she asked.

'She's good, thanks. Working, of course. There's an exhibition in Liverpool so she's there at the moment. She'll be back tomorrow morning.'

It was difficult to tell what he thought of that, but she guessed he was glad that life was carrying on as normal. He wasn't the type to want a wife at home fussing around.

'Steve, I know you've been asked more than enough questions,' she began, 'but can you tell me exactly what Lauren Cole knew about you?'

He frowned at that. 'How do you mean?'

'Did she know the route you walked? The time you'd be out walking? That you sometimes carried an axe or a saw with you?'

'Well, yes,' he said after a moment. 'She knew all that. One day when we met up, she asked what was in the sack. I had an axe and half a dozen logs in it. She laughed, I remember. Said she would have thought twice about speaking to me if she'd known I had an axe.' He sighed loudly. 'Given what's happened, it's not very funny, is it?'

'And she knew that you walked the same route

at the same time every day?'

'She knew where I liked to walk with Cally, yes. But sometimes that route took me an hour and sometimes two. Why do you ask, Jill?'

'I'm just trying to piece things together,' she answered, deliberately vague. 'What about Charlie? Was he the sort of dog to go off with strangers?'

'No, he was utterly devoted to Lauren. Although if someone had food...' He smiled, a sad sort of smile. 'She told me that when she found him, or rather he found her, he was starving. A stray, he was. She didn't think he'd ever got over that and was always hungry. He had a good nose on him, too. Once, he ran off quite a distance. When we caught up with him, he'd found a sandwich that someone had dropped. He must have been able to smell that from a hundred yards away.'

If Steve, who only saw the girl now and again, knew all this about Charlie, it stood to reason that any acquaintance of Lauren's would, too.

'What are you getting at, Jill?'

'I'm not sure,' she admitted. 'I'm trying to understand what happened that morning. Is it possible that someone could have enticed Charlie away from Lauren, knowing that you would split up? Is it possible that someone set you up?'

The question clearly shocked him.

'But why would anyone – I mean, why me?'

'Why not?' Jill responded.

To escape blame, the killer wouldn't care who he put in the frame.

'Do you think it's possible?' she asked again.

247

'Not really, no. It was my suggestion we split up to look for Charlie. No one could have known I'd say that. I dropped my sack and no one could have known I'd do that. In fact, no one could have known that I'd even have it with me.'

He was right, of course. The killer couldn't have known those things.

But if Jill's theory was correct, this had been a spur of the moment attack. Their man was an opportunist. He was an amateur, albeit one who, so far, was clever enough to get away with murder. Perhaps he'd followed Lauren that morning. Perhaps he'd seen her meet up with Steve, enticed the dog away with a Mars bar or anything else he happened to have in his pocket.

It sounded far-fetched, and she certainly couldn't see Max falling for it.

'I think someone wanted Lauren out of the way, Steve, and I think you were an easy target for the blame.'

'I can't see why. Or how.' He looked so weary of it all. 'Thanks, though. For believing I'm innocent, I mean.'

'I never doubted it,' she replied.

'Chief Inspector Trentham did. Still does, I shouldn't wonder.'

'He's keeping an open mind,' she said lightly.

To give credit to Max, he always kept an open mind. He would never send an innocent man to a cell.

'If you remember anything else about that morning,' she said, 'let me know, will you?'

'I will, yes. Of course.'

He showed her to the door and she took the

unfamiliar car keys from her pocket.

'You seem to be coping well,' she couldn't help saying. He looked desperately tired, but he appeared more confident than she'd ever seen him. He looked as if he could take on the world and win.

'I've had a lot of time to think about things,' he said. 'I've realized that the small stuff doesn't matter.'

'You're right there. Be seeing you, Steve.'

Instead of driving straight to headquarters, she drove to Todmorden Moor and parked there. The wind strength was increasing and it buffeted the car.

Deciding the planet would have to take care of itself, she kept the engine running for warmth. She leaned back in her seat, closed her eyes and tried to picture what had happened the morning Lauren Cole met her end.

'Right,' she murmured to herself, 'tell me what you did. You followed Lauren to her dad's house, didn't you? You saw her leave and you knew she was in a temper. Her dad said she drove off in such a state that she knocked the wheelie bin flying. So you wondered where she was going, didn't you? You followed her. So you must have a car.'

Jill smiled to herself as she thanked God her mother couldn't see her talking to imaginary nutters. Except this particular nutter wasn't imaginary. He was out there somewhere. All they had to do was find him.

'So, for some reason, you wanted Lauren out of the way,' she continued. 'Why? What did she know? Ah, perhaps you'd both been stealing from her father and Lauren wanted to end it. You wouldn't want to stop, would you? Was she threatening to tell someone? The police perhaps?'

She needed to give him a name. It was easier to get on the same mental wavelength if it was personal.

'You're Josh, aren't you?' she decided. 'So, Josh, you followed her up the hill. There were plenty of walls so you could keep out of sight. You were angry with her. You were going to teach her a lesson. And then Steve Carlisle appeared and the show was over. Until he left her...'

The dog wasn't enticed away from Lauren. Charlie's nose told him that someone he knew was in the area.

'Charlie sought you out. You couldn't hide from the dog, could you? You tried to send him away, but he was too pleased to meet a friend. Perhaps you even had food on you. Chocolate or chewing gum. Lauren saw he was missing and panicked. She called him, but the thought of food made him deaf. Then, like a gift from above, Lauren and Steve split up to look for him. You saw Lauren alone.'

Jill drummed her cold fingers on the steering wheel as she wondered how he could have known the perfect murder weapon was in Steve's sack.

'Of course. You would have looked in the sack because you're a common thief. You'd already stolen from Lauren's dad, hadn't you? If someone leaves something lying around, you instinctively see if there's anything worth pinching. This time, you got really lucky and found an axe. You

250

killed her and legged it. Charlie wouldn't have followed you, he would have stayed with Lauren. By the time Steve got back, you would have been long gone.'

She wasn't even convincing herself, but she forced the car into gear, turned around and drove into Harrington.

Jill had plenty of work to keep her occupied for the remainder of the day. By the time she closed her office and went in search of Max, ready for a lift to her temporary home, the briefing was coming to an end and only a few officers remained.

She decided to join them, belatedly realizing that one of those was Phil Meredith. That he was in a foul mood and taking it out on a young constable was nothing out of the ordinary.

He turned to the room in general to bark out, 'You have all the resources you need, the overtime bill would keep the whole bloody country in luxury and yet still you're getting nowhere. It's not good enough!'

With that, he barged out, almost knocking Jill over.

'Don't mention it,' she muttered as his back vanished along the corridor.

'Phew,' someone said with evident relief that he'd gone.

'Penis envy,' Jill decided.

'You what?' Fletch said. 'I thought women had that.'

'It's most likely that Meredith has a very small penis. Minuscule, in fact. Invisible with the naked eye I shouldn't wonder.'

251

A few snorts of laughter had everyone relaxing.

'I don't suppose you've got anything useful, have you?' Max asked. 'Other than the size of Meredith's dick, that is?'

'Possibly,' she replied, but she wasn't confident. 'We're all ears.'

'OK, I think you're looking for a young male, about twenty years old–'

'Blimey, that's narrowed it down a lot,' Fletch scoffed.

'Who may have a record. Not murder, possibly not even anything violent. He could well be on file for burglary though.'

Her interpretation of the events surrounding Lauren's death was wrong, she knew that. Unfortunately, as she couldn't find the missing piece of the jigsaw yet, she could only give them her possibly half-baked theory.

'He'd known Lauren for a few years and thought he was on to a good thing,' she said. 'He knew she went to her father's for money that morning and he was annoyed that she didn't get any. I think she was going to tell someone – her dad, the police, her priest perhaps – what she and our man had been up to, stealing from her father, getting money from him. So he followed her. At the time, he wasn't thinking of murder, just exerting power over her, bringing her round to his way of thinking. The dog wasn't enticed away. Charlie knew him. When Lauren and Steve Carlisle split up, he was made. He's a thief, so it would have been second nature to look in Steve's sack. He found the axe. So, not only could he get rid of Lauren permanently, he could lay the blame at someone else's feet.'

She had their interest, but she could see they weren't convinced.

'He took the key from Lauren, the one to her dad's house,' she went on. 'Remember, he's an opportunist. He broke in, thinking he could take what he wanted while Vincent Cole slept in his bed. But Vincent was too distressed to enjoy a good night's sleep. He confronted our man and suffered a blow to the head that killed him.' She shrugged. 'That's my theory.'

She waited for the usual ridicule. It didn't come, but she could see that Max was looking bemused by something.

'What?' she asked him.

'I'm just wondering why Lauren didn't keep the key to her dad's house on the fob with her car and house keys. Or are you suggesting that our killer removed that one key from the bunch? And if so, why? She was dead. He knew she didn't need her car keys.'

She hadn't thought of that.

'She obviously kept her dad's key separate,' she said, although that didn't make much sense. Still, that was their problem. 'Now, I have no idea how he came to be friends with Lauren,' she went on, 'but something will have happened, something that helped them bond. She trusted him because she believed they were alike. My guess is that she got to know him after her mum died. She was at her most vulnerable then. Something might have happened to him around the same time.'

There were a few raised eyebrows, but no one spoke.

'OK,' Max said at last. 'The graveyard shift needs to gather mug shots of all likely suspects. Male. Late teens, early twenties. Local. On file for burglary. Take them out in the morning and show them to people who knew Lauren. Cole's cleaner, Mrs Hollingsworth, will be a good place to start. She might be able to recognize someone.'

As he barked out orders, Jill prayed she wasn't wasting everyone's time.

Chapter Twenty-Five

It was almost one o'clock when Steve Carlisle heard his wife's car pull on to the drive. He'd been about to make himself something for lunch, but that could wait. He didn't have much of an appetite; he was simply acting on auto-pilot.

He stayed where he was, sitting at the kitchen table, the *Daily Mail* open in front of him.

'I'm home, darling!' she called out.

The greeting echoed with falseness, and he felt his heart start to race.

'In here,' he called back.

She came into the kitchen, dropped her handbag and laptop case on the table, gave him a casual peck on the cheek and went straight to the coffee-maker. She'd be expecting him to rush out and fetch her clothes from the car as he usually did.

'The motorway traffic was murder,' she said.

'Really?' His radio had been tuned to BBC Radio Lancashire all morning and nothing had been mentioned. It was rarely too bad on Saturdays.

He could see her mind ticking over, trying to fathom out why he hadn't leapt to his feet when she came in, why he was being distant. And still his heart raced with anger. All the anger he'd felt for the last twenty years was gripping him now. He made a conscious effort to breathe deeply and calm himself.

'Everything all right?' she asked.

He folded his newspaper and stood up.

'I'm leaving you,' he said simply.

'You're–' She'd been about to reach into the cupboard for a cup and her hand froze an inch from the door. 'You're leaving? To go where? What do you mean?'

'I'm renting a flat in Harrington,' he said, surprised at how calm he was managing to sound. 'It belongs to a friend, an ex-customer of mine. The rent's reasonable and, most important, he doesn't object to Cally being there.'

'But I don't understand.'

'I can't live with you, Alison, so I'm moving out. I've packed some stuff. The rest can be sorted out later.'

She stood across the table from him, her knuckles white as she gripped its edge.

'But – what's happened?'

'Nothing's happened. I just thought it courteous to let you know. I'm going now.' He couldn't wait to get out.

'You won't go until you've told me what the fuck is going on!'

This was the Alison he was used to. The one

who barked out orders.

She looked as she always did. Immaculate. Expensive highlights in her blonde hair caught the light from the window. Her beautiful face was carefully made up, the perfect advertisement for the cosmetics she was so good at selling. Black trousers fitted perfectly, as did her white blouse. Several hundred pounds worth of jewellery sparkled from her fingers and wrists.

'Dad believes you're having an affair,' he said, and he saw the blush creep up from her neck.

'Oh, for...' She shook her head, probably to hide her heightened colour. 'And what, pray, makes him think that?'

'He saw you with the man in question. You were meeting him on the Burnley Road.'

This statement brought more colour. Now, even the tips of her ears were scarlet.

'What complete nonsense,' she said. 'He's obviously made a mistake. It's ridiculous, I tell you. You know that, Steve. Now, if that's what this little tantrum is about, we can forget it and get back to normal. It's all right for you sitting here all day, but I've been working. I'm whacked.'

'I don't really care if you're having an affair or not,' he said. 'That's the sad thing, isn't it? It no longer matters to me. I want out, Alison. And I want a divorce.'

'What?'

From blushing scarlet, she was now deathly pale.

He'd known how she would react to mention of the d-word. It didn't fall in with her plans. If it had, she would have dragged him through the courts long ago.

'You're being ridiculous, Steve. Petty and downright spiteful, too. What do you want, hm? What do you want me to do or say? You know as well as I do that we can't get divorced.'

'Plenty of couples do. What's so different about us?'

'You know damn well.'

'That's just it, I don't.'

'Well, I'm sure as hell not volunteering to tell Uncle David!'

'Ah, dear old Uncle David. He won't like it, will he? Hell, he might even cut you out of his will.' Steve shrugged. 'It doesn't mean we can't get divorced.'

'Of course it does,' she hissed. 'I'm all he's got!'

'He'll still have you. And I'm more than happy to tell him. All I know is that I'm sick of you. I can't live with you. In fact, I wish to God I'd walked out years ago. Instead, I took the blame for our misery. I accepted that Maisie's death was all down to me. It wasn't, though. At least I was here for her when she died. Where were you? Working. You were staying in a hotel overnight, probably with your man of the moment.'

'Shut up!'

He felt the bitter, angry smile tug at his mouth.

'Shut up,' he repeated. 'How very apt, my dear. Those were the last words you said to your daughter, weren't they? "Shut up," you said. Do you remember the last words you said to me before you left that day? You said, "You'll have to figure out a way of shutting the little brat up because she's doing my head in." How the hell—'

He had to break off as the memories flooded in. At the time, he'd tried to put Alison's hostility towards their daughter down to post-natal depression. All these years later, it still sickened him.

'You never wanted her anyway, did you?' he went on furiously. 'Children get in the way, don't they? No one was supposed to get in the way of your perfect life.'

The only thing that surprised Steve was that he'd put up with her for so long. And why? Because he loathed conflict. Because he hadn't wanted his parents to know that he'd made the biggest mistake of his life in marrying her. Nor had he wanted anyone's pity. Or to appear a failure in the eyes of that hypocrite, Father David Gosling. Dear old Uncle David.

'I narrowly escaped being sent down for murder,' he reminded her, 'and, while I saw how little that meant to you, it meant one hell of a lot to me. It gave me time to think. It made me appreciate my freedom. And that's all I have now, my freedom. I'm free to live where I choose. Free to take life as it comes. And that's exactly what I'm going to do.'

He walked upstairs and carried down two holdalls. The rest of his stuff was already in the back of his car, along with Cally's bed, blankets and toys.

Alison was standing at the bottom of the stairs, arms folded across a chest that was rising and falling rapidly as she took each furious breath.

'You can't fucking leave me,' she screamed at him. 'I won't stand for it!'

'Watch me!'

DS Grace Warne could have done without working on a Saturday. Her favourite shoe shop was having a pre-Christmas sale and she would have liked to have been first in the queue.

But work she must. She enjoyed her job, she liked her boss and she got along well with her colleagues. Well, most of them. Also, she considered this area of Lancashire as her patch and no way would she rest while someone out there thought he could get the better of her.

So this Saturday morning found her driving out to Longman Drive and the home of Mrs Hollingsworth. She had DS Fletcher for company, and they had the grand total of eight photographs for inspection.

The trouble with police mugshots was that everyone looked guilty. Even Mother Theresa would have looked like a mass murderer if she'd ever had the misfortune to be photographed at the nick. And since they'd been taken, the subjects could have dyed their hair, grown beards and picked up scars.

'We'll call on Lauren Cole's flatmate after we've done Mrs H,' Fletch said. 'I know she claims she never saw Lauren with anyone, but she must have. These might jog her memory.'

'Good idea.'

As soon as she stopped the car, Grace took the photos from Fletch and shuffled them.

'What are you doing?'

'If Jill's right – and I know it all sounds like a load of crap, but I bet she is – my money goes on him as our likeliest candidate.' She pointed to the photo of the young man now in the middle of the stack.

'Why?'

Grinning, she tapped the side of her nose. 'Come on. Let's hope she can recognize someone.'

Mrs Hollingsworth must have been watching out for them because the front door was opened before they reached it.

'Come in,' she said.

'Thank you. And thank you for seeing us,' Grace added. 'We do appreciate it.'

'That's all right,' she replied, 'but like I said on the phone, I'm not sure I'll be able to recognize the young man. As I told the Chief Inspector, I only saw him once in town. I might have seen him visit Mr Cole's house with Lauren, but I can't be sure of that.'

'That's OK,' Grace assured her. 'We'd still like you to take a look.'

She hunted for her glasses and Grace took the opportunity to look around a sitting room that was crammed with junk. Christmas decorations vied for space with china animals. It resembled an Oxfam shop that was in dire need of expansion.

When Mrs Hollingsworth had found a pair of worryingly thick spectacles, Grace handed over the photos.

'Take your time,' Fletch said.

Grace watched the woman closely as she discarded first one, then two, then three.

At the fourth, she stopped. She carried the mugshot to the window and examined it closely in a better light.

'This is him,' she announced. 'This is the person I saw in town with young Lauren.'

Grace could have punched the air with joy.

'You're sure? You don't want to look at the rest?'

'I'm sure. Yes, this is definitely him.'

'Thank you, Mrs Hollingsworth. You've been a great help.'

'I'm not sure if it's the same one who came to the house with her, though,' she reminded them. 'I couldn't really say what he looked like because he was wearing a hood.'

'That's OK. Thank you,' Grace said again.

If it hadn't been so icy, Grace would have skipped down the drive to the car.

'OK, fez up,' Fletch said, fastening his seat belt. 'Why did you think it was him?'

'Just a stab in the dark, Fletch.'

She fired the engine and drove down Longman Drive. But she felt sorry for Fletch and knew she had to explain.

'Maurice Temple, the one in the photo? He's twenty-one and has been in trouble for nicking stuff since the age of twelve. Oh, and his mother died,' she added.

'So?'

'So she was at the same hospital as Lauren Cole's mum. They died within a couple of weeks of each other. Both had breast cancer.' She grinned at him. 'Looks like Jill was on to something after all.'

Chapter Twenty-Six

As a rule, Colin Pierce liked these jobs. Whenever a new tenancy agreement was signed on one of the flats, Colin had to check the electrics. It was a doddle. The estate had been built twelve years ago, a mix of flats, or luxury apartments as they were called, town houses, and small detached homes. The wiring was relatively new so he only had to take a quick look, sign the forms to confirm that the necessary regulations were satisfied and send in his invoice. Wesley Housing Group were prompt payers so it was money for old rope.

This appointment had been arranged through the landlord.

'Can you do it early morning?' Jackson had asked. 'It's just that the tenant is going to be out and about this week so he wants it out of the way.'

'Nine o'clock on Monday morning?' Colin suggested.

'Great stuff. Thanks for that. And you'll let me know if there are any problems?'

'Of course.'

There wouldn't be any problems though. The properties had been built by established reputable builders. No corners had been cut. The wiring, like everything else, was spot on.

It was 8.55 a.m. when Colin rang the bell and waited for the security phone to crackle into life.

All was silent so he rang it again.

This was typical. Tenants wanted the early appointments and half the time they weren't even out of bed.

Colin stabbed a finger at the bell for a third time.

This job would take fifteen minutes tops, and that included filling in the paperwork, but if he couldn't gain access to the property, he would be putting in a bill for time wasting.

'Come on,' he muttered, 'open the bloody door!'

He read the notes on his clipboard and realized that for once he had a phone number for the tenant.

Back in his van, his gaze not leaving the front door, he called the number from his mobile. There was no answer. It was possible, he supposed, that the tenant was in the shower and unable to hear either bell or phone.

The dashboard clock read 8.58. Colin decided to smoke a cigarette and then try again. He had a busy day ahead and he didn't want to have to call back later.

The nine o'clock news came on the radio when he'd smoked half of it. Knowing his luck, he'd be moaned at for being late now.

He tossed the butt out of the window and left his van.

Three times he rang the bell, but no one answered.

It was the ground floor apartment so he walked round the back of the block and peered in through the kitchen window. No one was there. He couldn't see signs of movement through the bathroom's frosted glass either.

When he looked into the lounge, the first thing he saw was a dog. Odd that it wasn't barking.

The second thing he saw—

'Bloody Nora!'

He ran back to his van, grabbed his phone and punched in 999.

'I need an ambulance,' he gasped out. 'And the police, too!'

Chapter Twenty-Seven

After the morning briefing, Max took the stairs to Phil Meredith's office to update him on their progress. There *was* progress, but it was going at the speed of an injured slug. Blink and you'd miss it.

He tapped on the door and stepped inside.

'Right. Let's hear it.' Meredith took three Polos from a packet and tossed them in his mouth together. 'You must have something by now, Max.'

'Yes,' Max said, taking a positive stance. 'First, the Yasmin Smith case. A photograph of her taken at a friend's party was put on the internet.'

'Bloody internet,' Meredith muttered. 'The damn thing should be banned for people under eighteen.'

Max knew where his boss was coming from. He also knew that his sons would be lost without it. Not so long ago, Ben had told Max he ought to get himself a page on Facebook.

'Then we could be friends,' Ben had said.

'Sorry. We'll just have to be friends in real life,' Max had told him.

'We don't know which site it was put on,' he told Meredith now. 'Her friend thought it was Facebook. Then she wondered if it could have been SeeYouThere. That's yet another social networking site. Anyway, we have the girl's computer and Mel's going through it now.'

Meredith nodded at that. Even he knew that Mel was more than an IT wizard; she was a genius.

'We've got a lot of CCTV footage from Blackpool,' Max went on. 'We're looking for Yasmin or the white Mercedes.' He didn't add *any* white Mercedes or hint that they still didn't have anything to mark that particular car from any other of the same model.

'So that's moving along a bit,' he said, still being Mr Positive.

'Good. But what about these bloody murders? The press know damn well that Cole was murdered. If we haven't called suicide within twenty-four hours, they know we're looking at murder. They're spreading rumours about serial killers being on the loose now.'

Max knew that, and he wasn't surprised. Serial killers sold newspapers like nothing else.

'Going on Jill's theory,' he explained, 'we gathered mugshots of people in the right age bracket on record for burglary. One of those was a Maurice Temple. Vincent Cole's cleaner has identified him as the man she saw with Lauren in town one day. The owner of the corner shop that

265

Lauren sometimes used recognized him, too.'

'And where is this Temple?'

Good question, and one for which Max had no answer.

'We're tracing him now.'

Having crunched his way through his Polos, Meredith put three more in his mouth. Max wondered if his boss was suffering from indigestion. It wouldn't surprise him. Meredith didn't cope well with stress and was a likely candidate for ulcers or a heart attack.

'So really, it's going OK,' Max pointed out.

'Hm.' Meredith wasn't getting excited. 'You need to run this by the book, Max. If Jill's theory turns out to be a load of baloney, you're going to look like bloody imbeciles.'

'Jill only offered us a short cut by telling us where to look. We've had two positive IDs for Temple.'

'Being seen with a victim doesn't make you guilty of murder,' Meredith said, crunching on each syllable.

That was true enough, but when you had as many other leads as Max – i.e. none – you were grateful for anything.

Without ramming cars out of the way, something even DS Warne wouldn't do, there was nowhere to park on Dale Street. She drove into a side street, finally found a gap that only blocked half an entrance, and headed for the jeweller's.

The shop looked as if it had been there forever. The facade was clean enough, but it wouldn't have looked out of place on a film set from the

266

forties or fifties.

There was no doubting the quality of the items for sale though, and there were no price tags on the slim gold watches or antique rings. Grace guessed that if you needed to ask the price, you couldn't afford it.

A tiny bell tinkled as she pushed open the door.

'Good morning,' an elderly man greeted her.

'Mr Atwood?' she asked.

'Yes.'

'DS Warne.' Grace flashed her ID and he examined it closely. He'd been looking at a small silver plate and still wore an eyeglass. 'We spoke on the phone earlier.'

Grace had drawn up a list of the most likely places a thief would try to offload booty from Vincent Cole's home. Atwood's shop had been fourteenth on that list.

'Indeed we did.' He removed the eyeglass. 'I thought at the time there was something suspicious about the items that man was selling. I'm afraid to say that isn't unusual, though.'

'Oh?'

'No. Because I deal in antique jewellery and silverware, people think I'll pay cash for anything. They're wrong. Unless sellers can provide me with certificates of ownership, I'm not interested.'

Like the shop, the owner's suit could have featured in an old film. The lapels were wide, and the fabric was a dark grey that had worn thin. In its day, it would have been quality. Sadly, its day had passed a couple of decades ago.

'Can you recall the items mentioned?' Grace asked.

'The only thing the chap actually showed me was the silver rose bowl that I told you about. A large one, and a very fine example. It was ten years old.'

'You say that was the only item he showed you?'

'Yes, but he described other items. A milk jug, a stem vase, a silver-backed hairbrush...' He rubbed a finger down the length of his nose. 'Several pairs of cufflinks. One was gold, he said. I think he guessed from the start that I wasn't interested in buying, but he wanted to know how much the items were worth.'

Grace looked around the shop.

'Do you have security cameras?' she asked, already guessing the answer.

'I don't. The shop, however, as I keep telling the insurance company, is very secure. There are metal shutters on external windows and doors, and, at night, everything is locked away in the safe.'

She wasn't too interested in security, more in catching a glimpse of the man trying to sell stolen property. 'Could you give me a description of him?' she asked.

He closed his eyes briefly as if trying to bring the image to mind.

'Twenties, I'd say. Early twenties. Scruffily dressed. That in itself speaks volumes, dear. He was wearing the uniform of today's youth. Jeans that were in need of an iron's sole-plate, not to mention a good wash. They dragged on the ground by at least two inches. One of those shapeless tops. It was grey with a hood. He had very short fair hair and his face was slightly pocked as if he'd suffered from acne at some stage. Oh, yes, and he wore an earring. A cheap little cross, gold coloured, hanging from his right ear.'

Grace was impressed with his powers of observation. Who needed CCTV?

'That's great.' She handed him a photo of Maurice Temple. 'Would you say this is him?'

'That's him. Without doubt.'

'Would you be prepared to officially identify him?'

'I certainly would. The items are all stolen, I take it?'

'They are, yes.' She returned the photo to the envelope and gave him a bright smile. 'You've been most helpful, Mr Atwood. Thank you for your time. We'll be in touch. Oh, and if he happens to call on you again, please let us know.'

Grace left the shop in an optimistic mood. For all he wore the uniform of the young, Maurice Temple got himself noticed. People remembered him so it couldn't be too long before they found him. And once they found him, it wouldn't take long to nail him.

Grace couldn't wait.

Jill was about finished for the day and was hoping Max was, too. She wanted a lift, preferably one that went via her cottage so she could pick up some clothes. She could, of course, insist on moving back home, but, for some reason, she'd made an unconscious decision to leave it a few days.

The first person she saw as she set off in search of Max was Clive White. Damn it all. Was there a day when he *wasn't* in the building?

'Clive–'

'Jill, hi. How's things?'

He had no idea how he was annoying her. The genial smile, the delight at seeing her – he had no idea at all.

'Clive,' she began again, 'when you were suspended from duty, the idea was that you had a rest and stayed at home. At home, Clive. It's one thing calling in occasionally to try and raise some sponsorship, but you're here every day.'

'Aw, I know.' He gave her one of those looks that said he was about to come clean. 'I called in to see if anything was happening in the Yasmin Smith case,' he admitted. 'I was dead chuffed with myself for spotting her on the CCTV.'

CCTV that he shouldn't have been anywhere near.

'That was good,' Jill said, 'but you're not supposed to be here. What's the point of suspending you, Clive? The way things are going, you'll be facing another couple of months away from the job. Unless you can prove that you–'

'I know, I know,' he cut her off. 'The thing is...' He shuffled from one foot to the other. 'Angie's moved out.'

It took a moment for Jill to realize that Angie was his wife. She recalled meeting her once. Slim, dark-haired, stunningly attractive with a brain the size of a pinhead.

'How do you mean, moved out?'

'Things have been a bit difficult between us for a while,' he admitted, 'and she's packed up and moved back in with her mother. I expect she'll come round, but, at the moment, the house is feeling a bit empty.'

'I'm sorry to hear that, but it doesn't alter the fact that you're not supposed to be here. Perhaps you'd be better occupied talking to your wife.'

'I'm going to. In fact, I'm on my way there now.' He put up his hands in a gesture of submission. 'I'm gone. And you won't see me again until my assessment.'

'Good.'

Smiling, and striding along the corridor as if it was his own personal domain, he went on his way.

Jill let out her breath on a frustrated sigh. She'd meant it; if he didn't stay away, she would recommend that he was suspended for a further couple of months.

She carried on towards Max's office and met Grace coming from the opposite direction.

'Christ, what a bloody day!'

'Has something happened?' Jill asked.

'Haven't you heard? Steve Carlisle was found this morning with stab wounds. I've just come from the General.'

'What?'

'Yeah. An electrician called at his flat–'

'But Steve doesn't have a flat. He lives in Kelton.'

'He moved out on Saturday apparently,' Grace said. 'He's now living in Harrington. A flat. Ground floor, thank God, or he wouldn't have been found. The electrician called to check the wiring this morning and was nosy enough to look through the windows when no one answered the door. Steve Carlisle was lying in a pool of blood. Stabbed and left for dead.'

271

Jill was struggling to keep pace. None of this made any sense.

'How is he now, Grace?'

'Not good. It's touch and go, I gather.'

'Any idea who—'

'Not a bloody clue! Catch you later, Jill.'

As Grace raced off in the direction of the CID room, Jill stood for a moment to try and take in what she'd just heard.

Then, gathering her wits, she headed out of the building. It was a nuisance not having her car with her and, really, she couldn't see much point in having it parked outside her cottage. Her favourite prankster might assume she was in and play more tricks, thus getting caught on camera, but she didn't think that having her car parked on the drive would make an iota of difference.

Fortunately, it was only a ten-minute walk to Harrington General and, although it was cold, it wasn't actually snowing.

As she'd missed news from the Kelton Bridge grapevine over the last few days, she hadn't heard about Steve moving out. Gossip would be rife because, of all the couples in the village one would expect to split up, the Carlisles weren't one of them.

Moving out was one thing, though. Being stabbed and left for dead was another matter entirely. It made no sense at all.

The lights from Harrington General were bright in front of her and, as she walked through the car park, she saw the usual signs of frustration. First, visitors couldn't find a parking spot. Then they had to beg, borrow or steal enough money to feed the machines. Not a week went by when people didn't complain to the local newspaper about the situation.

Perhaps not having her car wasn't such a disadvantage as she'd thought.

She walked up to the main desk and waited until the receptionist ended a phone call.

'I'm a friend of Mr Steve Carlisle,' Jill explained. 'I gather he was admitted this morning.'

Without needing to check records, the receptionist nodded.

'He's in the intensive care unit, but I'm afraid you won't be able to see him. Immediate family only.'

'That's OK. Thanks.'

Jill walked along sterile corridors and then took the lift. The ICU had a small visitors' room and, through a square of glass in the door, Jill saw Ruth and Frank Carlisle.

She went inside and Ruth rushed forward.

'Oh, Jill...' Tears welled in her eyes and she hugged Jill tight.

'How is he, Ruth?'

'I don't know. Alison is in there with him now. They'll only let one person in at a time, you see.'

'He lost a lot of blood, they say,' Frank explained.

Jill joined them on the row of blue plastic seats.

'Does anyone know what happened?' she asked.

They both shook their heads and Jill saw the way Frank reached for his wife's hand and gave it a squeeze supposed to convey that everything would be all right. Jill hoped it would.

'He's wired up to machines,' Ruth said, her

voice shaking. 'He's only just come out of the operating theatre and they said they're keeping him sedated.'

Jill's heart ached for them both. They looked small, lost and very confused in this harsh environment. In other parts of the hospital, relatives were treated with as much respect and kindness as the patients. In the intensive care unit, the patient was the only priority and everyone else had to fend for themselves.

'I just want to be here with him,' Ruth added. 'I know he won't know whether we're here or not, but I'll feel better.'

That was understandable and Jill would feel exactly the same. They couldn't do anything other than rely on the power of their will to pull him through.

'I've been staying at a friend's over the weekend,' Jill said, 'so I had no idea Steve had moved out. Is it a temporary thing or–?'

'He'd finally come to his senses,' Frank said. 'I don't believe in divorce. Weakness I call it. Couples today have their first quarrel and head straight to a solicitor. They can't seem to grasp that marriage is all about compromise, and about considering the other half of that marriage. But in Steve's case, I think it's justified. It's never been a happy marriage and now–'

He broke off and his lips clamped tight.

'Now?' Jill prompted.

'Nothing.'

Jill wondered what he'd been about to say. She guessed she wasn't going to hear it, though. Not while Ruth was within earshot, at least. She'd have to catch Frank alone.

'I think this trouble he was in,' Ruth said, 'gave him a chance to think. I think it dawned on him that life was too precious to waste. If he'd ended up in prison, I don't know what he would have done.'

'His moving out was a bit sudden, wasn't it?' Jill said.

'He went on Saturday morning.' Frank spoke as if it wasn't a moment too soon. 'He found that flat through a friend and, as the chap was happy to have Cally there, Steve signed the lease. He waited till Alison got back from Liverpool and then him and the dog left.'

'He did warn us that Alison wasn't happy about it,' Ruth confided. 'He thought she might cause trouble, but she hasn't said a word to us. Not a word.'

'Literally,' Frank said scathingly. 'We barely got a hello out of her.'

As if his words had conjured her up, Alison, looking as well groomed as ever, appeared in front of them. There wasn't a hair out of place or a smudge of make-up.

'I didn't expect to see you here, Jill.' She spoke sharply, taking Jill by surprise.

'I was at work when I heard about Steve,' she told her, 'so I thought I'd call in and see how he was.'

'If you lot hadn't suspected him of killing that girl,' she spat out, 'none of this would have happened. He'd still have been at home. He wouldn't have been in that hateful flat in the first place!'

'And perhaps if you'd spent more time at

home,' Frank challenged her, 'he might have had something to stay for!'

He stood up and gave his wife's shoulder a squeeze. It was as if he couldn't bear to be in his daughter-in-law's presence.

'I'll go and see if Cally's all right,' he said, adding for Jill's benefit, 'The dog's staying with us for the time being. I've got her in the car.'

Jill wanted to go with him, to see if she could find out what he'd been about to say earlier, but he was already out of the door. In any case, with things so strained in the family, she wasn't sure Ruth would appreciate being left alone with Alison.

Ruth, however, had other ideas.

'Alison, if you're not sitting with Steve then I will.' And she took herself off to be with her son.

As Jill wasn't in the mood for Alison's company, and Alison didn't appear to be in the mood for *anyone's* company, Jill decided to leave her to it.

'I'm nipping out for some fresh air,' she said.

Instead of waiting for the lift, she skipped down the stairs to the main reception area.

When she got out to the car park, Frank was walking the dog back through the main gates. She crossed the tarmac to join him.

'At least she doesn't need much exercise,' he said, giving the dog a pat.

They walked together and when they reached Frank's car, Cally was more than happy to jump in and curl up on the back seat.

'What do you know that Ruth doesn't?' Jill asked as they headed back to the hospital.

Frank stopped walking to look at her, surprise

on his old face.

'I know Alison has been cheating on him,' he said at last.

'Are you sure?'

'I am. Well...' He sighed loudly. 'I thought I was. I saw her, you see. She got out of her car and met a bloke who was parked in a lay-by. I saw her kiss him, and it wasn't the sort of kiss you'd give someone you hadn't seen for a while. She's one of those who has to kiss everyone, men or women, I know that. But this was different. The bloke's hands were all over her.'

'I see.'

'And I told Steve,' he admitted quietly.

She could believe that. Frank and Ruth were good honest people and they would have no time for dishonesty from anyone.

'How did he take it?'

'It's hard to say. He seemed OK about it. And he said he wasn't surprised.'

'And that's why he moved out?'

'I don't know, Jill. Partly, I suppose. But I think she's led him a merry old dance for years. This is only my opinion, but I think it got too much and he wanted a fresh start for himself.'

'Alison isn't happy about it,' she pointed out. 'She must love him, Frank.'

'Love?' Frank kicked out at a piece of gravel. 'She doesn't know the meaning of the word!'

Chapter Twenty-Eight

A strong north wind carried in a sub-zero temperature the following morning. Not that DS Fletcher cared. He'd been in this small room with Maurice Temple for over an hour and, as yet, had been able to elicit nothing more from him than 'No comment' and 'Mistaken identity'.

Fletch's stomach grumbled loudly reminding him it was lunchtime. He terminated the interview and arranged for a sandwich to be taken to Temple.

Pie and chips would have been welcome, but Fletch didn't have time for more than a sandwich and a bar of chocolate. This job played havoc with his health. Everyone said his diet was appalling, but what choice did he have? There was never time for a decent meal. At home, he ate healthily, too healthily for his liking, his wife made sure of that, but he spent more hours at work than at home.

With a bacon roll in his hand and two Mars bars in his pocket, he set off to find Max. His boss wasn't going to be pleased.

Max was in the car park, pacing as he smoked a cigarette. At least Fletch didn't smoke. He never had been and never would be the kind of idiot who forked out a small fortune to kill himself. Not that Max was an idiot, but he *was* someone who could kick the habit for months, even years at a time, and then, within a week, be back up to thirty a day.

'Well?' Max asked him.

'Nothing,' Fletch admitted. 'I can't get a squeak out of him. He does look nervous, though.'

'Isn't he saying anything?'

'Zilch.' That wind was whipping round the side of the building, chilling Fletch. 'What worries me is that we only have Atwood's word that he's the bloke who tried to sell him some stuff. Atwood's old, he could easily be wrong. I know Mrs Hollingsworth says he's the one she saw with Lauren Cole, but so what?'

'I know. It's not what you'd call conclusive, is it?'

'And now, with Steve Carlisle at death's door–'

'It makes you wonder if we're barking up the wrong tree,' Max finished for him. 'We were assuming this all centred around the Coles. The attempt on Carlisle's life has put us right back to square one.'

Max ground out his cigarette but made no attempt to return to the windproof, warm building.

'How is Carlisle anyway?' Fletch asked.

'Still critical. I gather the last rites have been delivered.' Max spun round on his heel. 'We'll see what Jill thinks. The fact that Temple's photo was shown to anyone in the first place is all down to her.'

Which is exactly what Fletch had been thinking. Jill had dreamt up a profile, they'd gathered together a few mug-shots, and two elderly witnesses, one of whom wore bulletproof spectacles, had picked out Temple. It was far from convincing.

'Not,' Max added, 'that I'd dare to question her judgement right now.'

Jill was in her office and Fletch envied her. It was the warmest room in the building by far. These days, when aesthetics was all, the workplace looked more like a flashy hotel than a police station. It was all open plan, a gleaming mass of glass and chrome. In the summer months, despite the air conditioning, it was a hothouse. In winter, the heating system was worse than useless.

'We're drawing a blank with Temple,' Max told Jill, getting straight to the point. 'What's more, we're not even sure we're on the right track.'

Jill didn't look very confident either.

'Perhaps he's not our man after all,' she said. 'But he must be, mustn't he? The jeweller swears he's the bloke who tried to offload that silver. And Mrs Hollingsworth saw him with Lauren.' She chewed on her bottom lip. 'All the same, I was expecting our man to be called Josh. I was confident that he'd been putting Lauren under pressure.' She tapped her pen between her fingers. 'We still haven't found anyone called Josh?'

'No.'

'OK,' she said. 'What exactly happened to Steve Carlisle? How much do you know?'

'There was no sign of a break-in,' Fletch began.

'So it was someone he knew?'

'Not necessarily,' he pointed out. 'He probably didn't know people in the other flats. Anyone posing as a neighbour could have been invited inside.'

She nodded acceptance of that.

'What time was the attack?' she asked.

'Around eight that morning. No later.'

'Early for a neighbourly call,' she pointed out. 'Are there no security cameras?'

Fletch saw Max roll his eyes at such a stupid question before snapping out, 'If there had been, we'd have seen any callers, wouldn't we? No, there are no cameras at the property and none anywhere on the estate.'

'Right,' she said. 'Go on, Fletch.'

'The flat's furnished, and whoever attacked him used one of the knives from a set of six in the kitchen. An eight-inch blade. No prints on it.'

'So it wasn't premeditated,' she murmured. 'Someone called on him and an argument followed.'

'We're assuming that, yes,' Max said, 'but we have to accept the facts. One, Carlisle gets himself involved in Lauren Cole's murder.'

'He didn't.'

'He did,' Max argued, 'which is why he spent hours in this building. He may or may not be guilty of her murder, but he was involved in some way. Two, he then leaves his wife of twenty years and moves to Harrington.'

'According to his father, he went because his marriage had never been happy. That and the fact that his wife was having an affair.' She ran her hands through her hair, a sure sign she was confused. 'Alison Carlisle could be your chief suspect.'

'For the attempted murder of her husband? I know that.' Max's voice was clipped. 'Not for the murder of Lauren Cole, though. Alison Carlisle was in Leeds when she was killed.'

'Have you checked that?'

'Of course we have.'

Fletch felt a knot tighten in his stomach. He wasn't sure that they had. Her colleague, Mark Radley, had said he and Alison travelled over the Pennines together. If he was the bloke she was supposedly having an affair with...

'Perhaps we should double-check that, Max,' he said. 'From what I recall, Mark Radley confirmed that he and Alison travelled together and arrived in Leeds shortly before nine o'clock that morning. He could be lying for her. If they're having an affair–'

'Then bloody well check it, Fletch!'

All Fletch wanted to know was what he was supposed to do with Maurice Temple. He might as well watch the grass grow as sit in that interview room with him.

He wasn't going to argue though. He'd make sure they really *had* checked Alison Carlisle and Mark Radley's alibi. If they hadn't, they were going to look pretty stupid.

On the way back to his office, Max stopped to see how Mel was getting on hacking her way through all the so-called deleted files on Yasmin Smith's friend's computer.

'I was coming to see you, guv,' she said.

'Oh?' Hope sparked.

Judging by the office grapevine, Mel had no social life at all. Rumours were rife that she was a lesbian, but no one could either confirm or deny that, mainly because she was attractive in a geek sort of way and none of the male officers had, as yet, managed to get a date with her. She lived in a large house on the outskirts of town with mortgage payments that should have been far beyond her reach.

But her personal life was her own affair. Max was more interested in her IT skills.

'The photo of Yasmin Smith was put on SeeYouThere just three weeks before she disappeared,' Mel said. 'Despite Mr and Mrs Smith claiming that Yasmin insisted on having the picture removed, she exchanged a lot of messages with users of the site about it. She even gave one person a phone number, and it wasn't the same one the Smiths had. I'd guess she had another phone, one she didn't want her parents knowing about.'

'Can we trace it?'

'It hasn't been used since she disappeared,' Mel said, 'but we're waiting for the records to come through.'

'This person she gave the number to,' Max asked, 'who's that?'

'Someone who goes by the name of DaddyO.' She pulled a face. 'I'm hoping SeeYouThere will give me details for him. And for everyone else she had contact with.'

'That's great,' Max said, encouraged.

'It will be if they'll give us the info,' she agreed. 'This Data Protection Act has a lot to answer for.'

'Let me know how you get on.'

'Will do.' She spun round on her chair and was totally engrossed in the screen before her.

Max carried on his way, did a detour through the main reception and realized that the woman standing at the desk with her voice raised in anger was none other than Alison Carlisle.

'Is there a problem?' he asked, and she swung

round to face him.

'Too right there's a problem.' She stood with her hands on her hips. 'Perhaps *you* can tell me why I'm not allowed inside my husband's home.'

Several people were waiting to have problems solved, or, more likely, complaints heard, but they all seemed to be enjoying the spectacle Alison was providing.

'Shall we step into my office?' Max suggested.

Most women whose husbands were in intensive care would lose interest in their appearance. They wouldn't care if their hair needed brushing or if they were seen with no make-up on. Alison Carlisle didn't have an eyelash out of place. She was wearing a long, red woollen coat with black knee-length boots.

'This is farcical,' she said, following him. 'That I can't collect his belongings is just plain ridiculous.'

Max pushed open the door to his office.

'Do you have a key to the property?' As far as he was aware, the two keys that Steve Carlisle possessed were being held by the force.

'Of course I don't. That's why I'm here. I need to get his things. To take them home.' She spoke slowly and carefully, as if trying to get through to a dementia patient.

'Sit down,' he suggested, and she threw herself down in the chair opposite his desk.

'Look,' she said, striving for calm, 'as you know, Steve and I had a bit of a tiff and he moved out. But everything's changed now. I need to take his things home.'

'I'm sorry, but I can't let you do that.'

'Why not, for God's sake?'

'The main reason is that your husband's flat is currently a crime scene. I can't allow anything to be removed.'

'Ridiculous!'

'Mrs Carlisle, have you any idea who might have attacked your husband?'

'Bloody hell!' She looked as if she wanted to scream. 'You've already asked me that fifty times. I'll tell you again, I have no idea at all. Let's face it, he didn't move to the best neighbourhood in the country, did he? It could be anyone.'

'You believe it was a stranger?'

'Of course. No one who knew Steve would do that to him.'

'We'd like to think not,' Max agreed pleasantly.

'Of course it was a stranger.'

'Rumour has it you've been having an affair, Mrs Carlisle.'

Her eyes, glittering with anger, bored into his.

'That's come from Steve's father, and he's nothing but a gossip-monger. Holier than bloody thou. I've had a bit of a fling, yes, but who hasn't? It means nothing.'

'A bit of a fling with Mark Radley?'

'So what? What does that have to do with you or anyone else?'

'Quite a lot. It suggests that Mr Radley might be willing to lie for you by providing you with an alibi.'

She got to her feet, then leaned across his desk. 'Are you arresting me, Chief Inspector?'

'Not yet.'

'Then, if you'll excuse me, I need to be with my

285

husband.' She strode to the door and turned. 'And for your information, I didn't attack my husband. Nor do I have any idea who did. If you concentrated on your job instead of harassing innocent people, perhaps you'd be able to find out!'

She yanked open the door and slammed it shut behind her.

As soon as Jill heard that DS Fletcher was paying Maurice Temple's father a visit, she glued herself to his side.

'Temple left home four years ago,' Fletch warned as he drove them through Harrington, 'so don't expect too much.'

'I won't.'

'So...' Fletch grinned at her while they queued at the traffic lights. 'How's the Thai boxing coming along?'

She knew he thought it ridiculous. In Fletch's view, women should be at home taking care of the children, the house and their husband's needs. And not necessarily in that order.

'It's good,' she replied. 'My instructor is one of the best in the country. And it's not just the self-defence aspect, it's an excellent way of keeping fit and fending off the effects of the Mars bars,' she added with a wry smile.

'Perhaps I'll look into it,' Fletch said. 'Then again, perhaps not, eh? I can't see much point to all this keep fit malarkey.'

He stopped the car outside the Temples' home. It was on a local authority housing estate, surrounded by a hundred identical properties.

'We don't usually get a warm welcome round

here,' Fletch warned her as they walked up the icy path to the front door.

While Fletch showed ID to the woman who opened the door, Jill repressed a shudder. The new Mrs Temple must weigh in at more than twenty stone. A cigarette was gripped in her fingers. Hair was dyed blonde. Black leggings were straining at the seams as they fought to cover enormous thighs. Her feet were encased in mauve slippers.

'What do you want with Sid?' she asked, resting her weight against what Jill hoped was a sturdy door frame.

'Just a word about his son,' Fletch said. 'May we come in, please?'

She shrugged, then waddled up the hallway, leaving them to close the front door and follow.

Sid was in the sitting room, stuffed into an armchair. The TV's remote control was on his lap. He was the same size as his wife.

'Which son?' he demanded, lowering the TV's volume.

'Maurice,' Jill said.

'Why? What's the little shit done now?' Before anyone could answer, he added, 'And what's it got to do with me? I haven't laid eyes on him for years.'

Christmas decorations were bright and gaudy. All colours of the spectrum were there. The tree, however, was black and decorated with white baubles. If Mrs Temple had been aiming for taste and elegance with that, she'd missed in spectacular style.

A huge pub-type ashtray on the coffee table was overflowing.

'Maurice is being questioned in connection with the murder of a Lauren Cole,' Fletch explained.

'Murder? Bloody hell!'

'Does the name mean anything to you?'

'Of course it doesn't. Why the hell should I know her?'

'We believe she was a friend of Maurice's,' Jill said.

'So? I don't know his friends. Why the hell should I?'

People who claimed that blood was thicker than water ought to pay the Temple family a visit, Jill thought with despair.

'Was Maurice close to his mother?' she asked. 'How did her death affect him?'

'You just get on with life, don't you?' Mr Temple replied.

His new wife had stubbed out her cigarette and was in the process of lighting another.

'Get me a beer, Tash,' Temple said.

She waddled off and returned with a can that she handed to her husband.

'Murder?' Temple said again. 'Bloody hell!'

'To get back to Maurice's friends,' Fletch said as Sid tugged on the ring pull, then licked the froth that had sprayed out of the can and landed on his arm. 'Don't you know any of them? The people he's been living with, for example?'

'Of course not. Why the hell should I?'

It was clear that they might as well have stopped a stranger in the street and asked him about Maurice Temple. Jill wasn't sorry when they were leaving.

'One more thing,' she said. 'Does the name Josh mean anything to you?'

'Eh? Well, of course it does. That's him, innit.'

'Sorry?'

'Maurice. A few folk call him Josh. Or used to.'

Jill couldn't believe this.

'Your son, Maurice, is nicknamed Josh? But why?'

'When Barry was born,' Temple explained, 'he couldn't talk properly. There was Maurice and John and the daft little bugger called 'em Mosh and Josh. Then the lazy sod just called 'em both Josh. It stuck, that's all.'

'Well I never,' she murmured in amazement.

They'd found Josh after all. She could hardly believe their good fortune.

As Fletch drove them back to headquarters, Jill was aware of the sideways glances he kept giving her, looks that said he considered her some sort of witch.

She might have been tempted to gloat, after all she'd bet them their man was called Josh, but she wasn't confident enough for that.

She ignored Fletch, and kept her gaze on the town's streets. The imagination that inspired some of the snowmen amazed her. As kids, she and her sister would have rolled two huge snow-balls, put one of top of the other and fashioned a face from a carrot and two lumps of coal. Today, they passed a long-legged snowman sitting on a bench and, even better, a snow-horse.

They were soon in the car park at headquarters.

'You got lucky back there,' Fletch said at last.

'Let's hope so, Fletch.'

289

Chapter Twenty-Nine

Jill had begged Max to let her talk to Maurice Temple alone but now that she was actually in the room with him, she didn't know where to start.

The room was small, just one table and three chairs. The only window had a view of an adjacent brick wall. It definitely lacked atmosphere.

Fletch had been right about one thing: Temple was very nervous. A vein was throbbing at his throat and his hands were trembling.

'I'm Jill Kennedy,' she introduced herself. 'I thought we could have a chat about Lauren.'

'I don't know who you're talking about.'

'Come off it, Josh. May I call you Josh?'

His eyes widened at that, and Jill saw fear in them. He shrugged it off, but he looked out of his depth.

'Call me what you like,' he muttered.

'So let's talk about Lauren, shall we, Josh? It's her I'm interested in, not you. I know you were friends with her. You've known her for years, haven't you?'

He didn't answer.

'How was she when her mum died? Distraught, I suppose. The same as you were. It's cruel, isn't it, to lose your mum when you're still at school? Mums are supposed to be there to watch you get married and then babysit your kids. They're not supposed to leave you when you're still at school, are they?'

'It's life,' he said. 'Nothing you can do about it.'

'That's true enough,' she agreed, 'but it doesn't mean to say you have to like it. Life or not, it still makes you angry. And sad. Depressed.'

'You a psychiatrist or what?'

'Psychologist,' she said.

He smirked at that, a private little smile.

'Don't worry,' she said, 'I won't get the ink spots out or ask you who the prime minister is. I'm more interested in Lauren. I'd like to know what she was like when her mum died.'

'Why?'

'I'm curious. Was she close to her dad, Josh? Would she have turned to him when her mum died?'

'He didn't want to know.' He flushed at the admission and scowled at Jill as if his stupidity was her fault. A small part of her felt sorry for him. Born to a father like Sid Temple, Maurice had never stood a chance.

'Are you saying he wasn't interested in her?' she asked.

'She might not have existed as far as he was concerned.'

'Is that when you became good friends?' Jill asked him. 'I suppose it is. An awful tragedy like that brings people together, doesn't it? It's easier to cope when you can share the pain.'

'She didn't have no one else.'

He kept tugging on the sleeves of his sweater with fingers that showed well-bitten nails. When he wasn't doing that, he was scratching at those fingers or biting on the inside of his mouth.

Had this young man killed Lauren in such a brutal way? Jill couldn't see it at all. Lauren had been killed with a passion that Temple lacked.

'That's sad, isn't it?' Jill murmured.

'She had her dog,' he added.

'Ah, yes, Charlie. He was devoted to her, wasn't he? Just as she was devoted to him.'

'Yeah.'

'But a dog's not the same, is it? She'd need real friends, people she could talk to, and people who could talk back. I bet she was as mad as hell with her dad, wasn't she? For not being there for her, I mean.'

'Yeah.'

'What did she do after her mum died, Josh? She didn't move out for quite a while, did she?'

'She wanted to.'

'Oh?'

'She'd got no money, had she?'

'Ah, I see.'

Jill didn't speak. She wanted Temple to do the talking.

A pigeon flew past the window and they both turned to look as it landed on the sill and peered through the glass at them.

'She got a job at the supermarket,' Temple said as it flew away, 'so she had money then. She moved in with a couple of mates for a month or so, but then wanted her own place. Her boss was a right bitch though and, once, when Lauren was late for work, she sacked her. Just like that.'

That was one version of events. They'd talked to the 'right bitch' and, according to her, Lauren had been late for work many times and, sometimes, simply hadn't turned up at all. She'd been given two verbal and three written warnings. Few employers would have been as tolerant as the 'right bitch'.

'So Lauren had no money again?' Jill guessed.

'No.'

'Her dad was well off, though, wasn't he?'

'Yeah, but he was a tight-fisted bastard.'

'He wouldn't give her any?'

'No. Well, a bit. Not a lot.'

That wasn't what Vincent Cole had said. Or Mrs Hollingsworth. According to them, it was rare for Mr Cole to say no to his daughter's demands. Perhaps Lauren hadn't liked to ask for as much as Temple thought she should.

'Someone said she took some silver candlesticks from her dad's,' Jill said. 'Is that true?'

'Why not? He kept telling her they'd be hers one day. She just took what was hers. Why shouldn't she have them?'

Maurice Temple had many previous convictions for theft and didn't see the world as others did. He had no respect for property or possessions. He'd once stolen a car just for the hell of it. When questioned, he'd been surprised that anyone cared. 'No one was using it,' he'd said.

'Lauren was changing, wasn't she?' Jill said, assuming his question had been rhetorical.

'Dunno.'

'I expect she was healing,' Jill said. 'She was finally getting over her mother's death, wasn't she?'

'Dunno,' he said again.

293

'Did you go to church with her?'

'Me? You kidding or what? I wouldn't be seen dead in a bloody church.'

'Some aren't so bad.'

'That one she went to was bloody awful. Dark and creepy. Everyone lighting candles.'

'So you did go?'

Again, he looked at Jill as if she was making traps for him to fall straight into.

'Once. She wanted me to see what it was like. As if I didn't know what a bloody church was like. They're all the same. People were going in and lighting candles. I left her to it.'

'Why was she changing, Josh? Why was she suddenly going to church?'

'Dunno.'

'Did she start worrying about the way she'd behaved towards her dad? Did she regret asking him for money and stealing from him?'

He didn't answer, just shrugged his shoulders and started pulling at the sleeves of his jumper.

'I expect she did,' Jill pushed on. 'Once you get inside a church, they go banging on about not stealing, don't they?'

'Dunno.'

Jill believed that Lauren had experienced a rush of guilt for the way she'd treated her father. Perhaps she'd gone to the church for forgiveness. She'd been turning, very slowly, back to her father. And Temple hadn't liked that.

He was fairly happy to talk about Lauren as she'd been. The new Lauren, the one who went to church, was a stranger to him.

'The morning she was killed,' Jill said, 'she

294

asked her dad for money.'

'She didn't get any though, did she?'

'Didn't she? I wouldn't know. How do you know that, Josh?'

'Dunno.'

'Perhaps she did then.'

'Yeah. Perhaps she did. I dunno.'

'Perhaps you spoke to her that morning and she told you he hadn't given her any?' Jill suggested.

'I never spoke to her. I was at the hospital all morning.'

'Sorry?' He had an alibi? 'The morning Lauren was killed, you mean? You were at the hospital? Where? Harrington?'

'Yeah. Having two teeth out under anaesthetic.' He opened his mouth and showed her a gap at the back of his mouth.

Before Jill could press him, Fletch tapped on the door, stuck his head round and indicated that he'd like a word with Jill.

'They've found a key to Vincent Cole's house at Temple's place,' Fletch announced with a grin.

'Yeah? That would be great, Fletch, if only–'

'If only what?'

'I've got him to admit to knowing Lauren, but he claims he was at the hospital having two extractions under anaesthetic when she was killed.'

'What? No way. I'll get it checked, but I bet the little sod's lying.'

Jill wasn't so sure he was.

Max needed to get away from headquarters. Temple was enjoying dinner courtesy of the generous British taxpayer, so Max was nipping across

295

the road for a coffee, a sandwich and some peace.

He lit a cigarette and smoked it as he walked the hundred yards to Starbucks. He'd give up again after Christmas. Come the new year, that would be it. No more cancer sticks.

Just as he stubbed it out, he spotted Jill striding along the icy pavement, presumably heading back to the office. He waited until she reached him.

'Are you getting a coffee?' she asked him. 'What a good idea. You can get me one, too. And a chocolate muffin. I was going to have an hour round the shops, but it's manic. I'll try again tomorrow.'

They stepped into the warmth of the cafe.

'I'm waiting for Temple to be fed so I can have another chat with him,' Max explained.

'Do you know if he was definitely at the hospital?'

'Not yet, no.'

While Jill chose a table near the window, Max went to the counter to order their coffees and Jill's muffin.

This branch of Starbucks had only been open a month so Max had never seen the place without Christmas decorations. Huge green and gold baubles hung from the ceiling, smaller ones were dotted on a fake tree.

He carried the tray to the table and sat next to her.

'Hello, Jimmy,' Jill said, and Max turned to see a teenager with earphones attached to an iPhone dangling round his neck.

'Er, hi, Jill.'

Jill was set for conversation, but the lad was having none of it. He couldn't get out of the building fast enough.

'You know Pat who gives the Boxing Day parties?' Jill asked Max.

'I remember carrying you home from the last one.'

'Yes, well–' She laughed at the memory. 'That's her son. Usually, he doesn't stop talking but, lately, you can't get a word out of him. He was skipping school, too.'

'Kids only respond to text messages these days.'

'True. But something's bothering him.'

They watched the boy walk down the street with his earphones firmly in place.

'So when's your dad arriving?' Jill asked when the lad was out of sight.

'Tomorrow.' And Max was dreading it. 'Unless he decides to stay at home,' he added. 'He phoned me this morning to say he was a bit worried about the weather.'

Max saw her surprise, and understood it. Not so long ago, his father wouldn't have thought twice about it. He'd been a decisive man. If he'd made up his mind to visit Max and the boys, that would have been that.

'Ten minutes on the phone to him almost drove me mad,' Max told her, 'so God knows how I'll cope with him for days.'

'Keep him occupied,' Jill replied, munching on her muffin. 'Make him see that life won't stand still, no matter how much he wants it to. Take him somewhere special. He loves art and he likes being out in the fresh air, so Antony Gormley's

Another Place would be perfect. A day at the Yorkshire Sculpture Park would be great for him, too. He'd enjoy all the Henry Moore stuff.'

It was worth a try, Max supposed. If his dad liked art, though, his sons definitely didn't. Max couldn't say it excited him, either.

'We'll see,' he said.

He couldn't think about Christmas right now, and he didn't want to think about his dad's visit.

'What about Maurice Temple?' he asked her, and she sighed.

'I don't know, Max. My bet is that he was at the hospital all morning. He's a nasty piece of work, but I can't see him caring enough to murder Lauren. Even if they'd had a quarrel. Even if she was threatening to come clean and tell her father or the police what they'd been doing.' She finished her coffee. 'I don't know.'

'I don't, either,' he said, 'but I need to find out. And fast.'

They walked back to headquarters together.

The temperature had dropped still further as the darkness had descended and although Max lit a cigarette as they walked, it was far too cold to enjoy it.

Ten minutes later, he was sitting opposite a well-fed Temple and longing to punch the smile from his face. He didn't look as nervous as he had earlier. Perhaps that was because he'd enjoyed Jill's easier style of conversation.

If that was the case, he was out of luck because Grace was sitting beside Max. She had a good interview technique, one that fellow officers could learn a lot from, so long as she didn't lose patience. Grace's only problem was that she was too easily frustrated. It was a fault Max shared.

She dangled a small plastic bag in Temple's face.

'When was the last time you used this?' she demanded.

'What key's that? They all look the same to me.'

'They do,' she agreed, 'so let me enlighten you. This key was found in your bedroom. It fits the front door of Vincent Cole's house.'

'Who?'

'Vincent Cole. You know him. He's your friend's father. You visited the house once with Lauren. It's a nice house on Longman Drive. Now, let me ask you again. When was the last time you used this key?'

'I've never seen it before.'

'It was found in your bedroom. Don't tell us the key fairy put it there.'

'Oh, yeah. I remember now. Lauren gave it to me ages ago.'

'How many ages ago?' Max asked.

'Can't remember.'

'Why?' Grace asked and he looked confused by the question. 'Why did she give you a key to her father's house?'

Temple looked from Grace to Max as if he might have the answer. Works of fiction clearly didn't come easily to Maurice Temple.

'Dunno,' he said at last.

'Perhaps she didn't give it to you,' Max suggested. 'Perhaps you stole it from her.'

'Course I didn't.'

'OK,' Max said, 'we're going to stop playing

299

games now. You used the key to let yourself into Vincent Cole's house. We know that and we know you tried to sell the stuff you stole from there.'

'Didn't.'

Max sighed heavily. 'We have a witness.'

'OK,' Temple agreed. 'Yeah, you're right. Lauren had given me the key, so I helped myself to some stuff. That's all.'

'That's not all,' Grace snapped. 'Tell us about Vincent Cole. He was in the house, wasn't he?'

'So?'

'So what happened?' Max demanded. 'Where was he?'

'In bed.'

'How do you know that?' Grace asked. 'Did you go into his bedroom?'

'No.' Temple drummed worried fingers on the table. 'He heard me. He came out of his bedroom, that's how I know.'

'He threatened you?' Max guessed.

'Yeah. Yeah, that's right. So I hit him. Self-defence.' Temple looked delighted with the invention.

'What did you hit him with?' Grace asked.

'One of them brass lamps. Like miners used to have, you know? He had a couple of them. So I belted him with one, but he was all right when I left him.'

'All right?' Max repeated. 'What does that mean? What was he doing?'

'I hit him,' Temple said, 'that's all. He woke up and caught me in the act so I belted him one and scarpered. But he was all right.'

'Rubbish,' Grace scoffed. 'You killed him.'

'I did not!'

'Yes, you did,' she said. 'You hit him, possibly a bit too hard, and realized you'd killed him. Then, knowing he was upset about the loss of his daughter, you had the bright idea of stringing him up and trying to make it look like a suicide. The thing is, Mr Temple, we know that he was already dead before he was tied to the beam. Now, dead men don't–'

'That's it. I'm not saying another word until you get me a lawyer. I know my rights!'

He swung his face round to look at the wall behind him. If he couldn't see them, he wouldn't have to talk to them.

Chapter Thirty

The following morning, Harrington was in complete chaos. Despite the heavy snowfall being forecast, no one seemed prepared for it, least of all the council. There was no sign of a plough or a gritter, and the morning rush hour was gridlocked. Max and Jill sat in the car for ten minutes without progressing so much as a yard.

Max could have screamed with frustration. Instead of wasting his time going nowhere, he wanted to be dragging the truth from Maurice Temple.

'It'll be quicker to walk,' Jill said.

'True, but we need to find somewhere to park first.' They moved twenty yards in the next ten minutes. It was enough to allow him to pull into a side road.

'Bloody council,' he muttered. 'I can't see what the problem is. It's winter. It happens every year.'

'Not like this, it doesn't. Come on, it'll be lovely to walk in.'

They abandoned the car and set off. It was hard work but, as Jill had said, it held a certain appeal. Plenty of others were doing the same. Children were being pulled on sledges and one chap had even donned a pair of skis for the morning commute.

'Sensible footwear would have been a good idea,' Jill said as they slid on their way.

'Some grit on the roads would have been even better.'

'Well, yes.'

The walk was a slow one, but not unpleasant, and they finally arrived at headquarters. Judging by the lack of vehicles in the car park, a lot hadn't.

Jill headed off to her office and Max went to catch up with the team. The incident room was like something from a spoof horror show. Christmas decorations that Grace insisted on having about the place sat next to photos of a dead Lauren Cole. Max had put his foot down so at least the battery-driven Santa that insisted on screeching 'Ho, ho, ho' every time someone walked in the room had been banished.

Today, it looked as if Christmas had come early for Grace because she was standing by Mel's desk, punching the air in celebration.

'What's happened?'

'Barry Foreman,' Grace said. 'You know, DaddyO? The bloke Yasmin Smith contacted on the internet? Mel's got a name and address for him from SeeYouThere. And tell me, what sort of tosser would call himself DaddyO? Anyway, it seems Foreman is known to us.'

Barry Foreman certainly was known. He'd been released from prison eighteen months ago after being convicted of kidnap. He'd bundled a fourteen-year-old girl into his car and been picked up ten hours later.

'How likely is it that this address is current?' he asked Mel.

'About fifty-fifty, I suppose.' She didn't care. She'd done her bit and now it was up to them.

'Nice work, Mel,' he said. 'Grace, someone needs to check him out. Do you fancy a trip to Blackpool?'

'I'm on to it, guv,' she promised.

'Take someone with you.'

'I will. It says here that he's six feet five...'

Max hardly dared to hope. More than anything, he hoped he could give the Smiths good news for Christmas. The alternative didn't bear thinking about.

At least it was a lead and that was good news. The bad news was that Maurice Temple's alibi checked out. Just as he claimed, he'd been at the hospital having dental work the morning Lauren Cole was murdered. Having said that, he hadn't arrived there until just before ten-thirty. At a push, that gave him long enough to kill Lauren Cole and race back to Harrington.

An hour later, Max and Jill set off to interview

303

Temple once more. This time, Temple's lawyer was sitting in the room with them.

As defence lawyers went, Max quite liked Sam Allerton. They rarely saw eye to eye, however. Max was paid to bring criminals to justice and Sam was paid to do his damnedest to make sure that scum like Temple walked. It made for an uneasy relationship.

The best thing about Allerton was that he liked Jill. She would get away with things that would have Sam reading the riot act to the rest of them.

The four of them sat in that room like poker players hiding their hands.

'Josh,' Jill began amicably, 'tell us who might have followed Lauren Cole out to Kelton Bridge the morning she was murdered.'

'Now look here!' Sam Allerton was completely taken aback by the question.

Max wasn't surprised. Sam had thought his client was being questioned in connection with the burglary at Vincent Cole's house.

'I'm sure Josh is willing to help, aren't you?' Jill continued. 'Who would have followed her, Josh?'

'I dunno. Her old man probably.'

'Her father?' Jill asked, as surprised as Max. 'What makes you say that?'

'He liked following her. Snooping on her.'

'When did he follow her?'

'Dunno. She reckoned he did.'

'Why would he do that?' Max asked.

'So he could tell her how pathetic she was and how she couldn't cope without her mum.'

'What about you?' Max asked him. 'Did you follow her the morning she was killed?'

'Of course not,' Temple said in astonishment. 'Anyway, I already told you I was at the hospital.'

'Not until half past ten,' Max said. 'That gave you plenty of time–'

'That's enough,' Allerton said, glaring at Max. 'My client is more than willing to–'

'OK, OK,' Max cut him off. 'We'll talk about the burglary on Longman Drive and the murder of Vincent Cole. Mr Temple, how did you know that Mr Cole had refused to give his daughter money on the morning she was killed?'

'I didn't know.'

'But you told me she didn't get any from him,' Jill reminded him. 'You must have known.'

'I just knew he wouldn't give her any.'

'How?' Jill asked.

'For one thing, he was a tight old bastard and getting tighter. For another thing, Lauren didn't try hard enough.'

'Ah. Why was that? Because she was starting to feel guilty about it?'

'Yeah.'

'Is that why you decided to help yourself to Cole's possessions? Because Lauren wasn't being any use?'

'Yeah.'

'My client,' Sam Allerton reminded them, 'has admitted breaking into a property on Longman Drive and stealing several items. He also admits to hitting the occupant in self-defence. He's guilty of no more than that.'

'Self-defence,' Max murmured. 'Hm. The thing is, Mr Cole suffered one blow to the head. Just one. And it was enough to kill him.'

'My client hit him in self-defence,' Sam said again. 'But he didn't hit him hard enough to kill him.'

'So you're claiming someone else went to the house, used a key to get in, killed Cole and tied him to a beam, and then locked the house again?' Max asked. 'I can't see a jury falling for that one.'

'My client—'

'Is being very helpful,' Jill said, giving the lawyer her sweetest smile. 'And you don't mind telling us about Lauren's dog, do you, Josh?'

Temple looked at his lawyer, then shrugged. 'OK.'

'Did you get on well with Charlie?' Jill asked. 'You like dogs, do you?'

'Well, yeah.' Temple was frowning, not sure what she was talking about.

'Did Charlie come running up to you whenever he saw you?'

'Yeah.'

'I thought so.' Jill was smiling as if this was a thrilling game she'd just invented. 'I bet I can tell you something else about Charlie. I bet his collar was loose.'

Temple's head flew up and his eyes were wide with surprise.

'Am I right?' she asked.

'How d'you know that?'

'When Lauren's body was found,' she explained, 'Charlie was by her side. The thing is, he wasn't wearing a collar. Some dogs don't, of course, but Lauren loved that dog and she would have bought a nice shiny collar for him. I bet he had the best dog collar in Harrington.'

'So?' The puzzled frown was still there.

'So whoever killed Lauren Cole followed her up the hill. But then she met up with someone so he had to keep out of the way. The dog found him, though, and ran up to him. Our killer grabbed Charlie by the collar. When Lauren and her companion split up to look for the dog, the man goes off in the opposite direction and Lauren returns to Clough's Shelter. Charlie, seeing her, struggles free and slips his head out of the collar.'

Sweat was pouring down Temple's face, and he was visibly shaken. Whether that was because Jill had the scenario exactly right and he knew it, or whether he simply thought Jill was raving, Max couldn't tell for sure.

'What would that person do with Charlie's collar, Josh?' Jill pushed on. 'Would he put it in his coat pocket? Or do you think he'd throw it away?'

Every item of clothing that Temple possessed and, surprisingly, there were a lot, had been bagged up and taken to the lab. Had Charlie's collar been taken there?

'I don't know what you're talking about,' Temple said, but his voice was struggling to function.

Guilt? Or was he frightened of being banged up for a murder he didn't commit?

'I was at the hospital,' Temple reminded them. 'Anyway, I wouldn't have followed her. She was my friend.'

'She was never your friend,' Jill argued. 'She was just someone foolish enough to trust you. Her dad had a bit of money and you did well out of that, didn't you? But she was changing. Was she threatening to tell her dad how much the two

307

of you had stolen? Or was she threatening to tell the police–?'

'That's enough,' Sam Allerton cut her off. 'My client has nothing further to add. He has admitted to breaking into a property on–'

'He has,' Max agreed pleasantly, not wanting to hear Sam's speech yet again. 'We'll take a break, shall we?'

He and Jill left Temple with his lawyer.

'Oily sods,' Jill muttered when they were in the corridor.

'I quite like Sam. Don't you?'

'That's neither here nor there, is it?' She sighed heavily. 'Temple's not our man. No way did he kill Lauren Cole.'

'You don't know that. Come on, Jill, we've even found a hole in his alibi. He would have had time to get back to his flat, change his clothes, and still keep that appointment at the hospital.'

'I know, I know, but he's not our man.' She gave him a weary smile. 'As daft as it sounds, Max, you need to find that dog's collar.'

Chapter Thirty-One

Ruth Carlisle sat by her son's bed and held his hand. No one seemed to know for sure if he could hear anything, but nurses had advised her to keep talking to him. She would have done that anyway.

He wasn't conscious, but she'd been told they

were keeping him sedated because of his internal injuries. Maybe, one day soon, he would open his eyes, talk to her, laugh with her...

'Cally's made herself at home,' she told him. 'She's taken over your dad's chair. Not that he minds,' she added quickly. 'He's gone right soft with that dog. He was even feeding her roast chicken last night.'

It was difficult to know what to talk about, but Ruth was sticking to easy subjects. She wanted to know what had happened that morning, of course she did, but there was no point talking about that yet.

She'd spoken to the electrician who'd found him. Ruth thanked God the lad had been impatient enough to walk round the back of the building and peer in through the windows. He said all he'd seen was a leg sticking out from behind the sofa. If he hadn't, Steve would have been dead.

'Everyone's coming to us for Christmas,' she said, squeezing his hand, 'just like they always do. We'll have a house full but it will be good.'

It wouldn't. How could it be when Steve would be lying here? She was determined to sound cheerful, though.

She thought about Maisie as she so often did. Her granddaughter would have been twenty now and Ruth would have loved to have seen her sitting at the table for Christmas dinner. Perhaps, at twenty, she would have brought a young man with her. Or perhaps not. These days girls seemed more interested in careers than men.

Ruth didn't blame them for that. There would

be plenty of time for marriage when they'd seen a bit of life.

'Christmas will be a squash, but we'll manage. We always do, don't we? Joyce and Dennis are going to their son's this year so we've borrowed chairs from them. They're good neighbours.'

Ruth was glad of this quiet time with Steve. Alison was working today and said she'd call in this evening. Frank had taken himself down to the canteen to get a sandwich.

'I wish you were coming to us for Christmas,' she said softly, and her eyes filled with tears.

She blinked them back. There was no point crying until she knew what she had to cry about.

The news from the hospital seemed more optimistic today. They hadn't said anything different, not in so many words, but Ruth had gained the impression they were slightly less worried.

Oh, she hoped she was right.

The address Grace had for Barry Foreman turned out to be the end of a run-down terrace that backed on to an equally scruffy row of terraced houses. Wheelie bins had been left out on the pavement but there was more rubbish lying in the snow than in the bins.

Max's dislike of Blackpool was legendary, probably, she guessed, because his sons loved the place and it cost Max a small fortune every time he was blackmailed into bringing them. Grace would willingly give Harry and Ben a day out here. In fact, she'd suggest it to Max.

She loved everything about Blackpool and was always first in the queue at the annual switching on of the famous illuminations. The town brought back memories of happy childhood holidays. Years later, she had often been falling out of the clubs in the early hours with a gang of friends.

Unlike Harrington, Blackpool could only boast a couple of inches of snow. It was enough to show her and the two uniformed officers a set of footprints heading from Foreman's front door to the road though.

Grace hammered on that door. Getting no answer, she peered in through grimy windows. The front window looked straight into a sitting room that was littered with newspapers, empty beer cans and very little furniture other than a huge plasma TV that was probably worth more than the house.

While PC Wilde waited by the front door, Grace and PC Jones walked round the back, let themselves in through a rickety gate, walked up the path and knocked on the back door. A window here showed them a kitchen where dirty saucepans and plates were piled high in the sink. A small yellow table was just visible beneath yet more newspapers.

She sent PCs Wilde and Jones back to their car and returned to her own.

The property at the other end of Foreman's street was twice the size of the others and was being used as a bed and breakfast. Grace suspected it was cheap lodgings. She also guessed that neither the bed nor the breakfast would be palatable.

For all that, several people left or entered the building during the next couple of hours. In con-

311

trast, no one went near Foreman's house.

She was beginning to fidget and couldn't decide what she needed most. Coffee, food or toilet. Probably the latter.

What, she wondered, had made her think that a job in CID would be glamorous? She was sitting in a cold car, she was hungry and thirsty and she really did need a pee.

Her phone burst into life, startling her.

'He's heading your way – just turned the corner. Black coat, overlong jeans and three Asda carrier bags.'

She slunk down in her seat and watched as Barry Foreman strode past her. He looked behind him before turning and walking smartly to his front door and letting himself in.

'Right, one of you round the back and one with me,' Grace told the uniforms. 'And he's a big bugger so be careful.'

As soon as PC Wilde was at the back of the property Grace and PC Jones walked up to the front door. There was no sound from within so Grace hammered on it. No response. She knocked again, harder.

PC Jones pushed open the letterbox. 'Police! Open up!'

Nothing.

'We'll bash the bloody door in,' Grace said, tired of this. 'We know he's in there.'

She heard the sound of breaking glass and instinctively put her hands over her head. It was coming from the back of the house though.

'He's smashed a window at the back. Come on, Jonesey. Quick!'

As they ran round to the back of the property, Grace was thankful it was the end property in the terrace. In the small yard, Foreman was lying face down on the ground while PC Wilde tried to get handcuffs on him. When PC Jones added his weight, they managed to contain him.

'Barry Foreman?' Grace yelled at him. 'We want to talk to you about a fifteen-year-old girl called Yasmin Smith. We know she contacted you via–'

Foreman twisted his head enough to spit at her.

For his trouble, he got a sharp kick in the ribs from PC Wilde who, with blood dripping from a cut above the eye, was living up to his name.

'Obstructing police officers, assaulting a police officer, judging by the state of PC Wilde's face – you're under arrest, sunshine.'

'Fuck off, pig!'

He continued to kick and spit until the two PCs finally had him under control.

'Right, take him in. Then you,' she said, nodding at PC Wilde, 'need to get yourself to a hospital.'

Barry Foreman wasn't going quietly but he was at least going. They marched him through his house and outside to the waiting patrol car.

When they'd gone, Grace looked round the house, pulling open cupboards and checking under beds, but there was nothing of interest to be found.

'Asda carrier bags,' she murmured to herself.

He'd walked in with three but they were nowhere to be seen.

Then she spotted another door. It was half

hidden behind a wardrobe in what was a ground floor bedroom of sorts. Apart from the wardrobe and a narrow single bed that was covered in boxes and assorted junk, the room was bare.

Thankfully, the wardrobe was fairly easily shouldered out of the way. All she needed now was the key to the door, and that was probably on the way to the nick with Foreman.

She went to the kitchen, found a small vegetable knife and began unscrewing the lock. She was still desperate to use the toilet, but she didn't fancy venturing into Foreman's bathroom.

Eventually, the lock came free. She should have guessed these properties had cellars. There was a switch at the top of the stairs and although the light from it was dim, it was enough to stop her falling headlong into the cellar.

The smell as she descended was something she couldn't identify. Perhaps it was merely damp.

When she reached the ground, she saw three Asda carrier bags. There was a single mattress on the floor and it took Grace a moment to realize that the mounds beneath the grubby quilt were human. Two girls lay side by side.

'Holy shit!'

She put a finger to their necks. Both were breathing.

Chapter Thirty-Two

When Max reached his office the following morning, he didn't bother opening the blinds. He swallowed two aspirin, put his feet on his desk and closed his eyes. It had been after nine o'clock last night when he'd suggested they call it a day and have a couple of drinks at the Green Man to celebrate one of their more successful days. Max rarely suffered from hangovers, but when he added vodka to the equation, a drink he didn't even like, he gave himself real problems.

If Mel made it to the office today, he'd be amazed. She'd been last seen staggering through her front door singing 'Yellow Submarine' at the top of her voice. For her sake, Max hoped she had understanding neighbours.

That she'd been knocking back Jack Daniels as if it was water had taken them all by surprise. Maybe she was finally seeing herself as part of the team.

He supposed it was difficult for her. While the rest of them were out in the field talking to people, she was staring at a computer. A lot of the time, she only had the flimsiest of background information for a particular inquiry. Added to that, she was a naturally reserved person.

It had been a good day, though, and Max had saved the best job for himself. He'd been the one to phone the Smiths and organize the car that

315

took them to the hospital and their daughter.

Max hoped Foreman was put away for a very long time. Better still, he wished Adam Smith could be allowed five minutes alone with the man. It would be a long time before the word forgiveness found its way to Smith's lips. He'd lost sleep, lost his job and almost lost his sanity.

As yet, they had no idea of the extent of the abuse suffered by the girls. It would come out later perhaps. Meanwhile, trained counsellors were doing all they could.

Yasmin's companion had been a young teenager from Arbroath, Angela McCann, who, like Yasmin, had been fooled enough by Foreman to take a train from her home in Scotland.

It was too easy for men like Foreman. With so many young people chatting with virtual friends, it was simple for Foreman to prey on the naive and vulnerable. Online, Foreman had been a fun-loving, caring nineteen-year-old who wanted nothing more than friendship. The reality was that he was a sick and very sinister individual.

In Yasmin's case, her love of ice cream and the cinema had taken her straight into danger. She'd expected to miss school for the day and see the latest blockbuster with a nineteen-year-old.

At least Foreman had fed the girls well and, thankfully, he'd only given them sleeping tablets. Heavy doses, but nothing that would do any permanent harm. The mental scars would take longer to heal than the physical damage.

As tempting as it was, Max knew he couldn't stay in his office all day. He was adjusting the blinds to let in the daylight when Phil Meredith

316

came inside.

'Yasmin Smith. Excellent work, Max!'

Meredith spoke as if it was news to him, yet he'd made sure he was on the small screen last night telling the public what an outstanding job his officers had done.

'All down to Mel,' Max replied.

'Yes, and I've already spoken to her,' Meredith said.

Max was glad she'd received some recognition from above.

'I wanted to let you know that Carlisle is conscious,' Meredith went on. 'So that's more good news. He's not allowed visitors yet but he's off the danger list.'

'That *is* good news.'

'No visitors before two o'clock this afternoon at the earliest apparently. Anyway, I won't keep you,' Meredith added. 'I'm sure you have plenty to do.'

He did. Like proving that Maurice Temple had killed both Vincent and Lauren Cole.

Perhaps Carlisle would be able to tell them something useful. Max would make sure someone was by his bedside at two o'clock sharp to see if he was up to answering questions. In fact, he might even go himself.

While he was almost certain that Temple was guilty of Lauren and Vincent Cole's murders, he could find nothing to link him to the attempt on Steve Carlisle's life.

Amazingly, Mel was at her desk, taking a sip of water from a bottle she always had with her.

'You OK, Mel?'

'Fine, thanks. You?'

317

'I've felt better,' he admitted, and she smiled.

'It was a good night, though, wasn't it?'

'It was.'

He was glad she'd enjoyed herself. They knew nothing more about her private life than they had the day she'd started working with them, but hopefully that would come in time.

'Any sign of Fletch?' he asked. 'Or Grace?'

'They were both in early, but – sorry, boss, I don't know where they are now.'

A search of the building didn't help, but Max guessed Fletch and Grace would be busy on something. It was Christmas Eve and, like everyone else, they'd be wanting to go home and start the holiday. They would both give the job everything until they finished for the day though.

Max was about to call Jill when Grace rounded the corner at a run.

'We've got him, guv. Temple, I mean.' She was breathless with excitement and struggling to get the words out quickly enough. 'They've found traces of blood on a pair of his jeans and I'll bet it's Lauren Cole's.'

'Let's hope so.'

Grace was another, it seemed, who didn't have the word hangover in her vocabulary.

'You feeling OK?' he asked.

'Dog rough,' she admitted, 'but this has perked me up. I knew he was guilty. It was just a matter of proving it. And we almost have.'

'*If* it's her blood,' Max reminded her, but Grace wasn't to be put off.

'Sure to be.'

Before Max could comment on that, Fletch

came over to them. He looked how Max felt. His skin was pale, his eyes bloodshot, and he walked very carefully so as not to succumb to motion sickness.

'You look like death,' Max told him.

'Yeah? I must be improving then. Anyway, you'll never guess–' He broke off and looked from one to the other of them. 'What's happened?'

'We've found blood on a pair of Temple's jeans.' Grace relished every one of those words. 'We're still waiting to hear from the lab, but it has to be Lauren Cole's.'

'Yeah?' Fletch didn't look too impressed. 'Well, this is what I've got.'

He held out an evidence bag. Inside was a red dog collar that was studded with mock diamonds. A matching red tag hung from the collar.

Max took the bag from Fletch. He didn't need to read the tag to know what was engraved on it, but he did anyway. Beneath the name Charlie was Lauren Cole's phone number.

'Please tell me this was found at Temple's place, Fletch?'

''Fraid not, Max. It was right at the bottom of Vincent Cole's rubbish bin.'

'What? Oh, shit. How the hell did it get there?'

'Maybe,' Grace said slowly, 'it had been in Temple's pocket for a week and he decided to dump it when he broke into Cole's house?'

Max would love to believe that, but it was on a par with thinking that a fat man in a red suit really *was* coming down the chimney tonight.

Jill was cold and tired, but, thanks to copious

319

amounts of coffee and a couple of paracetamol, her hangover had more or less gone. It was Christmas Eve, though, and she was finally in the mood for the festive period. She didn't want to be at work thinking of murder; she wanted to start the holiday. Her copy of the *TV Times* was still unopened so she had no idea what she'd be viewing over Christmas. *The Great Escape* would follow the Queen's speech, she supposed. *It's a Wonderful Life* was sure to be on, too. She'd bought lots of junk food, mostly chocolate. Max and the boys would attack the savouries. Jill longed to sit and watch rubbish on TV with a box of chocolates to hand.

Before then, though, she had to share the same air space as Maurice Temple. He'd asked to see her, and she needed to satisfy her own curiosity about his involvement in Lauren Cole's murder. He was innocent, she was sure of it, but he had to be involved somehow.

'How are you, Josh?' she asked when she'd taken off her coat, settled herself in the chair opposite him and switched on the recording equipment.

'What's it to you?'

'Wait a minute, have I got this wrong? I was told you wanted to speak to me.'

'Yeah.' He shrugged, and Jill wondered if he'd changed his mind.

'I suppose you're a bit upset because of everything that's happened this morning?' She spoke casually and pretended to search in her bag for something. 'That's understandable.'

'What happened?'

'Haven't they told you?' She knew damn well they hadn't, but she shook her head at the incompetence of coppers. 'They've informed your lawyer and he's on his way, but you'd think that someone would have seen fit to tell you.'

'What happened?' he asked again.

'They've found evidence,' she said, still speaking casually. 'Enough evidence to prove that you killed Lauren and Vincent Cole.'

'That's crap.'

His tone was scoffing, as well it might be.

'It's true. I'm only surprised no one's told you. I bet you could get them into trouble for that.'

'What evidence?'

'Plenty, I'm afraid. You know I was talking to you about Charlie's collar? They found that. You threw it out, didn't you? When you broke into Vincent Cole's house, you realized you still had Charlie's collar in your pocket. So, while you were lurking around the outside of his house, you chucked it in the rubbish bin, didn't you?'

'I – what?' Several times, Temple opened his mouth, but he couldn't force any more words out.

'They also found a pair of your jeans,' she went on. 'They've got blood on them.'

Except the lab results were back and it wasn't Lauren Cole's blood. It was his own.

Temple didn't even attempt to speak. His whole demeanour changed and tears welled in his eyes.

'I didn't kill her. You have to believe me. I promise you, I didn't kill her. Someone's trying to frame me.'

Jill did believe him. His alibi was worthless, as

he could easily have killed Lauren and raced back to the hospital for his appointment, but she knew in her heart that he was innocent.

All the same, he had to be involved. He had to know something about it.

'I'm sorry they haven't told you,' she said. 'I assumed that was why you wanted to see me. And it's why I came as I soon as I could, to see if you were all right.'

'But I didn't kill her. They've got it wrong. That blood on my jeans – it's not hers. How the fuck can it be?'

'Whose is it then?'

'What?' He looked at her as if she was mad. 'How the fuck do I know? They must have planted it. Fuck, I don't know.'

'So if you didn't kill her, who did?'

'I don't know!' He screamed the words at her.

'How did you get the key to Vincent Cole's house?' she asked him.

'I told you. Lauren gave it to me ages ago.'

'I don't believe you.'

'OK,' he admitted. 'She didn't give it to me. I had a copy made.'

'Why?'

'Just in case– Look, he had some valuable stuff there.'

'And you thought you were set up, didn't you?' Jill went on. 'You let yourself into her dad's house–'

'I didn't mean to kill him!' Temple buried his face in his hands and began to sob. 'It was a mistake!'

The sudden display of emotion took her by

surprise. It wasn't for his victim, obviously. It was a mix of fear at the prospect of a life sentence and regret that he'd finally admitted to his crime. Even so, she hadn't expected tears from him.

She didn't care, though. They finally had a confession from him.

'You hit him too hard, did you?' she asked, her voice calm.

'Yes.'

'And then tried to make it look as if he'd committed suicide?'

He nodded, tears and snot running into his mouth.

He must have panicked on realizing he'd killed Vincent Cole, but would have thought himself little short of genius to come up with the suicide idea. He would have hunted for a length of suitable cable, tied it around Cole's neck, grabbed a couple of chairs from the kitchen, stood on one and hauled Cole, a big man, close enough to the beam to tie him up. Josh didn't look strong enough, which proved how potent adrenalin could be.

Satisfied with the picture of suicide he'd created, he would have returned one chair to the kitchen and put the other on the floor as if it had been kicked away by Cole. Jill could picture him admiring his handiwork.

'But I didn't kill Lauren. I swear to you, I didn't do it.'

Jill sat back in her chair, arms folded as she tried to decide how to play this. If he hadn't killed Lauren, and Jill believed him, who the hell had? She needed Temple's help, which meant treading very carefully.

'OK, Josh, you're in a lot of trouble. You know that, don't you? Now, if I were you, I'd be as helpful as I possibly could. If you offered them information about Lauren's killer–'

He lunged forward and, if Jill's reactions had been any slower, his head would have crashed against hers.

'I don't fucking know anything! Got that, you stupid bitch? I don't fucking know who killed her!'

Jill was thinking about taking an early lunch when her office phone rang. Temple was having his lunch, and she thought she may as well do likewise. She was feeling better now, and her appetite had returned.

She picked up her phone. 'Hello?'

'Merry Christmas!'

The connection was cut immediately, leaving her to stare at the instrument. His call hadn't come via the switchboard. Her stalker had come direct to her extension number and that really was a disturbing thought.

There was something else, too. He'd only said two words, yet something in his voice had sounded familiar. She closed her eyes and tried to bring the sound to mind again, but it was too late. It had gone.

Forgetting lunch for the moment, she set off in search of Max.

'He's at the hospital,' Grace told her. 'Apparently, Steve Carlisle wanted to speak to him.'

'So early? I thought no one could see him

before two o'clock. Is he all right? Steve, I mean?'

'I suppose he must be if he's able to talk to people.'

Jill began walking to the hospital. The wind cut through her like a machete and she pulled up her coat's collar as she walked. She didn't mind winter, so long as she could keep warm, but she hated the short days. It hadn't really got light today.

The hospital was as warm as ever. No cold air, or even fresh air, managed to penetrate the building, and it was always stifling.

A tall Christmas tree with twinkling lights stood in the corner of the main reception area and decorations hung from the ceilings and above framed pictures, but they did little to add cheer. There could be few things more depressing than a hospital at Christmas.

She took the lift to the intensive care unit, only to be told that Steve had been moved to Watling Ward on the second floor.

She went back down the stairs and followed the arrows to Watling Ward.

Before she reached it, she came to a small room filled with chairs and tables, magazines and children's toys. Sitting in the corner were Ruth and Frank Carlisle. Ruth was clutching a teddy in her hands, but she rushed forward on seeing Jill.

'Hello, love.' Ruth gave her a hug.

'How is he?' Jill asked.

'He's going to be all right.' Ruth's voice was shaking as she fought to keep her emotions in check.

'He hasn't said much,' Frank put in, 'but he

told the nurse he wanted to speak to that young man of yours.'

In other circumstances, Jill would have howled with laughter at the description. *That young man of yours.*

'Is Max with him now?'

'He's been with him for almost a quarter of an hour,' Ruth said.

'Has Steve talked to you about what happened?'

They both shook their heads.

'That flat of his had been empty for a few weeks,' Frank said, 'so I'm assuming someone was hoping to take up squatters rights.'

Jill nodded, and hoped he was right. Perhaps he was. Perhaps someone had wanted a home for a while and, not realizing a new tenant had moved in, thought they'd take up residence.

'I just want him to come home with us,' Ruth said. 'He'll have to come to us when they let him out, won't he? We've got Cally and he won't be able to take her for walks. He'll be better with us.' She broke off, looking uncertain. 'I'm sure he won't want to go back to Alison.'

'Of course he won't,' Frank said, patting her hand.

'He's all right, that's the main thing.' Jill sat beside them. 'I'm sure everything will work out for the best.'

Perhaps Steve and Alison would be able to patch up their differences and enjoy a stronger marriage. Jill doubted it because Steve seemed so determined to end it, but it was possible.

Above all, she hoped he could remember

326

everything about the morning he was attacked. It sounded promising. Why else would he want to talk to Max?

'I can't believe it's Christmas Day tomorrow,' Ruth murmured. 'It doesn't seem two minutes since I took last year's decorations down.'

'Too true,' Jill agreed, happy to make conversation.

They spoke of Christmases past, the weather, the kindness of the hospital staff, the way the building was decorated, until finally, Max emerged through the double doors.

'He's fine,' he told Ruth, giving her shoulder a squeeze. 'Go in and see him.'

'We will. And thank you. Did he tell you–?'

'He did,' Max cut her off. 'And don't worry. Everything will be fine.'

Realizing that Max wasn't about to say more, Ruth and Frank stood up.

'Thank you,' Frank said gruffly.

'And a happy Christmas to you both,' Ruth added.

'And to you, too.' Jill gave them both quick hugs before they made their way to Steve's room.

'Well?' she asked Max when the other couple were out of sight.

'I'm off to arrest a man for attempted murder,' he said, looking pleased with himself. 'Coming?'

'Me? Well, yes. But who? Where are we going?'

'To see a hypocritical little shit who thinks he can stick a knife in anyone who doesn't share his views on life.'

'Who?' she asked, having to skip to catch him up as he strode along the corridor.

Grinning, he tapped the side of his nose.

'Max!'

'All will be revealed.'

'Is this mysterious person likely to get violent?' she asked.

'Why? Are you hoping to practise your Thai boxing skills?'

She was hoping it wouldn't come to that.

Chapter Thirty-Three

When Max stopped the car outside St Mary's Church, Jill was beside herself with rage. It was the hypocrisy that angered her the most. Outside the church, easily seen thanks to an orange flood-light, was a huge sign welcoming people to worship. That Father Gosling had the cheek to stand in front of his parishioners and preach to them beggared belief.

'I suppose it was God's will,' she muttered.

Max switched off the car's engine and unfastened his seat belt. 'That'll be it, kiddo.'

Jill was impatient to confront Gosling, but they stayed in the warmth until a patrol car pulled up behind them.

'Come on,' Max said.

They walked up the path to the church but, although the building was well lit, there was no sign of Jill's favourite priest.

'We'll try the house,' Max said.

The four of them marched up the winding

driveway to the large house next to the church.

Max rang the bell and, seconds later, a dark-haired woman in her late forties opened the door. She gave an involuntary gasp at the sight of them. Uniformed police officers have that effect on people.

'We'd like to speak to Father Gosling,' Max told her, showing her his ID.

'Oh. You'd better come in then.'

They walked into a hallway that was steeped in furniture polish. In fact, Jill thought the house had the same smell as the church.

'Just a minute,' the housekeeper said awkwardly.

She left them filling the hallway and knocked on a door to their left before entering.

Jill took advantage of the housekeeper's absence to have a look round. Two antique tables and a dresser looked to be worth a few pounds and the carpet, although a little worn, was of the best quality. As might be expected, there were several effigies of Christ or the Virgin Mary to be seen. There was plenty of highly-polished silver on display, too.

The door clicked open and Father Gosling, dressed in a dark suit with those same brown shoes, came into the hallway.

'What's all this then?' Without waiting for a reply, he addressed his housekeeper. 'That's fine, Rebecca. I'll deal with this, thank you.'

She escaped through another door.

'You'd better come into the sitting room,' he told his visitors and the four followed him. Jill's heart was pounding with rage.

'Now then,' he said, 'what's all this about?'

'I'm here to arrest you for the attempted–' Max began, only to be cut off.

'Arrest me? I don't understand.'

'Oh, I think you do.' Jill couldn't keep quiet any longer. 'I suppose you thought, *hoped*, that Steve would die. Well, as you've probably heard, he's tougher than that and is going to make a full recovery. He's sitting up in bed, his memory as sharp as ever, able to recall every detail of the morning you called on him and left him for dead.'

A bible in a soft, black leather binding was sitting on the table and Jill picked it up to flick through it.

'You ought to read this,' she said. 'I'm no expert, but I'm sure it says something like "thou shalt not kill". Or perhaps you believe that doesn't apply to you?'

'He was going to divorce Alison,' he retorted, as if that was reason enough.

'And not before time by the sounds of it. He'd wanted a divorce for years but Alison wouldn't hear of it. I wonder why. Because she stood to inherit everything from you and wanted to keep on the right side of you?'

'It has nothing to do with that. The church is against divorce, Miss Kennedy!'

'And it's not against murder?' she cried in astonishment, hurling the bible across the room. 'Jesus, this is a bloody funny church you have here!'

'How dare you talk to me like that?' His eyes were dark slits and spittle landed on her face as he snapped at her. 'He was going to break her heart!'

330

'Break her heart?' Jill echoed with a hollow laugh. 'She's been too busy shagging her boyfriend to have her heart broken.'

'Father David Gosling, I am arresting you—' Max said again, but he got no further.

'I didn't mean to hurt him,' Gosling said, his voice softer.

'So what *did* you mean to do?' Jill asked.

He was looking at her as if he pitied her. There was an almost secret smile in his eyes, too. No remorse, just that smile. It made her sick, yet her mind was racing through the last conversation she'd had with the priest.

'You were friends with her mother, weren't you?' she said curiously and his smile vanished.

'Bloody hell!' She should have guessed. 'Alison's your daughter, isn't she?'

'I would die for her,' the priest spat out. 'Just as I would have died for her mother. I couldn't stand by and let that man hurt her.'

Jill struggled to take her eyes from him. She wasn't religious but, usually, she had a great deal of respect for men, and women, of the cloth. This man, Father Gosling, was one of the most vile people she had ever met.

'You're a hypocrite,' she said at last. 'A lying, cheating hypocrite who thinks he's above the God he claims to worship. The vow of celibacy means nothing to you. Murder means nothing to you.'

'You think I care what *you* think? Yes, it's true. Alison is my daughter.'

'Does she know?'

'Of course she knows, you stupid little fool.'

331

'Steve doesn't, though, does he?'

'What does it matter to him? He was going to divorce her, that's all that matters. I went there to frighten him. I didn't have a weapon, but the knife was there–'

'Yeah, yeah,' Jill cut him off. 'Remind us never to have dinner with you.'

Max nodded at PC Wilde. 'Cuff him.'

He went quietly, almost proudly, and was soon sitting in the back of the patrol car. Even as it pulled away, his eyes bored into Jill's.

When the car was out of sight, she let out her breath on a long sigh.

'I hope they throw away the key,' she muttered.

'He won't be leading his flock for a while.'

'How dare he?' she demanded. 'How dare he preach his sermons and listen to people's confessions?'

'He hasn't proved a hit with you, has he?'

She smiled at the understatement. 'What a hateful man.'

As Max drove them away, she gazed out of the window and tried to forget Father Gosling. It was impossible. She'd like to believe he'd acted out of love for his daughter, but she couldn't. He was Alison's father, yet he hadn't wanted what was best for her.

She'd always believed Alison too shallow to worship in Harrington every Sunday. So why had she? To be near her father? Or to make sure he didn't cut her out of his will?

She wondered what lengths a father would go to to give his daughter the life he believed she should have. What about Vincent Cole, for example? He'd loved his daughter, Jill had no doubt, but she hadn't been living the life he'd wanted for her.

'Forget him,' Max broke into her thoughts. 'He isn't worth it.'

'Gosling? He's forgotten. Actually, I was thinking about Vincent Cole.'

'What about him?' He accelerated to overtake the car in front of him.

'I don't know,' she admitted, but something was niggling her.

Belatedly, she realized that Max was driving out of the town.

'Where are we going?'

'I thought you wanted to call at your place and collect some clothes.'

'I did. Yes, thanks.'

'We'll do that, and then I'll run you home. It'll give them time to process our favourite priest. I'll nip back to deal with him and then, that's it. Finished for Christmas.'

'Thank God for that!'

Jill's thoughts returned to Vincent Cole. Temple had claimed that Cole constantly told his daughter she was pathetic. That wasn't the impression Jill had gained. She'd thought him saddened to see Lauren losing her way in the world.

'Hell, I forgot to tell you about my late-night caller,' Jill said.

'What about him?'

'He's now taken to calling in the middle of the day, it seems. But it came through direct to my office extension, Max.'

'What did he say?'

'Merry Christmas.'

Max slapped the steering wheel. 'I'll give him merry bloody Christmas when I get my hands on him.'

Jill never knew whose decision it was to take a walk up the hill, hers or Max's. Neither of them were dressed for it, but at least the wind had dropped and the temperature had risen slightly. It would soon be dark, though, and only a fool would be out on the hill then. For all that, they walked on, their gaze on Clough's Shelter. Bleak and lonely, it was no place to die.

Perhaps coming out on to the hill was their way of making some sort of promise to Lauren Cole. As yet, they hadn't found her killer. But they would.

'Temple's alibi is worse than useless, you know,' Max said as if he could read her thoughts.

'True, but he's not guilty. He killed Vincent Cole, not Lauren.'

'What makes you so certain? It was your profile that put us on to him in the first place.'

She was fully aware of that, but she was certain he was innocent of Lauren's murder. Her profile had led her to someone who knew Lauren well, better than most people did–

'Who's that?' she murmured. 'What the devil would anyone be doing up here at this time of day?'

'The same as us maybe?' Max suggested drily.

As they walked on, Jill recognized the figure. It was Jimmy Walker. Jill had only seen him once, that afternoon in the cafe, since the day Pat had been called to school to explain his truancy.

'How odd,' she murmured.

'What?'

She shook her head, unable to explain because Jimmy was within earshot.

'Hi, Jimmy, how's things?' she asked as they met on the narrow track.

'OK,' he murmured.

'Where have you been? Up to the shelter?'

'Yeah.' Unless she was mistaken, tears had dried on his cheeks. It was cold, but the wind wasn't strong enough to make his eyes water. So why had he been shedding tears?

'You know Max, don't you? A policeman,' she added for the benefit of his blank expression.

At that, Jimmy took an involuntary step back.

Something had been bothering the boy for a while, Jill had known that, but if the sight of a copper had him looking terrified, and it did, this was serious. Jill wished now that she'd quizzed Pat more. But Pat had put the problems down to Jimmy missing his dad.

'Do you come up here a lot?' she asked him.

It would be the ideal place for a boy who wanted to get away from it all, from his mother, from the village, from the pain of missing his father.

'Sometimes.'

'A young woman was killed here,' Max said. 'I suppose you heard about that?'

Jimmy nodded. As long as they blocked his path, he couldn't escape. It was obvious he wanted to though.

'Would you know anything about it?' Max

asked him.

Jimmy, panic in his eyes, looked at Jill.

'Jimmy?' she prompted.

He knew something, she was sure of it. The trouble was, he was too frightened to say anything.

'If you know anything,' she said, 'you should tell us, you know that, don't you?'

'I–'

'What do you know, Jimmy?' she asked. 'Did you know Lauren?'

He nodded, terror in eyes that had filled with tears again.

'Tell us about it,' she suggested.

She thought he was about to make a run for it, but he reached, very slowly, into his pocket and brought out an iPhone.

'Is that the one your dad bought you?' she asked lightly, and he nodded.

He hit a couple of buttons, looked at Jill, then at Max. Finally, he hit another button and handed his phone to Max.

Jill was at the wrong angle so she couldn't see anything other than glare on the screen. Max, though, she could tell, was looking at something very interesting.

Eventually, Max hit a button and handed the phone to her.

To her complete amazement, she saw a shaky video of Lauren Cole walking up the hill, her white dog running alongside her. And that's all she saw. Lauren Cole walking. The distance was too great to see her in close up, but there was no mistaking her. She was wearing a red coat and dark blue jeans.

Was Jimmy looking so upset because he'd had a crush on the dead girl?

The camera angle changed so that it showed someone else with Lauren. It was impossible to tell who it was. Was it Steve Carlisle?

Then the angle changed again and half of the screen showed a stone wall. The right half showed Lauren Cole having an argument with someone. There was still no way of recognizing the person.

It was easy to hear his voice, though.

'You can't cope with your mum's death, can you?' that voice was saying. 'I know you can't. You never have coped and you never will!'

'It's you I can't cope with!' That was Lauren's voice, raised in despair. 'Why do you have to keep following me?'

Jill watched, both horrified and fascinated, as the camera followed Lauren. She bent down to Steve's sack and took out an axe. The shouting that followed was impossible to make out.

There was a fight, a struggle, then the axe changed hands.

Again that voice, wild, hysterical, 'You can't cope, Lauren. Your mum's abandoned you. I know because she abandoned me, too. She left us. And you can't cope!'

The camera swung round and focused on the man's face. It caught it as he was about to bring down the axe on his daughter's head.

Lauren had been followed out to Kelton Bridge that morning. By her own father. He'd followed her and killed her. The knowledge had Jill shaking. She felt sick, too, and grateful that she'd had to skip lunch.

'We need to take this,' Max told Jimmy. 'You'll get it back as soon as possible. You should have told us, you know that, don't you?'

'Too scared,' Jimmy said.

'There's nothing to be scared of,' Max promised. 'Right, run along home now. Someone will be along to talk to you later, OK?'

The lad nodded, and he looked relieved to be away from them.

They watched him as he half-walked and half-ran down the hill.

'You were right then,' Max said at last. 'You said that, if we found Charlie's collar, we'd find our killer.'

'Yes, but–'

'Bloody amateur dramatics,' Max said, shaking his head. 'He should have been a pro.'

'But to kill your own daughter.' Jill still couldn't take it in. 'To him, of course, it will have been an act of kindness. He truly believed she would never cope with her mother's death and he couldn't bear to stand by and watch her throw her life away. But she *was* coping. She *was* healing.'

'It seems to me it was him who couldn't cope,' Max said, and Jill couldn't agree more.

'The poor kid spent years craving love. In the end, it was love that killed her.'

For Jill's sake, Max would be glad when Christmas arrived. She looked sick of it all, and he couldn't blame her. Her friend and neighbour, a man she trusted and respected, had been banged

338

up on a murder charge and then left to fight for his life. One father had almost killed his son-in-law, another had killed his daughter.

Max parked his car on Jill's neighbour's drive-way, just behind the caravan they were using for surveillance. Darkness had fallen quickly as it always did at this time of year.

'This is a waste of time,' Jill said. 'He must know I'm not staying there. Why else would he have phoned me at the office?'

'We don't know, do we?'

He knew that, at the moment, she wasn't too concerned about her mysterious caller. She was still too shaken. It was one thing to learn a killer's identity, and another to see the murder taking place before your eyes.

She felt bad, too, he knew that. As always, she believed she should have led them to the killer.

What was done was done, and there could be no bringing back of the dead. As far as Max was concerned, there was nothing but good news. They had Lauren Cole's killer, and her father's. Yasmin Smith was back at home with her family. They even had the odious man responsible for Steve Carlisle's spell in hospital.

Max was still concerned about the man intent on frightening Jill, though. There was no knowing what a person capable of killing a cat could do. Look at any psychopath's history and you'd see a history of cruelty to animals.

'Call this off, Max,' Jill said. 'It's a waste of time. He knows I'm not there.'

'We can't be sure of that.' He switched off the engine. 'Come on, let's go and see if anything's

339

been happening.'

They crossed the garden to the caravan and, after knocking briefly, stepped inside PC Glover's temporary home. There was only one very tiny light, not visible from the outside, so it was impossible to see much at all.

'Welcome,' the PC greeted them. 'Come in and make yourselves at home. Sorry, I only warranted the mini-caravan but there's just about enough room to stand and drink a coffee if you want one.'

'We'll pass, thanks.' Max stared out into the darkness at Jill's cottage. Lights were on in the hall and the sitting room. 'Anything?'

'Not so much as a stray cat in the garden.'

Max felt Jill shudder beside him, no doubt recalling the way the little stray had been killed.

'What with this weather,' PC Glover said, 'it's not surprising the world's deserted.' He broke off, stared into the darkness and then shook his head. 'In the end, you start imagining there's someone out there.' He tapped his fingers on the table. 'Dammit, I'm sure I just saw something.'

Max peered out, but could see nothing.

'By the front door,' PC Glover said, his voice urgent now.

Still Max could see nothing.

'The security light would come on if anyone was there,' Jill reminded them.

'Yeah, perhaps it was my imagination,' Glover said. 'Sit here long enough and you go a little bit crazy.'

They all stared into the darkness and Max knew that after an hour of this, you would be seeing aliens. Or vampires. Or any damn thing you chose.

'What time do you finish tonight?' he asked Glover.

'Ten. And then I'm off till after Christmas. A whole four days and I can't wait.'

'Have a good one,' Max said. 'Thanks for the offer of coffee, but we'll leave you to it. We're going into the cottage to collect a few things, so don't send the dogs in.'

'If only I warranted a dog,' he muttered. 'Oh, and a happy Christmas to both of you!' he added.

They left the relative warm of the caravan and walked up the lane. Just as they were about to turn into the drive, Max spotted movement. There was no doubt in his mind. He grabbed Jill's arm and put a hand over her mouth as he pulled her close to the hedge.

Max had his eyes on the cottage and, this time, there was no mistaking it. There was definitely a dark moving shape at the side of her cottage.

Any minute now, the security light would come on.

They stood quite still, trying not to breathe deeply. Still no light came on. Max knew it was either faulty or had been put out of action, and he suspected the latter.

There was something else. An odd smell was being carried towards them on the cold air.

The figure moved. All in black. In the dark.

Just as a tiny spark of light appeared, Max realized what that smell was. Petrol.

'Shit!'

He ran forward and hurled himself at the moving figure.

341

He was aware of a huge, heavy-duty torch being raised. He even saw it coming down at great speed towards his head.

It was the last thing he did see.

Chapter Thirty-Four

It had been a strange Christmas morning. Without Max in it, his house had seemed quiet and empty, and given that there were two adults, two boys, three dogs and three cats in residence, that was ridiculous.

Getting through the morning had been a struggle. Jill was exhausted, too. She hadn't slept for more than a couple of hours. She couldn't stop shaking, either.

One good thing had come from this, though. Max's father had woken up to the knowledge that life was to be lived whether he liked it or not. His son could have been killed last night. No one knew what was lurking round the corner so each moment had to be lived to the full.

'Tell you what, Jill,' Miles Trentham had said when lunch was over, 'you can drop me and the boys off at Judy's. We'll hand over the presents and walk on up to the hospital. It'll give you and Max some time alone,' he'd added with a wink.

Jill, wanting that time with Max, hadn't argued. She'd dropped them off at Judy's house and arrived at the hospital alone.

Laden with carrier bags bulging with presents,

food and a bottle of wine, she made her way to Max's room.

When she pushed open the door, she was in time to see a very attractive nurse laughing with him. Typical, she thought. He'd be the star turn.

'I'll leave you to your visitor,' the nurse said, giving Jill a smile that was difficult to return.

His room looked like Santa's grotto. There were cards, balloons, a huge inflatable Santa and a big banner above his bed that read: The miracle of Christmas: a copper with a day off.

'My God— Oh, don't tell me, Grace has visited.'

'How did you guess?'

'Female intuition.' She bent to kiss him. 'How's the head?'

'No permanent damage and at least it's stopped hurting.'

'A pity. And the next time I tell you that one of your officers is unfit for the job, damn well listen to me.'

He patted the side of his bed. 'How's your cottage?'

'Fine, thanks.' She dumped her bags on the chair and sat on the edge of his bed. 'It stinks of petrol but at least he didn't have time to put a match to it. And I was thinking of getting a new carpet anyway.'

The stupid thing was, she was still shaking. If PC Glover hadn't come to their aid...

'It's a good job you've done that Thai boxing,' he murmured.

'Ha. My instructor would have died of embarrassment if he'd seen me kick the bastard in the balls.'

Max laughed at that, and she relaxed a little.

The kick had been good enough to have him doubled up in pain and retching. She still hadn't recovered from the shock, though. When PC Glover had removed that balaclava, she'd been horrified to find herself staring straight into Clive White's face.

'You?' she'd cried in astonishment.

'You jumped up prissy cow!' He'd spat at her – and missed, thankfully. 'You think you're bloody God, don't you? You think you can mess with people's lives.'

'No. I just recognize a bloody arsehole when I see one!'

Max reached for her hand and held it. Why, she wondered, did she always feel so vulnerable with him? And how long would it take for the sight of him, lying on the floor with blood pouring from his head, to start to fade?

How long, too, before she recovered from the shock of knowing that Clive White had wanted her dead? He'd planned to burn her cottage to the ground, thinking she was inside.

It was over. There was no point in tormenting herself. Yet she was still trembling.

'A pity you missed lunch,' she told Max, moving to easier subjects.

'Oh, I don't know.'

'You had turkey? With all the trimmings?'

'I certainly did. Served by the lovely Patricia, too.'

'You always smell of roses, don't you, Trentham?'

He smiled at that. 'So how was your lunch?

Please don't tell me you cooked it. I have two sons and a father that I'm rather fond of.'

'Me? Ha, I was promised lunch cooked by your fair hand. Instead, I had to ring round every blasted restaurant in Harrington. I started at the top and worked right down to the greasy spoons.'

'Oh, dear.'

'It was OK in the end.' Sometimes there was nothing more enjoyable than a good gloat. 'Tony's rang me back late last night to say they had a cancellation.'

'Tony's?' He whistled at that.

'Yep. It was the best Christmas dinner I've ever had. Turkey with everything. The most delicious pud and you had to see the chocolates that came with the coffee to believe them. Pricey mind. It's a good job I've had some decent winners lately. Oh, yeah, and even Ben and Harry enjoyed the champagne.'

He rolled his eyes at that.

'No crackers?' he asked.

'Of course.'

Despite the easy banter, he looked pale and she guessed he was still in some pain.

'I called in last night, but you were sleeping off the painkillers.'

'I know. Sorry. And thanks. For coming I mean.'

She didn't know what to say to that. There was something in the atmosphere that she couldn't fathom.

'I've brought you some wine,' she said. 'Can you drink it?'

'Easy, kiddo. You just put it in your mouth and swallow.'

345

Perhaps it wasn't the atmosphere. Perhaps it was the way he was looking at her. It was an all-knowing sort of look as if he could read her every thought. It was damned unsettling too.

'There are a couple of small Christmas presents, too,' she said, 'but we thought we'd save the rest till we're all together at home.'

She caught his sharp gaze and knew he was as surprised as she was that she'd said 'at home'. She'd meant at 'his' home. Now that Clive White was under arrest, she and her cats could return to her cottage any time she liked.

He was looking completely relaxed, and that confused her. Usually, he was too impatient to be still.

She'd wanted this time alone with him but she found herself wishing that his father and sons would arrive to ease the tension a little. Tension on her side, she acknowledged. She knew that, for some reason, her face was the same shade as the Christmas balloon tied to his bed.

'Are you concussed?' Perhaps that would account for his relaxed, smiling demeanour.

'A bit. Not concussed enough to forget your present, though.' He reached into the small locker.

'Blimey, what have you bought me from your hospital bed? Someone's appendix that was going spare? A year's supply of Elastoplast? Piles ointment?'

'Better than that. Close your eyes.'

She did, but her heart was racing at a ridiculous pace.

'You can open them now.'

In his hand was a ring. Fake gold with a plastic

'ruby', it had clearly come from a Christmas cracker.

'No expense spared,' he murmured, as he slipped it on to the third finger of her left hand. 'Let's get married, Jill.'

Knowing he was serious, she could only stare at him. And he stared straight back.

She tried to utter some clever, amusing little witticism but couldn't. Her voice wouldn't work for the huge lump that had found its way to her throat and decided to lodge itself there for the duration. Tears had sprung to her eyes causing an unpleasant stinging sensation.

'Well?' he asked.

Still the clever quip didn't spring to her lips.

She was trying to think logically. Christmas was a time when people acted out of character. There was too much goodwill to all men about. Added to that, they'd had a stressful time of it lately. They'd found a killer, reunited a teenager with her parents, and arrested a priest for attempted murder. On top of that, Max was lying in a hospital bed when he should have been enjoying Christmas with his family. And that was thanks to the actions of a man he had trusted, a member of his team. It was no wonder that neither of them were thinking straight.

'Well?' he asked again.

The door crashed open, and Miles Trentham arrived with Harry and Ben.

'Wow, cool balloons, Dad!'

'That's a wicked scar you're going to have, Dad! And you only got hit with a torch. That's amazing.'

Everyone tried to talk at once and Jill put her hands in her pockets. Surprisingly, the ring was a perfect fit.

Over an hour passed before the nurse came to evict them all.

'He needs to rest,' she told them sternly.

They grabbed coats and said their goodbyes.

Max held Jill's hand longer than necessary.

'Well?'

'When are they letting you out?' she asked, evading his question.

'The Clarets are playing Bolton tomorrow. A three o'clock kick-off at the Turf.'

Jill supposed that answered her question. It would take a great deal more than the NHS to keep him from the Boxing Day football fixture.

Miles and the boys had deserted her. She could hear them outside in the corridor, laughing at something.

'If you don't like the ring,' Max said, 'we can choose another. Marry me and I'll fill your every waking hour with happiness. I'll dispose of all wildlife your cats bring in, keep you warm at night, cater to your every sexual need, let you have the TV remote.'

'Well, if you put it like that–'

The door banged open.

'Come along, come along!' the nurse chided, shooing Jill out of the room.

'I'll, um, see you tomorrow, Max.'

This Large Print Book for the partially sighted, who cannot read normal print, is published under the auspices of

THE ULVERSCROFT FOUNDATION